MW01235445

Forgetting With You

Robin Clairvaux

Copyright © 2023 Robin Clairvaux

Cover Design by Rachel Bowdler

Edited by Victoria Grant

All rights reserved. No part of this book may be reproduced or used in any manner without the express written permission of the publisher except for the use of brief quotations in a book review.

This is a work of fiction. Names, characters, businesses, places, events and incidents are either the products of the author's imagination or used in a fictitious manner. Any resemblance to actual persons, living or dead, or actual events is purely coincidental.

ISBN: 9798869595935

FORGETTING WITH YOU

1

Camryn Durant detested bars. Especially crowded ones. The swarm of overheated bodies, dim lighting, and drunken laughter were all too chaotic for her quiet-loving brain.

Tonight, however, quiet was the last thing her brain needed. After spending all day obsessing over *should haves* and regurgitating every decision of the past six years of her pathetic career, she couldn't stand to be alone with her thoughts for another second. That's why she'd given in when Britt had pestered her to go for drinks when they'd gotten off work.

Britt was in the media planning department of the advertising agency where Cam was a graphic designer. She was a few years younger than Cam's thirty-three, so the downtown Dallas night life drew her in every weekend like a moth to the flame. Cam preferred to be more like a moth that contentedly fluttered around the bulb of a living room reading lamp. Despite their differences, Britt was Cam's favorite coworker, and she'd never appreciated the constant badgering to get out and be more social than she did tonight when she was craving distraction.

Cam waved to get the bartender's attention, but the tattooed man in his late twenties didn't look in her direction. Instead, he smiled at three pretty younger women at the other end of the bar. Cam swept her eyes over the trio, who were all wearing tight dresses with low-cut necklines. She couldn't blame the guy for not wanting to abandon them for a tall-to-the-point-of-gangly woman who was clad in business casual and a bit on the butch side.

Britt returned from the bathroom and swept onto the empty barstool beside Cam before waggling her fingers at the bartender and calling, "Excuse me" in a loud but sweet tone.

The bartender tilted his head and grinned at Cam's elegant, raven-haired coworker before coming over to take their orders.

"Thanks for that," Cam said after the bartender left. "I might have died of thirst waiting for him to turn around."

"You're not assertive enough, Cam. That's your whole problem," Britt chided. "That's why you got passed over for the senior designer promotion for that dork Finn Harper, you know?"

Cam groaned. This uncomfortable little outing was supposed to help her forget about the promotion. "No. I don't know."

"He couldn't design a coupon book. You and he aren't even in the same league! But all he does is brag about his minor accomplishments to Logan. Heck, I'll bet Logan promoted him just to get him to shut up!"

Britt accepted the colorful cocktail the bartender set in front of her with a smile, took a long swallow, and kept right on chattering. "You have real accomplishments to brag about, but you never say a word."

"I shouldn't have to brag. I do the work. I basically finished the last two projects by myself and drafted the ideas for the new Glass-Hardy campaign, all while onboarding two new designers. Why isn't that enough?"

Cam pulled her beer close but didn't drink yet, worried the bile in her throat would mix with the beer and make her choke.

"It would be enough, if you had a good manager who noticed your work, but let's face it. Logan is a crap manager. That's how Mr. Braggy Pants gets recognition instead of you."

Despite her sour mood, Cam smiled at the nickname. It was fitting. Finn's illustrations were lackluster at best, but they'd probably improve exponentially if he spent the same amount of time polishing them that he spent bending Logan's ear about how great he was.

Of course, Cam had her doubts about Logan's skill and eye for detail too, but she never dared voice them in the office. She didn't feel like voicing them now either. All she wanted was to put Finn, Logan, and her job at the Propagate Agency out of her mind for a few hours. She was on the verge of asserting herself enough to announce those feelings to Britt so they could change the subject when Britt's phone emitted a loud ping.

She grabbed the device from its place on the bar beside her and checked the screen. "Ooh. Haley and Jon are at that new bar a few blocks from here. It's the one that opened two weeks ago, and everyone's already raving about it!"

Cam was certain she didn't personally know anyone who had raved about it, but she nodded.

"They said they found a table, and there's room for more. You wanna go?" Britt asked, her brown eyes sparkling.

"No, thanks. You go on. I'm going to finish my beer and head home."

"Come on, Cam. Don't be such a senior citizen! This place is supposed to be amazing. Plus, since it's so popular, I'll bet there will be a few queer ladies there too!" Britt gave Cam a playful elbow to the ribs.

Ugh. The last thing Cam needed was a woman to further derail her life. "Nah. Not tonight. I'm not in the right headspace for that."

Britt's expression sobered, and she studied Cam's face. "You want me to stay and keep you company?"

"Thanks, Britt. You're the best, but no. Go on. I'll hang out a minute and then go home to cuddle up with my e-reader."

A fond smile lifted the corners of Britt's mouth. "And be perfectly content, right?"

"Yep." And Cam meant it…for the most part.

"All right. Whatever you say." Britt gave her a quick hug before flitting away.

Once Britt was gone, Cam slumped on her barstool and took a sip of her beer. She closed her eyes, letting the smooth, faintly fruity flavor of the locally made brew wash over her tongue.

The overlapping voices of the other bar patrons faded into a dull background roar, and when she opened her eyes again, a pleasant sight greeted her. The bar area had mostly cleared out, and the other bar patrons had taken their drinks and dispersed to the various tables, worn leather chairs, and billiard tables that populated the interior of the establishment.

Maybe staying a bit longer wouldn't be so bad after all. She might even be able to get a refill later without having to make a scene.

The thought made Cam scowl as she recalled Britt's words.

'You're not assertive enough, Cam. That's your whole problem.'

Cam was 99 percent sure that wasn't her *whole* problem. Like the small family that had raised her—her mom, grandmom, and auntie—Cam was quiet but hardworking. But that's where a lot of similarities ended.

In a complete departure from their expectations, Cam had decided to leave rural Oklahoma and the benevolent bubble of her tribal community to attend a large university in the Dallas/Fort Worth metro and eventually work in the area.

Where had all that ambition gone? These days, Cam found herself taking a "wait and see" attitude for most things in life.

A rustling sound from further down the bar caught Cam's attention. She turned, and did an exaggerated double take like a cartoon character.

Four seats away, a willowy redhead in her early-thirties climbed onto a stool then gave the bartender a friendly grin as she ordered. The woman was dressed in a tasteful black dress that accentuated her slender frame without clinging to it. Once she'd settled onto her stool, she shifted and crossed long, tantalizing legs. In general, Cam tried not to ogle women, but something about the redhead captured her full attention.

Finally, Cam jerked her gaze away from the woman's body and studied her face. Her complexion was fair-skinned, probably even freckled under her makeup, although she didn't appear to be wearing a ton of it, and her features were soft and graceful.

Resisting the urge to prop her elbow on the bar and rest her chin in her hand like a smitten adolescent, Cam looked away and took another sip of her beer. If she were the "assertive" type Britt was blabbing about, maybe she'd sidle over to the redhead and strike up a conversation.

Just when that notion was turning into a nice daydream, a brown-haired man dressed in jeans and a sweater approached the redhead. The woman stood up to give him a peck on the lips.

Hmph. That figures.

Naturally, the redhead was in a relationship with a guy.

Cam had a gift for letting her head be turned by the wrong women. Women like Tina, whom she'd dated the last two years of college. Tina who had dumped her and married a guy instead. After two whole years of love, passion, and making plans, Cam hadn't been good enough for her.

Cam shook off the memory and studied the man who'd joined the redhead. He certainly hadn't put in much effort to match his date, clothing wise. After watching the detached way he'd returned her kiss, it wasn't difficult to imagine he wasn't her equal in other ways too.

With a wince, Cam turned away. *Wow, Cam. Judgmental, much?*

The couple at the other end of the bar was none of her business, and there was no point in embroiling them in her foul mood, even if it was only in her imagination.

Cam's resolve to ignore the couple lasted all of two minutes before her ears began to tingle at the sound of the redhead's bright, melodious voice as she recounted her day to her partner.

He was staring at his beer bottle instead of her.

"I can't believe I even beat you here, honey," the redhead said. "After school, I went shopping for the twin's birthday present, and I barely had time to go home and change to get here by six."

She reached down to grab a shopping bag sporting the logo of an educational toy store and began rummaging through it. She pulled out a box with a picture of a remote-controlled drone on the side and held it up to the man with a proud grin. "Isn't it great? They'll think they have the coolest uncle any eleven-year-olds could ask for!"

The man spared the box a glance and mumbled, "Yeah, it's great." Then he took a swig of his beer and set it down. "Look, J, I need to talk to you."

The redhead's smile dimmed but didn't fade completely. "We'll talk at dinner. I booked us a reservation at a nice, quiet place because I wanted tonight to be special. I know we need to talk. To reconnect." She placed her hand on top of his, but he pulled it away.

"It's not going to work, J." The man ran his hand through his hair and avoided her eyes. "*We're* not going to work. There's someone else."

"What?" The redhead's voice squeaked. "What do you mean? We've been together two and a half years! We were committed! We were making plans. Marriage and a family and—"

"That's the problem, J!" the man shot back. "With you, it was always about our future plans. You never wanted me. You only wanted a husband. I was filling a role for your dreams or your father's or whoever's. But I'm done with it."

The man stood to go, and the redhead reached for him. "Rob, wait. I'm sorry. We can work this out. I'll do better."

He pulled away. "It's over, J."

With that, he bent to pick up the toy store shopping bag then turned and stalked out the door.

Cam turned to watch the man go, and her jaw went slack. *He dumped her?*

Besides reeling from the fact that she'd just witnessed a breakup, Cam was equally floored by the man's clear lack of good judgment. What was wrong with him? This glorious woman wanted a future with him, and he said, 'No, thanks'? Did he think those kinds of opportunities came around every day? And if they did, did he honestly think he was such a great catch that he could take advantage of them?

Cam took another swig of her beer to keep from grinding her teeth. Why was the world only being kind to morons today?

After stewing a few seconds, she peeked over at the redhead again. The woman's formerly confident, energetic posture was gone. Now she leaned on the bar, head lowered with her hands wrapped around the edge of the bar like she was hanging on for a ride she didn't want to be on.

A pang of empathy shot through Cam's stomach. She'd been in that woman's place before: stunned and hurt with all her hopes shattered around her. The shock would soon be followed with a sense of utter worthlessness. At least, that's what had happened to Cam. She hoped that wouldn't be the case for the woman at the other end of the bar.

Cam didn't know a thing in the world about her other than what she'd seen tonight. Yet she couldn't manage to quell a startling conviction stirring deep inside.

The woman deserved better.

After another gulp of beer, Cam stood. Her long legs straightened and carried her forward as if of their own volition.

What am I doing?

This was a bad idea. So far from the cautious, thoughtful approach she'd learned to take toward life ever since Tina dumped her all those years ago. But, tonight, it didn't matter. Tonight, she was all alone except for depressing thoughts about her stagnant career. Maybe it was time to assert herself, after all. Just a little.

What did she have to lose? It wasn't like she was risking her heart.

2

Jackie stared at the glass of clear liquid on the bar in front of her for several minutes then shoved it away. She was going to need something a lot stronger than seltzer water. Motioning the bartender over, she ordered a scotch and soda.

As she watched him make her drink, she massaged her temples. The bartender had probably overheard the entire humiliating scene that had played out between her and Rob. At least there hadn't been a lot of customers around to witness it.

Her eyes squeezed shut. What was wrong with her? Her boyfriend of more than two years broke up with her five minutes ago, and all she could think of was whether anyone had seen it or not?

You never wanted me. You only wanted a husband.

Was he right?

She'd loved him, hadn't she? She must have. She'd told him she had during their time together. So what if she couldn't describe in detail what that even meant? They'd been good together. They had been working toward a future, or so she had thought.

Now it was all over. All the progress she'd been making toward her dreams: a home, a marriage, and a family of her own. It was all over.

Dejection settled deep in her stomach followed by an avalanche of dread. Just wait until her dad heard about this. How hard would it be to leave her teaching job, pack up, and move out of the country before that could happen?

The bartender set the drink in front of her, and she thanked him before muttering. "Keep them coming, please."

He nodded and left her alone, and she picked up her glass to take a sip.

"Are you sure you want to do that?" a low, husky voice asked.

Jackie whirled around and looked into a pair of dark brown eyes.

A tall, lanky woman around her age stood beside her. She had a full head of black hair that was clipped short and her skin was a tawny beige color that Jackie couldn't help but admire even in the bar's low light. This woman probably hadn't gotten a dozen sunburns every summer the way Jackie had as a teenager.

She returned her attention to the stranger's eyes, which held a startling mix of warmth and intensity. "Excuse me?"

"I asked if you're sure you want to get drunk alone and wake up with an epic hangover in the morning. Will that really help?"

"Help…what?"

The woman leaned an elbow on the bar and shifted sideways to face Jackie head on. "Help you forget that guy."

"You saw that?" Heat flushed over Jackie's face, but she wasn't sure if it was from embarrassment or from being the focus of this stranger's pointed attention.

The woman moved closer to Jackie, right to the outskirts of her personal space. She smelled nice, a mixture of clean linen and a faint musky fragrance like men's cologne. "Yeah, I saw."

Something like distaste colored her tone as she said it.

Jackie's cheeks heated again, and this time, it was definitely from embarrassment.

Great! She and Rob really must have made a scene. What's more, this random person had watched and was talking to her about it. What did she want?

Folding her arms, Jackie demanded, "So what is your prescription for forgetting the fact that you've been humiliated in a public place, if not alcohol? I mean, we are in a bar, you know."

Her growing irritation didn't faze the stranger. Calmly, she looked away for a moment, eyes scanning the various clusters of bar patrons around them. "Other things happen in bars too. I'll bet anyone here would jump at the chance to help a gorgeous woman like you forget for one night."

Jackie's eyes widened. It was a nice, if unexpected, compliment, but she definitely didn't feel like a hot commodity right now. She laughed and reached for her drink. "Any guy here, hmm?"

The stranger nodded then met her eyes again. "Some of the women too."

Jackie coughed on the liquid she'd just consumed. "Oh, um. I'm not like that. Into women, I mean."

"Not that there's anything wrong with it," she added quickly.

The woman shrugged and flashed a winsome grin that drew Jackie in, practically against her will. "I'm not sure labels matter so much for a simple night of forgetting."

Jackie's pulse picked up. Curiosity stirred in some deep, forgotten part of her. Well, of course, she'd thought about it a time or two. Wondered what it would be like. Most straight women did at some point, didn't they? There were times when she'd have the oddest dreams: images of the smooth, sensual curves of a woman in her bed and—no! Jackie shook her head at herself or the woman, maybe both. "I-I don't think…um. I mean, I'm not…"

The smile on the stranger's broad, tan face widened. She wasn't reveling in Jackie's confusion, per se, but she did seem amused by it. "No? That's okay. But the drink is on me, if you'd like. May I sit?"

Jackie found the woman's shift into a friendlier approach reassuring, so she nodded. Besides, she wasn't ready to give up the company yet. The last thing she wanted was to be alone with her thoughts.

"I'm Camryn Durant, by the way. But most people call me Cam," the woman announced, holding out her hand.

"Jackie," she replied, placing her hand in Cam's, who gave it a firm shake. "Jackie Webster, which probably won't be changing any time soon."

She sent Cam a tiny grin, belying the bitterness of the statement.

There was a soft, knowing look in Cam's eyes. "Hey, you don't have to act like everything's fine. You had a crappy night, and I elbowed my way into it. The least I can do is listen if you want to vent."

"That's kind of you," Jackie said. "But I think I'd rather wallow in the denial stage a while longer. Why don't we talk about something else?"

"All right."

"What do you do, Cam? I mean, when you're not chatting up pathetic women in bars?"

Cam leaned forward and pulled an exaggerated sad face. "Don't talk about my new friend like that."

Jackie giggled despite her mood. "Sorry, I'll try to do better. Anyway, what do you do?"

"I'm a graphic designer for an advertising firm," Cam said.

"That sounds like interesting work."

"Sounds can be deceiving," Cam retorted, making Jackie laugh again. "What about you?"

"I teach high school English."

Cam beamed. "Now, *that* is interesting!"

"Is it?"

"Well, it is to me," Cam said with a self-deprecating roll of her eyes. "My stereotypical first crush was my high school English teacher, Ms. Donovan."

Jackie chuckled. "That must have made it hard to focus on your Shakespeare."

"You don't know the half of it! But it wasn't just that she made my adolescent hormones go gaywire, she was nice, you know? She was patient and attentive. Shoot, she didn't even laugh the time I got tongue-tied during a presentation and said my favorite Shakespeare play was *Much Doo Doo About Nothing*."

"You did not!" Jackie tried to hold in her own laugh by covering her mouth.

Cam held up her right hand as if taking an oath. "Honest truth! And Ms. Donovan—bless her—she didn't even crack a smile."

Jackie shrugged. "Well, you learn to develop a good poker face, since you never know what will come out of those kids' mouths. Some of them seem to make it their personal mission to shock or dismay their teachers on a daily basis."

"That has to be hard to handle."

"It can be…" Jackie mused as she toyed with her glass. "But at some point, you figure out how to look under the surface. Some of my kids come from tough homes, and all of them are under a lot of stress trying to grow up in this chaotic world. Sometimes a kid acts out because they're grieving, or feel invisible, or they're just plain hungry because they don't get enough nutrition at home. Even though I'm trying to teach them about literature or how to write good essays, I feel like my main job is to make them feel seen. That's what everyone wants, isn't it?"

"Wow." Cam's intense focus was almost tangible as she listened. "You really care about them, don't you?"

"Yeah. Even on the days they drive me up the wall, I love my kids."

Jackie stared into her drink. She didn't even have to ask herself if that was true. Not the way she'd questioned herself about Rob a few minutes ago. Sure, it was a different kind of love, but some days it felt more real. A lot of days, if she were being honest. Maybe her father was right when he said her work was the only thing that mattered to her.

She started to take a sip of her drink then slammed it back down. "You know what one of the most absurd things about this whole breakup is?"

Cam raised her hands, palms out, as if to disarm her. "Whoa! Looks like we went from denial to anger, huh?"

"Yes, but mostly anger at myself. I realized that one of the first things to go through my mind when Rob walked out is, 'How am I going to tell my dad?'"

She leaned on the bar closer to Cam, once again finding herself appreciating her scent. "What does that say about our relationship?"

"Don't tell me your dad really liked *that guy*?"

"No, of course not. Dad doesn't really like anyone."

Cam coughed out a laugh. "Then what's the problem?"

"He's been bugging me to get married for years, mostly so I won't embarrass my older brother, the politician, with a spinster sister," Jackie said. She mimicked her father's hard, cheerless voice, "An unmarried woman always raises questions, Jacqueline."

"Oh yeah. I know all about those questions. Even worse," Cam leaned in and lowered her voice, which made it even huskier. "I know some of the answers too."

Jackie's heartrate picked up at the increased closeness, but she covered her response with a playful slap to Cam's arm. "Oh, stop it!"

The fun gesture felt oddly natural. Like they already knew each other well enough for banter. "I really don't think my answers are the same as yours. I've had boyfriends, some of them serious. Like Rob. But none of them ever worked out."

A dull, lonely ache spread through Jackie's heart. "No matter how hard I tried, they always left."

They left, and it wasn't fair. Despite what her dad thought, Jackie really did want a future and a family of her own, separate from her dad's stifling, controlling world where appearances mattered more than love or authenticity.

Frustration and hurt bubbled up to her throat, making her voice shake. "I'm sorry to unload on you like this, Cam. You probably came here for a nice, relaxing night, not to listen to some basket case whine about her problems."

"Hey, hey. It's all right." Cam's tone was soothing. She reached out and trailed a gentle hand up and down Jackie's bare arm.

Jackie's skin tingled, actually tingled where Cam touched it. What was that? Was it the effect of a little alcohol and an overwrought brain? Or maybe she was touch starved. God, it had been so long since she and Rob had…

"It's okay to be upset," Cam continued, interrupting her thoughts. "You've had a lousy night."

Cam rested her hand on Jackie's arm. It was grounding yet somehow exciting. Jackie's skin was heating up, and she didn't seem to have any say about it.

What were they talking about? Oh yeah. A lousy night.

But Jackie wasn't thinking about the night right now. Didn't want to think about it. The skin-on-skin contact felt so good, even though it was only a friendly, comforting gesture.

Maybe she *was* touch starved. What would it be like to feel more? Not only Cam's hand, but her arms, her whole body against hers? Her long body and small but firm breasts. What would it be like for Cam's heat to completely envelop and overwhelm her for a little while?

Suddenly, that spark of curiosity she'd always had was in danger of igniting into a flame.

"Cam?" Her voice came out low and breathless. Was she really going to ask?

"Hmm?" Cam prompted. Those dark brown eyes looked into hers and searched.

"W-what would you do?"

Cam's brow furrowed. "Do?"

"Yeah," Jackie swallowed. "To help me forget?"

She stared at Jackie for a few seconds. Cam's gaze was even more intense now. She seemed to be plumbing the depths of her very soul. Then, as if finding the answer to whatever question she'd had, she shifted on her stool until she completely faced Jackie. "First, I'd start with kissing."

Without thinking, Jackie stared at Cam's lips. They looked soft and inviting. "Kissing is nice."

"Hmm," Cam agreed. Slowly, she slid her hand to Jackie's and lifted it toward her lips, she turned it over and placed a single kiss to the tender skin of Jackie's wrist.

Jackie's breath hitched, and Cam sent her a serious, questioning look.

"Go on," Jackie said shakily.

Cam smiled. "Yes, kissing is nice. So nice that I like to take my time with it and be thorough."

She pressed her lips to Jackie's wrist again and started delicately nibbling. The tingles that had begun to form earlier now scattered through Jackie's entire body. Jackie released a light moan then glanced around the bar, her face hot. Fortunately, no one was nearby.

"Then what?" Jackie whispered. Her voice had gone hoarse.

Cam glanced around too then leaned in until her mouth was level with Jackie's ear. Jackie shivered at the sensation of Cam's breath brushing over her earlobe.

"Then," Cam murmured, "I'd politely relieve you of all your clothes."

Jackie giggled, despite the tension and heat of the moment.

Cam's own chuckle was short before she continued in a whisper, "Then I'd take you in my arms and make you forget. Over..." Cam's lips brushed her ear. "And over. And over."

Jackie's fingers clutched the side of the bar, worried she might fall off the stool. "So, what they say is true? Women make each other...you know...multiple times on the regular?"

"It can be true." Cam pulled back and grinned. "With the right pairing. But the same could probably be said for a man and a woman too, not that I'd know. Hasn't it ever been that way for you?"

Looking away from Cam's penetrating dark eyes, Jackie shook her head. "No, but maybe that's my fault."

Jackie's thoughts trailed over the times one past boyfriend had accused her of being a frigid bed partner.

Cam scoffed. "I seriously doubt it."

"How do you know?" Jackie demanded, staring into Cam's eyes once again.

The corners of Cam's mouth lifted in a wicked grin that made Jackie's insides contract. "There's only one way to find out."

3

I can't believe I'm doing this.

Jackie stood beside Cam as they silently rode the elevator to Cam's apartment. Her palms had been sweating ever since they'd entered the building, but she wasn't sure if it was from anxiety or arousal.

I can't believe I'm doing this.

Once the elevator arrived, Cam led Jackie down a short hall then into her apartment. The door closed behind them with a thud that made Jackie's pulse quicken. She stood fidgeting in the doorway leading into Cam's living room, too distracted to take in her surroundings except to notice the room was illuminated by a single lamp beside a large sofa.

"Do you want some water or something?" Cam asked.

"That would be great, thanks."

"Have a seat while I grab some."

Jackie sat on the plush sofa and listened to the sound of Cam rustling through her refrigerator. From where she was sitting, Jackie could see the open door of a dimly lit bedroom with a neatly made bed, ready and waiting in the center of the room.

I really, really can't believe I'm doing this.

Cam returned to the living room carrying two bottles of water. Jackie accepted hers and brought it to her lips. It was then that she realized her hand was shaking. She managed to steady it and take a short sip before setting the bottle on the coffee table. The last thing she needed was to spill water all over Cam's furniture.

"Hey."

She turned to see Cam standing beside the sofa and regarding her with a frank, open expression. "We don't have to do this, if you don't want to."

She must have picked up on Jackie's nerves, not that Jackie was doing a great job of hiding them.

When she didn't answer right away, Cam continued to study her. She sat down beside Jackie. "We can keep talking or I'll wait with you while you order a rideshare. Whatever you want."

Jackie's tension began to ease, and she shook her head.

"Okay." Cam reached up and brushed a strand of Jackie's hair away from her face, skirting her jawline with her fingers. "But if you change your mind at any point, let me know, and we'll stop. It's perfectly fine."

Warmth suffused Jackie at the gesture and the words. This was already a completely different experience from any she'd had in the past. Cam's gentleness and reassurances soothed her nerves to the point that excitement was taking over again. Cam was a complete stranger, yet somehow, Jackie knew it was safe to explore with her.

She drew in a long breath like a swimmer preparing to dive into the ocean. "I want this, Cam."

To drive the point home, she leaned over and planted her lips on Cam's.

Cam froze for a fraction of a second before kissing her back. Even though Jackie had been the one to instigate the kiss, she gasped. Cam's lips were so soft and warm as they moved against hers. Jackie closed her eyes and savored the sensation, moaning slightly.

The kiss ended and Cam pulled back. "Everything okay?"

Jackie could only nod, so Cam kissed her again. This time, it was slower and more purposeful. Cam's arms slid around Jackie's back and pressed their bodies closer together.

Jackie reveled in the feel and heat of Cam's body, oblivious to everything else until Cam's tongue began to trace her bottom lip, coaxing her lips apart. Jackie opened her mouth, and Cam slipped inside.

As if on instinct, Jackie's tongue met Cam's and tangled with it in a sensual dance. Moaning again, Jackie threaded her fingers through Cam's hair. So luscious and thick despite being short.

Jackie leaned into Cam even more until she was practically on top of her. Cam pulled back. They stared at each other, both breathing hard. Then Cam flashed her an absolutely wicked grin and pulled her all the way into her lap. Jackie hiked up her dress and straddled Cam. Her center pulsed at the contact, as if telling her how much she needed this. The tension, the touching, the passion. Did it matter if it wasn't with a man? Tonight was about forgetting for a while.

She would let herself forget and *feel*.

Cam stared up at her. Undisguised awe gleamed in her dark eyes. "Damn, you're sexy."

Jackie swallowed. When was the last time she'd heard anything like that? What's more, when was the last time she'd *felt* it? Shaking off the questions, she swooped down and kissed Cam again.

Cam eagerly met her lips, tasting and exploring until Jackie's body was on fire. Cam hadn't been exaggerating earlier when she'd said she liked to be thorough. Jackie had the feeling that Cam would devour her, if she let her. And right now, Jackie wanted nothing more.

She pulled away with a groan. "Cam?"

"Hmm?" Cam began sliding her lips over Jackie's jaw and down her neck, nibbling on her skin.

"Can we...ohh!" Jackie shuddered as Cam found a sensitive spot at the base of her neck and licked it. "C-can we..."

Cam pulled away and studied her. "Are you still okay with this?"

"No," Jackie blurted out.

"Okay." Cam nodded before slowly releasing her grasp on Jackie's waist. "That's all right. Do you want to talk some more, or would you rather go home now?"

"No!" Jackie repeated, already missing the heat of Cam's hands. "I meant, can we...take this to your bedroom now?"

Cam's dark eyes widened. "Oh." That wicked grin returned. "Best idea I've heard all night."

Yet again, Jackie found herself chuckling as Cam helped her to her feet and led her to the bedroom. Although her arousal was still thrumming deep inside, Jackie's nerves had almost completely dissipated. Something told her this was going to be fun.

With quick, efficient movements, Cam pulled back the covers of her bed before turning to face Jackie. She stalked toward Jackie like a jungle cat approaching its prey and pulled her in for another kiss.

Jackie shivered as Cam's hands slid lower and lower down her back until one rested on her ass. Cam gave a squeeze then bunched up the fabric at the hem of her dress.

Pulling back, Cam met her eyes. "May I?"

When Jackie nodded, Cam pulled the dress over her head and tossed it onto a chair in the corner of the room. Fierce hunger sparked to life in Cam's eyes as her gaze roamed over Jackie's lacy black panties and bra. "Damn, woman. Do you always wear stuff like that under your clothes?"

Jackie's skin heated at Cam's unabashed admiration. "Not always. I was trying to make tonight special until…"

She shook her head. She didn't want to talk or think about the breakup.

Cam slowly traced Jackie's bra from the strap all the way down the outline of her breast and hissed, "He's a fool."

"But you're not."

Cam's eyes stared into hers. "Not when it comes to appreciating a breathtaking woman."

Jackie smiled. That remark deserved a reward. She reached behind her back, unsnapped her bra, and let it drop to the floor. She wasn't sure where her sudden boldness had come from, but the look on Cam's face made it worthwhile.

Cam drew in a sharp breath and sank onto the bed, and Jackie approached her on shaky legs. They were close now, but apparently not close enough for Cam's liking. She grasped Jackie's hips and lightly tugged until she stood between Cam's thighs. Then she trailed her hands up Jackie's bare back until her skin prickled.

Her breasts were at Cam's eye level now, and Cam leaned forward and pressed a soft kiss to one of Jackie's nipples, making it harden. Jackie released a strangled gasp.

"Okay?" Cam asked, looking into her eyes.

"I'm not sure 'okay' is the best word to describe this, but it's nice."

"Good." She reached up and brushed her thumb across Jackie's lips. "If anything doesn't feel nice, tell me."

"I will," Jackie whispered.

Cam gave a satisfied nod then returned her attention to Jackie's breasts. She brought her mouth to the nipple again, this time circling it with her warm tongue.

Jackie's hands flew to Cam's shoulders and dug into the fabric of her shirt. Cam hummed against her skin before taking Jackie's entire breast into her mouth, sucking and licking with abandon.

Jackie's breath caught and she felt like she might combust any second. When Cam switched to her other breast, she barely contained a shout. She clutched at Cam's shirt even harder, and Cam pulled away, leaving the tips of her breasts glistening in the dim lamplight.

Cam's breathing was as ragged as Jackie's as she regarded her. Jackie trailed a trembling finger down Cam's shirt collar. "Can we take yours off too?"

Her voice had sounded more shy than seductive, even to her own ears, but Cam didn't laugh at her. Instead, she quickly stripped off her shirt, sports bra, pants, and boxers.

Jackie didn't have long to contemplate Cam's tan skin or angular body before Cam's arms were around her and gently lowering her onto the bed.

Her entire body buzzed with excitement as Cam settled against her, skin against hot skin with Cam's thigh nestling between Jackie's legs.

Whoa.

For a second, Jackie forgot how to breathe. The sensation of being wrapped around a woman's body was entirely new. Entirely different. It was thrilling and unexpected.

She widened her legs, and Cam's thigh pressed deeper against her aching center, making them both groan. Cam brought their mouths together for a fiery kiss and, this time, Jackie immediately parted her lips to welcome Cam's tongue inside.

Jackie ran her hands up and down the incredibly smooth skin of Cam's back, and broke the kiss. "Cam, I need you to touch me. Please."

Fire ignited in Cam's eyes when she looked at her, but she didn't speak. She sat up and reached for Jackie's panties. Her long, slender fingers ran appreciatively over the lacy fabric, and Jackie's hips jerked at the contact. That made Cam smirk before she hooked her thumbs in the waistband of the panties and slid them down her legs.

Cam lay down beside her, and propped herself up on her elbow before leaning over to kiss her. As their lips met, Cam slid her hand over Jackie's belly and down to her short, damp curls. Jackie whimpered into Cam's mouth when Cam's fingers stroked her folds and found her clit. Expertly, she began massaging it between two fingers, and Jackie cried out.

Groaning, Cam brought her lips to Jackie's neck and kissed her skin. Her hand slid even lower, and she circled Jackie's entrance with her index finger.

"Yesss," was all Jackie could manage, but it was enough because Cam promptly slipped her finger inside, and Jackie's entire body gave a jolt. Cam added another finger or perhaps two and began to stroke her in earnest.

Jackie trembled at the onslaught, and Cam raised up to watch her face.

"Yes. More. Cam! Please!"

Cam added another finger while increasing the speed of her thrusts, and Jackie's hips met her rhythm. Her hands clutched at Cam's now sweaty back as they moved against one another.

Cam's hand moved faster, and her palm hit Jackie's clit making her see stars.

"Ohh," she moaned and her body began to quiver uncontrollably.

Cam continued stroking, even harder, prolonging the wild sensations exploding all through Jackie.

She released one last shaky cry then collapsed back onto the bed. *Wow.*

Whatever she'd been expecting, whatever she'd thought about, wondered about, questioned in quiet instances here and there over the years—this encounter had exceeded it all.

Life returned to her limbs as Cam slowly withdrew her fingers and caused one last tremor to slither through her.

Cam smiled down at her and brought her lips to Jackie's cheek. "That was the hottest thing I've ever seen," she murmured.

Jackie was fairly certain Cam saw things like this on the regular. She must. She was way too good. But it was nice to hear nonetheless.

They lay there tangled together for a few minutes, Cam giving her the silence and time to recover. Although her hips were rubbing against Jackie's leg the slightest bit, as if she were unconsciously seeking some friction.

Curiosity and arousal reawakened, and Jackie shifted so her leg pressed into the prickly hair between Cam's leg. She drew in a sharp breath at the heat and wetness that greeted her.

Cam's eyes squeezed shut at the contact. "Jackie…"

The raw need in Cam's voice sent Jackie's pulse skyrocketing. She pulled Cam closer until she lay on top of her. Cam straddled her leg, braced herself over Jackie, and began to grind against her. The feel of Cam's hot, wet center on her leg, the sound of her rhythmic pants, and the sight of Cam losing herself in pleasure—all while those fathomless dark eyes bore into her own—ignited her desire anew. By instinct, her hands clasped Cam's lean waist, urging her to move faster. Cam's movements grew increasingly erratic, and Jackie could feel her passion everywhere.

God. I'm going to…

Jackie's hands slipped around to Cam's ass and squeezed hard as she began to shake beneath Cam once again, and that seemed to push her over the edge too. Cam's eyes closed, and she croaked out Jackie's name before collapsing on top of her. For a second, both of their bodies trembled simultaneously before they finally grew still.

As her breath slowed, Cam pressed a kiss to Jackie's neck and slowly rolled off her. A chill shot through Jackie at the loss of Cam's body, and it only spread as Cam shakily climbed off the bed.

Jackie gaped at Cam's long, lithe frame as she stood up. Was that it? Did Cam always end her one-night stands this abruptly? It was a far cry from the patience and attentiveness she'd shown at the beginning.

"W-what…" But Jackie didn't know how to finish the question. What was she expecting? Cuddling and brushing each other's hair? Cam was clearly done with her.

But no sooner than that thought had sunk in, Cam shot her a cheeky grin. "I don't know about you, but I could use some water before Round Two."

Jackie's jaw went slack, and she stared after Cam's very naked back as she strode toward the kitchen to get water.

Once Cam was out of sight, Jackie threw herself back on the bed and lay prone, limbs and everything in between still vibrating from two orgasms.

Round Two??

She'd thought her night of forgetting was ending too soon. Now she wondered if she'd even survive it!

4

Jackie's eyes fluttered open, and she stared at an unfamiliar ceiling. She squeezed her eyes shut and tried again. No. It still didn't look like her bedroom.

What in the world?

As she began to stir, she grimaced. Her body was sore in places it hadn't been for quite some time. Her eyes widened, and she bolted upright. The covers of the bed she was in were in complete shambles, strewn every which way all around her.

Jackie's face went hot.

Had she really gone home with a stranger…a strange *woman* and slept with her last night? What had she been thinking? Yes, she'd been upset about Rob walking out on her, but she'd had breakups before without taking leave of all her senses. Why now?

She threw herself back on the bed and drew in a long breath. A musky scent filled her nostrils, and her body tingled all over.

Cam.

Cam was the reason she'd taken leave of her senses. The woman was obviously some kind of butch Casanova, using a disarming mixture of friendliness, humor, and confusing sex appeal to play off Jackie's vulnerability and get her into bed.

Jackie sat up again and looked around. Where was Cam? Now that their night was over, had she left Jackie to show herself out while she went on the prowl for another victim?

After fuming for a few minutes, she finally shook off the thought. Jackie was no victim. Cam might be a player, but Jackie had been a *very* willing participant in the game. Her heartrate sped up as memories flitted through her brain. It had been so hot.

Possibly the hottest sex she'd ever had.

What was that all about? Was it the excitement of getting it on with a stranger? Or maybe the novelty of being with a woman? Other possibilities sprang to mind, and Jackie swallowed. She was so not prepared to explore them right now.

Stretching, she climbed to her feet and began searching the room for her dress, but the first thing she spotted was a bathrobe neatly folded on the end of the bed. Was that for her? She may as well borrow it for a minute. Cam was gone, and Jackie may have abandoned all logic and shame the night before, but in the sobering light of day, she didn't fancy finding the bathroom and washing her face while naked.

Once she was wrapped in the soft, plush robe, she made her way to the adjoining bathroom and was surprised to find a toothbrush still in its package, some toothpaste, and a few other toiletries set out for her to use.

Cam was considerate of her flings. Jackie would give her that.

After she'd washed up, she located her dress and was getting ready to change when she heard a clanging sound.

Hurrying to the bedroom door, she flung it open. A rich, savory smell greeted her. She stepped into the living room, which shared an open floor plan with the kitchen and gaped.

Cam was standing over the stove with her back to Jackie and cooking something in a skillet. She wore a t-shirt and a pair of shorts that looked loose enough to be comfortable but short enough to show off her long, shapely legs.

Jackie shook her head at herself and cleared her throat. "Good morning."

Cam started and spun around, nearly knocking over her pan in the process. "Oh, hi. I didn't know you were up."

"I haven't been for long. I'm sorry I startled you."

Cam was wearing dark-rimmed glasses now, giving her a serious, nerdy vibe that hadn't been present the night before. Her eyes lingered on the V-neck of Jackie's robe for half a second, but she soon jerked her gaze upward. "No, you didn't. Or, maybe you did, but it's fine. I was in my own world, but that wasn't your fault. Uh, breakfast?"

Jackie smiled at her rambling. "I don't want to intrude on your Saturday morning."

"You're not, and I have plenty of food."

"All right, thanks."

"Do you have any food allergies?"

"No, I don't." Jackie fidgeted with the tie of the bathrobe. "Do you want me to set the table?"

"Yeah, thanks," Cam said without looking at her. "The plates are in the cabinet, and there's juice in the fridge and some coffee brewing."

Jackie sat at the small table, and Cam set down two plates, each with a massive omelet, toast, and a small serving of fresh fruit on it. Jackie's eyes widened. "This looks amazing. You really didn't have to go to all this trouble."

She nodded but didn't meet Jackie's eyes. "It was no trouble. I like to cook."

"I'm excited to try it." Jackie studied her with curiosity. Then she added, "I seem to have worked up an appetite."

Cam fumbled her coffee spoon. It was hard to tell with her tan complexion, but Jackie thought she was actually blushing. That was a surprise.

"Jackie, look. I'm really sorry about last night."

She regretted it? For some reason, that made Jackie's stomach drop. "Sorry for what, exactly?"

Cam lowered her eyes and looked stricken. "You'd been drinking and you were upset when you agreed to come home with me. If I took advantage of you…"

"No! You didn't," Jackie rushed to assure her. "I wasn't drunk. You saw me. I only nursed one drink the entire time we talked."

"And before Manure Brain showed up?"

Jackie snorted at the epithet for Rob then covered her mouth. She never snorted! "I didn't drink before that either. All I had was seltzer water. I was expecting us to go to a nice dinner with wine, and I didn't want to be buzzed. I'm not blaming alcohol for my—"

She didn't really want to say *bad decisions*. It felt unnecessarily rude. "For my unusual choices last night. And, yes, I was upset, but I also wanted to forget for one night. I was responsible for my own actions."

"Okay, good." Cam's tense facial muscles relaxed, and she dug into her breakfast.

Jackie took a bite of the perfectly cooked ham and cheese omelet and almost moaned. "Hey, this is delicious!"

Cam sat up straighter. "Really?"

"Absolutely. Much better than my usual breakfast. I'm always in a hurry to get to school, so I only get coffee on the way or maybe a cranberry scone, if I have time."

"Cranberry?" Cam's face scrunched up into a comical grimace.

"What? You don't like it?"

Cam shrugged. "I've never had a cranberry scone. Why would I when blueberry is right there?"

"Well, you should. Trying new flavors can be fun."

"That's what she said," Cam mumbled.

Jackie's head shot up and their eyes met for several seconds before they both burst out laughing. Jackie couldn't remember when she'd been able to laugh at herself like this so much. It was freeing.

As they went back to eating, Cam asked, "Does the teaching really keep you so busy that you don't even have time for breakfast in the mornings?"

"During the school year, yes. My dad would say that's why I can't hold onto a man. He says no potential husband would want to come second to a bunch of brats."

Cam's mouth dropped open. "He really says that? I mean, sincerely? His daughter has an important career that matters to society, and he says things like that about it?"

Jackie smiled. Cam's words were nice, and her shock was telling. Jackie was so used to that kind of talk from her father that she didn't even consider what it might sound like to an outsider.

They continued eating in easy silence until they'd finished. Jackie put down her utensils and dabbed at the corners of her mouth. "That really was scrumptious."

"Thanks," Cam said, looking down and fidgeting with her glasses.

Her embarrassment over the small compliment made Jackie mentally scratch her head. This woman didn't seem like such a butch Casanova after all. Had she misjudged her?

She started to blurt out, 'Are you always like this?' but at the last minute, she changed it to, "Do you always cook such an elaborate breakfast for your one-night stands?"

Cam's cheeks colored, and she took a long swallow of her coffee before saying, "I've never really had a one-night stand before. I don't know what the protocol is."

"What?" Jackie set her own coffee cup down with a thud.

"Yeah, it's not my thing. I tried it once after I broke up with my college girlfriend, but that turned into a three-month rebound relationship instead. I don't recommend that, by the way."

Jackie took several minutes to process the new information. "So…were you the one who had too much to drink last night?"

"I wasn't drunk. I was angry." Cam released a heavy sigh. "I don't normally do the bar scene, but my coworker dragged me out last night to cheer me up after I'd been passed over for a promotion at work yesterday. The designer that got the spot hasn't been there as long as I have, and in my opinion, his work quality shows it. But the boss likes him better."

"Ugh. I'm sorry, Cam."

"It's fine. Or now I see that it *will be* fine, but I was really upset last night. After my friend left, I was getting ready to leave too when I saw what happened with you and your ex. And…I don't know." Cam shrugged. "I guess watching this mediocre guy walk out on a beautiful, considerate woman made me angry all over again, so I came over and talked to you when I ordinarily wouldn't have done something like that."

Jackie chuckled. "I guess we were both acting out of character last night." Admittedly, by sleeping with someone of the same sex when she was straight, Jackie probably took the prize for most out of character, but that was a topic for later reflection.

"It did make me forget for a while," Jackie mused. "I guess I should thank you for that."

"My pleasure." Cam's gaze met hers, and Jackie thought a trace of the fire from the night before flashed through Cam's eyes, but it soon faded into a kind smile. "I know it will be hard for a while: getting over the breakup and your lost plans, but things will get better, Jackie. I know it."

Jackie's insides warmed. "Thanks for saying that. And they will for you too. With your job, I mean. I'm sure your work will get noticed sooner or later. Maybe you can spend time reconnecting with other things you're passionate about in the meantime."

Cam was silent for so long that Jackie covered her face. "Sorry. It's an occupational hazard. As a teacher, I sometimes delve into annoying motivational speaker territory now and then."

"It's not annoying. It's nice. Thank you." Cam sent her a shy grin before getting up to clear the table.

When Jackie moved to help, Cam protested. "That's not necessary.

You're a guest."

"No, I insist. You made a beautiful meal. The least I can do before I leave is help with the dishes."

Cam didn't argue anymore, so they washed up and straightened the kitchen.

Working together made the task go faster, and Jackie found herself sorry about that fact. For reasons she couldn't grasp, Jackie wished she could prolong her stay a bit longer. Maybe it was because she didn't understand how one-night stands worked, or maybe she was enjoying the distraction from Rob and the breakup.

Whatever the case, Jackie knew she shouldn't take up any more of Cam's Saturday, so she accepted her gracious offer to use the shower, quickly cleaned up, and said goodbye.

Chances were, she would never see Camryn Durant again, but Jackie had a feeling she wouldn't forget her anytime soon.

5

Cam stared at her computer screen on Monday morning, seeing but not seeing the colorful image in front of her. For at least the hundredth time since Saturday morning, her thoughts were replaying the events from Friday night.

In some ways, it felt like she was watching someone else in her memory. The Cam in those moving pictures was confident, laid back, yet passionate—all things Everyday Cam wasn't.

It was unbelievable what a combination of pent-up frustration and some recklessness could lead to with the right partner. And Jackie had been the right partner that night. That was for sure.

A shiver ran through Cam the way it had every time she'd thought of Jackie. That woman was something: gorgeous, sexy, and so responsive in bed. It had been ages since Cam had experienced a night that hot.

Absently, Cam picked up her coffee and took a sip. She grimaced. It had already begun to cool as she sat here daydreaming. When she set the cup down, her thoughts turned to Saturday morning. Jackie had been funny and sweet during breakfast. Easy to talk to as well.

Cam sighed. What would it be like to have a girlfriend like that?

Oh no. We're not going down that road!

Cam glared at her dark, distorted reflection in the computer screen, which had gone blank thanks to inactivity.

Why couldn't she enjoy the memory for what it was instead of wishing for more? What was the point in dreaming? Hadn't she learned her lesson about that a long time ago? Friday night had been an open and shut thing, which both she and Jackie had enjoyed before parting on good terms.

"With all due respect, I think you made a huge mistake!" Britt declared as she marched into Cam's office.

Cam jumped at the interruption. "What? No! It was only a little fun between two consenting adults who—" She stopped talking when Britt's eyes went wide. "Wait, what are you talking about?"

"I was giving you a good opening for when you go to Logan to protest his bad decision about picking Finn over you." Britt arched her eyebrows. "What were *you* talking about?"

Heat surged to Cam's cheeks. Thanks to Jackie and Friday night, she'd almost forgotten about the promotion. She had done as much temporary forgetting as Jackie had.

Cam repositioned her glasses and focused on Britt. "I'm not protesting anything. Logan made his decision and that's that. Another opportunity will come up if I'm patient and keep putting in the work."

A skeptical frown crossed Britt's face, but she finally held up her hands. "Okay, okay. It's your life. But I hate seeing you go underappreciated."

"Thank you, Britt. You're the best."

"Yes, I know," Britt returned, making Cam laugh.

Britt walked closer and studied Cam. "You look much better than you did Friday night. That must have been a phenomenal e-book."

More heat returned to Cam's cheeks. "The weekend was fine. I decided to hang out at the bar for a while after you left and—"

Britt interrupted her with a strident squeal. "Oh my gosh. You had a hookup, didn't you?"

Cam cringed. "Geez! You wanna say that a little louder? I don't think the guys on the top floor could hear you."

"That's not a denial! You totally had a hookup. I love that for you!" She walked around Cam's desk and squeezed her shoulders.

Britt was acting like Cam had won big at a casino. She'd never actually gambled, but Cam couldn't imagine the euphoria of winning being any better than watching Jackie come apar—

"Look at you, you're glowing!" Britt yelped.

Cam's phone alarm went off then, reminding her of an upcoming team meeting, and she silenced it with relief. "As much as I hate to end this fascinating conversation, I have to go do actual work stuff."

"Okay, fine," Britt said with a huff. "But I want some details later."

"You have a dirty mind, Britt Patel," Cam told her with an affectionate smile as she gently pushed her out the office door and hurried down the hall to her meeting.

She took her place at the conference table and immediately regretted not refilling her coffee. The meeting promised to be long and drawn-out, and Cam had no idea how she could face it without fuel.

As discussions on the latest advertising campaign began, her attention kept wondering until she was looking at the clear blue sky out the window more than she was at her coworkers or the large computer screen at the head of the table.

What's wrong with me?

Normally, it was easy to stay engaged, especially when they were working on a campaign that used one of her design concepts like they were today. Logan tended to lean on her designs more than on anyone else's in the department. It was one of the many reasons she'd been expecting that promotion.

But it hadn't been enough. That was probably why she couldn't focus today.

Despite the reassurances she'd given Britt, the disappointment of losing the promotion weighed in the pit of her stomach like a bucket of molasses. The work she'd poured into her projects hadn't been good enough for Logan, and that thought was making it difficult to muster enthusiasm for doing more.

Cam didn't want to sulk, but neither could she find it in her to care about the tasks in front of her. She'd do what was expected, of course, but she'd have to find a way to stay focused until the sting of discouragement passed.

As she continued to gaze out the window, her thoughts drifted back to Jackie. This time, she pictured her at the breakfast table, wrapped snug in Cam's spare robe. It had looked much better on Jackie than it had on Cam. But even more than that mental image, Cam's mind snagged on Jackie's kind, pretty smile as she'd said, "I'm sure your work will get noticed sooner or later. Maybe you can spend time reconnecting with other things you're passionate about in the meantime."

Maybe Jackie was right.

When the meeting was finally over, Cam hurried to her office and grabbed her cellphone.

The phone rang twice before her friend Wendy answered. "Hey,

Cam! It's been a while. What's up?"

"Not much. I was wondering if you could use some extra weekend help at the museum again."

Wendy laughed. "What brought that on? It's been two years since you volunteered."

Cam pictured the sprawling art museum where Wendy was assistant curator. Cam had volunteered there for several years, beginning when she'd first moved to the Dallas/Fort Worth area. She'd been so upset when Tina had dropped her that she'd given up on her plans of getting her Master of Fine Arts degree after college. But being around the delightfully eclectic mixture of contemporary and historical paintings and sculptures had filled a void in her life. Maybe it would again.

"Cam?" Wendy's voice cut into her musing. "Are you still there?"

"Yeah, Wendy. I'm here. I thought you might need extra help as the holidays approach. And…I don't know. I guess I could use a fresh outlook."

They agreed to meet later and discuss details, and Cam ended the call with a satisfied nod of her head. Maybe Britt had been right about her. For the second time in less than a week, Cam was stepping out and reaching for something she wanted, and it felt incredible.

6

Late Monday afternoon after school, Jackie slid behind the wheel of her sedan and let her head thump against the headrest instead of immediately starting the engine. Thank heavens the Thanksgiving break was only a few weeks away. She was exhausted. Too exhausted for it to only be the first day of the week.

Although she'd worked to put it out of her mind, here in the relative quiet of her car, she couldn't avoid the fact that some of her fatigue was a carryover from Friday night.

When she thought about the breakup, all she felt was numb. If asked, she would have said she was happy with Rob, but in retrospect, she didn't know what that meant. They'd seemed to have similar personalities and tastes. She'd thought they'd been on the same page about their future too. She'd poured a lot of energy into that relationship. But now, she wondered if she'd merely viewed all that work as an investment in the future, solidifying their commitment so they could build a life together rather than actually acting out of love for him. It was an uncomfortable possibility, but one she probably shouldn't ignore.

Ignoring it is easier though.

Forgetting was easier too. Not to mention fun.

Despite her best intentions, Jackie's thoughts swirled back to the *other reason* she was so tired today: her wild night with Cam. Now that a couple of days had passed, it all felt like a distant dream...a sexy dream, but still a dream. And maybe it was best it stayed that way. It wasn't like she'd ever do something like that again. So what if she'd enjoyed being with a woman? Cam had been such an attentive, passionate lover that Jackie imagined practically any woman would have appreciated it—straight or not. It didn't mean anything except that, after a night full of shattered dreams, Jackie had let go and enjoyed intimacy without thinking about the future or her goals or anything else but the pleasure of the moment.

Jackie's eyelids closed as she remembered. Cam's hands had been so gentle yet sure when she'd touched her, and her fingers had taken Jackie places she'd never remembered going before. Dear God, if she thought about it too long, she could feel herself getting—

Her cellphone started buzzing frantically from her purse, and Jackie sat up straight.

What was wrong with her? Fantasizing in her work parking lot? That wasn't like her at all.

She fumbled with her purse and pulled out her phone, groaning under her breath when she saw "Dad" on the screen. This couldn't be good. He never called. She dutifully called to check on him once every two weeks, particularly since his health had gotten bad, but he didn't call her.

Taking a deep breath, she answered the call. "Hello, Dad. How are you?"

"How do you think I am?" he demanded. "Do you know what Grady told me today?"

Jackie frowned. How could her dad expect her to know about the goings and comings of his longtime assistant? She and Grady were hardly friends. Much like her dad, the man had never seemed to approve of her. "No, what did he say?"

"He said he ran into Rob, who informed him that you two had ended the relationship."

Jackie rubbed her forehead. She'd been hoping to have more time before she had to break the news to him. "That's right. It didn't work out with us."

"Jacqueline, what is wrong with you? You're over thirty without so much as an engagement. How long do you intend to keep squandering your life like this? It's an embarrassment!"

"Dad, I-I wasn't the one to end things. I was committed. Rob decided to break it off," she stammered. "He said there was someone else."

Normally, she wouldn't expose the messy details to her dad like this, but as was often the case with him, she found herself on the defensive.

"Hmph. I'm not surprised he went looking somewhere else."

Jackie swallowed. Some delusional part of her had been hoping for a modicum of sympathy or even outrage at Rob's choosing someone else over her.

His sympathy was all for Rob, though. He drove that point home the longer he ranted. "He probably found a woman who gave a damn about him, instead of a frosty career woman who'd rather spend her time with snot-nosed kids instead of her partner."

The corners of her eyes began to burn, and she squeezed her eyes shut to avoid full-on tears. As she did, an image floated into her mind of sitting at Cam's breakfast table and mimicking her dad saying almost the exact same thing he'd just said. Cam had responded with kindness but not pity. The memory calmed her somehow, and she managed to be detached enough to keep listening without an outburst.

"I swear, Jaqueline," his tone was still angry, but it was getting thin, like he was wearing himself out and getting slightly disoriented. "Some days you're exactly like your mother. Flighty and unreliable!"

Jackie's mouth dropped open. Although she'd never known her mother, who had died shortly after Jackie had been born, everything she'd ever heard suggested Florence Webster had been a dutiful wife of seventeen years and a good mother to Jackie's brother Conrad, who was fifteen years older than Jackie. "What does that mean?"

He paused for a second then barked, "Never mind! The point is this is a major disappointment. I thought you were finally settling down. But not now. And you're timing is terrible. You know your brother has a fundraiser luncheon this weekend, and the whole family was meant to be there. I hope you don't plan on showing up now that you're single again!"

Clutching the phone hard, Jackie worked to keep her voice steady. "No, Dad. I don't."

Truthfully, she *had* intended to go to the luncheon with or without Rob. She'd been attending public events like this since she was a child, when her dad was the politician instead of her brother. They were always stressful, and she felt like she had to be *on* every second, but they were also rare instances of family togetherness. Like, for a little while, she, her father, her brother—and later her brother's wife—were all working together for the same goal, even if the goal was following runaway ambitions and contriving the perfect family image.

But now her father was all but ordering her not to attend. It hurt, but she was still committed to holding onto her composure. "Besides, I have plans this weekend. I need to start organizing a field trip for my class for after Thanksgiving break."

"Yes, I'm sure you do," he said with cold sarcasm.

"I have to go now, Dad. I'm…sorry you're disappointed. I'll talk to you later."

Surprisingly, her dad let her end the call like that. She suspected he'd worn himself out with his ire. His declining health had brought changes to his temperament and his energy levels. While he'd never been particularly affectionate with her when she was younger, he'd recently become blunter in his criticisms and generally more irritable. But the storms never lasted long because he also was easily fatigued.

Jackie tried to be understanding with her father because of his health problems even knowing, deep down, that she couldn't console herself after one of his tirades by saying, "He didn't mean it." If he were healthy, he'd prefer to express himself with the calmness and self-control he'd once prided himself on, but the sentiments would still be there: disappointment in her and anger at her failures.

Whatever credits she'd built with him by being in a stable relationship, presumably headed toward marriage, were now destroyed. It was probably best he'd told her not to come to the luncheon. She couldn't have handled being around him in this state right now. His constant barbs about her showing up single and alone again would have been too much to take while she was still reeling from her own disappointment.

Out of nowhere, the tears she'd been holding back during the phone call began pouring out. For years, she'd done her best to respect and conform to her father's old-fashioned ideals of respectability while still being true enough to herself to pursue her own dreams too, like teaching. She was beginning to realize how exhausting that had been.

What would it be like to stop? Give up the perfection charade? How would she even do that?

For a moment, she imagined arriving at the luncheon with her family and all their associates there. Instead of coming alone, she was with a woman like Cam: warm, approachable, and unabashedly herself.

It would be the ultimate subversion of all her father's expectations for her. Even daydreaming about it felt liberating. True, her father and brother would probably disown her the second they saw her, but at least she'd be free. And she and Cam could leave and Cam would take her mind off it all by—*Stop!*

This silly fantasy was getting out of hand. It wasn't like she wanted to be with Cam or any other woman! It was only a wild thought about how different her life could be. That's all.

But it wasn't reality.

Reality was she would stay away from the luncheon to avoid disgracing her family with her spinsterhood. And that was perfectly fine. She really did want to explore a couple of field trip ideas for her kids. In fact, she was looking forward to it. She could focus on creating a good experience for her students and forget all about her family, her pathetic love life…and Cam.

7

Cam hadn't had time to reacclimate herself to the layout of the Woller Museum before her first volunteer shift began, but she was looking forward to doing that afterwards. As far as she could tell, some of her favorite paintings were still there along with new pieces the museum had collected since the last time she'd volunteered.

The museum was eclectic, boasting a large collection of paintings and sculptures whose dates ranged from several centuries ago all the way up to the present decade.

As her shift neared the end, she stood behind the information desk studying a paper map of the museum floorplan and making notes of the areas that had been moved or rearranged in recent years. Since part of her duties would include giving directions to museum visitors, she wanted to have all the details memorized as soon as possible.

Wendy approached her and smiled. The sixty-something-year-old assistant curator's face had a few more wrinkles since the last time Cam had seen her, but her blue gray eyes twinkled as brightly as ever. "You look every bit as enthusiastic about this as you did the first time you were here."

Her smile faded. "Wait, you're not here because some woman broke your heart again, are you?"

"What?" Cam asked, dropping her map.

"Well, a few months after you started volunteering here the first time, I remember your admitting this was your way of reconnecting with art after your college girlfriend dumped you. I was only wondering if a woman was to blame for this time too. Not that I'm complaining.

It's good to see you here again."

Cam shook her head. "There hasn't been any recent heartbreak, at least not where women are concerned."

"That's good to know. Are you dating someone, then?"

Cam frowned. Wendy always did like to gossip. "No, there's nobody right now, but thanks for asking."

She bent down to retrieve her map and hoped her answer would put a stop to Wendy's inquiries into her sad, nonexistent love life.

"Excuse me, are you Wendy Suarez? I talked to you on the phone earlier about arranging a field trip for my high school English class," a familiar voice said from the other side of the information counter.

Cam straightened so fast it made her dizzy. Jackie Webster was standing in front of the desk!

Wendy said, "Yes, I'm Wendy." But Jackie wasn't paying attention. She was staring at Cam, probably frightened after seeing her spring up like a mole in a whack-a-mole game.

"Cam!" Jackie said, her mouth agape.

"Jackie. Uh…hi." It was all she could think to say. Was her face turning red? Why was she crumbling up the map in her sweaty palms?

"Hi," Jackie finally replied. "I didn't know you worked here."

"I don't. That is, I'm a volunteer. But it's recent. You know how you talked about exploring my passion the other day?" The map crackled in her hand as she squeezed it tighter. That hadn't come out right.

Jackie flushed. "Oh right. I-I'm glad you took it to heart."

Wendy cleared her throat. She raised one eyebrow at Cam and then returned her focus to Jackie. "We already penciled you into our calendar for next month, Ms. Webster, as we discussed on the phone. I have a couple of forms for you to complete, but you can take them home and mail them back to us, if you'd like."

Jackie's gaze snapped to Wendy. "Okay. Thank you. I was hoping to take a look around today too and maybe see the room where the Hilda Spaulding letters will be displayed."

"Of course!" Wendy said. "Let me get you those forms and then I can show you around."

She reached under the counter for the forms. Cam willed herself to stop looking at Jackie and do literally anything else, but she couldn't.

Damn, she looked pretty today. She was dressed in slacks and a simple blouse instead of the dress she'd worn the previous weekend, but she wore it with elegance. Her lovely red hair was pulled up in a loose bun, and a few loose strands caressed her cheeks the way Cam's fingers had that night.

Stop it!

Cam needed to get a grip and move on to something else right now. She looked down at her poor crumpled map and started straightening it back out.

"Oh shoot!" Wendy said, with a suspiciously dramatic slap to her forehead. "I forgot I have a video call with a patron in a few minutes, Ms. Webster, but here are your forms."

Wendy thrust the papers into Jackie's hands. "Cam will be more than happy to show you around the museum instead."

Cam gulped. "But, uh, Wendy. This is my first day. I can't—"

"Don't be silly. You were a volunteer for nine years the last time. You know your way around well enough. Now be a good sport and help me out. I have to go!" She turned until only Cam could see her and winked before mouthing, "You're welcome."

With that, she strolled away, leaving Cam and Jackie alone.

Jackie met her eyes for a moment then looked away. "You don't have to show me around, if you're busy."

Cam hesitated. Did Jackie want her to say she was busy so she could escape? She swallowed. Honesty was the best policy, wasn't it? "I'm not busy."

"Oh. You're not?" Jackie looked at her again.

"No. In fact, my shift is ending. I can escort you around, if you'd like. It might take me a minute to get reoriented, but I'm happy to help."

Jackie's smile looked relieved as she nodded. "Okay, thanks."

Cam stepped out from behind the desk and gestured toward the main gallery hall. "Shall we?"

As Jackie fell into step beside her, Cam glanced at her wrinkled map. "Which exhibit did you say you were planning to bring your students to?"

"The Hilda Spaulding Letters collection that starts next month."

"Right," Cam said with a shaky nod. "That will be in Exhibit Hall B, which is down this way."

They walked in silence.

Jackie turned toward her as if about to say something, so Cam slowed her steps. But right before she came to a full stop, Jackie faced forward again and picked up her pace.

This was awful!

Why hadn't Cam taken the out when Jackie had given it to her and left? Jackie was clearly uncomfortable and had no desire to interact, but now they were both stuck.

As they entered the exhibition hall, Cam resolved to behave professionally and end the tour as quickly as possible.

"Here we are," she gestured at the space. "As you can see, it's a good size to accommodate group tours."

Jackie didn't respond as she walked around the perimeter of the room, which was currently empty of visitors, and glanced at the temporary exhibits on display.

Cam made a last-ditch effort at conversation. "I was surprised when I heard Wolly was getting this letter collection."

"Wolly?" Jackie asked, still not looking at her fully.

"The museum. We call it Wolly for short."

That brought a smirk to Jackie's lips. "Oh, I see. But why were you surprised?"

"A famous author's letter collection is fascinating, of course, but I guess I don't see how relevant it is to a museum that mostly features visual exhibits like watercolors and sculptures."

Jackie's face lit up. "Ah, but you see, she was an amateur artist too. That is, she'd often make sketches of the characters and settings in her novels. But not only that, she'd send letters with drawings to her friends. Sometimes she'd share the story sketches, and sometimes she'd send other drawings: little jokes and caricatures, doodles of her flower garden and cats. That sort of thing."

The sight of Jackie's growing enthusiasm warmed Cam. "I see. The letter collection was gathered from the friends she'd corresponded with?"

"Yes," Jackie affirmed, "and a few lovers too."

Cam's palms started sweating again. *Come on, Cam, focus.* "Interesting. So you're bringing your students here to see the letters."

"That's right. I thought it might resonate with them. The way she sent letters and images back and forth with her friends, boyfriends, and girlfriends—"

"It's like the way people nowadays text and send memes!" Cam said with a grin.

"Exactly!" Jackie laughed. "I thought it might be fun for them." She dropped her gaze. "But I don't know. It's probably silly."

"It's not silly. I think it's great!" Cam argued. "You clearly put a lot of thought into helping them enjoy learning. That's incredible!"

Jackie returned Cam's smile. "Thank you."

They fell silent and looked at each other until Cam glanced away. "Okay, well. You've seen the space. Do you want to take a look around the rest of the museum too? See if there's anything else you want to show the kids?"

Jackie's eyes scanned the museum outside the exhibition room, before her focus returned to Cam. "I'd like that. If you're sure you don't mind."

"Not at all. Like I said, I have to refamiliarize myself with the layout anyway."

She gestured Jackie to go ahead of her as they exited the room.

The first exhibit outside the room was a large display of Pueblo pottery. Cam's heartrate picked up. "Ooh. This is new!"

The pottery appeared to be arranged chronologically, beginning with a few ceramics labeled with dates in the 14th Century and ending with some blackware pottery created by a Pueblo artist in the 1930s.

Cam looked up to see Jackie admiring the striking geometric patterns of a bowl.

"Beautiful," Jackie murmured. Then she looked at Cam and indicated one of the oldest pieces. "I assume these were archaeological finds. Do you know how they..."

"How they what?" Cam asked, turning to face Jackie fully.

Jackie stroked her chin. "Maybe it's naïve of me, but do you know if the museum came by them, um, ethically? I know so much of this process can be exploitative to the peoples the artifacts actually belong to."

"That's a great question." Cam took a step closer. "Wendy and Morris, the curators, you know, are very fastidious where that's concerned. They wouldn't directly get something from an unethical source, although the whole provenance of pieces this old can be more complicated, as I'm sure you can understand. In the 90s, in particular, there was a huge black market for Pueblo pottery, but the authorities became more vigilant in enforcing federal protections of Native American sites and artifacts to help with that."

Cam's attention returned to the displays, and she traced her fingers along the information cards in front of them. "It's remarkable, isn't it?

This is only a tiny cross section of the art these people have produced over the centuries, but it still tells such a powerful story. You see the shifting techniques and styles, and you can feel the imprint of the events that shaped the artisans throughout the generations: migration, conflict, the inevitable influence of the colonizers, birth, death, and rebirth.

She stopped in front of the newest piece, studying the pottery first and then the black and white photograph of the artist beside it. "Most importantly, it shows resilience."

"It does," a soft voice beside her agreed.

Cam's attention darted to Jackie who was standing closer than Cam had realized. Her face grew hot. "Sorry. I didn't mean to nerd out. It's just been a while since I've been around all this, and it's invigorating."

"Don't apologize. I'm glad for you, really," Jackie said, her tone sincere.

"Thanks." She stood taller. "Okay, are you ready to see the rest?"

"Definitely!"

They made their way through the exhibits, and even though Cam managed not to give any more lectures, the tour still took time. That was partly because Cam was still figuring out the museum layout, but it was also because they would stop to discuss various pieces.

While Jackie claimed she was no expert in art, she clearly had the education or, perhaps, upbringing to give her an informed appreciation of it. Plus, she had a natural curiosity and keen eye for aesthetics in general.

By the time the tour was over, almost two hours had passed without Cam even realizing it. Even more shocking, she was no longer thinking about what had happened between her and Jackie only a week ago. It wasn't until they exited the museum together that the initial awkwardness from earlier that day returned.

Dusk was beginning to set in as they stood outside the building's glass doors and faced each other, neither of them speaking. A light fall breeze played with the loose strands of Jackie's hair, and Cam struggled not to fixate on the sight. She shoved her hands in the pockets of her jacket. "I hope you got everything you needed to plan a great field trip for your students."

"Definitely. I really appreciate your help. And I'll fill out the forms Wendy gave me and send them back right away."

"Sounds good." Cam's fingers flexed in her pockets. What were they supposed to do now? Shake hands? Hug? Exchange air kisses? More importantly, were they really going to bring this day to a close without talking about…it?

Cam sighed. What was there to talk about? They were two people who'd had a one-night stand and then happened to run into each other again. It was time to move on.

She looked at her watch without actually comprehending the numbers. "Wow. It's getting late. I'm sure you're ready to go home."

Jackie took a half step closer. "Cam, do you want to get coffee with me?"

"Coffee?" Cam repeated like an obnoxious parrot.

"Yeah, or tea or hot chocolate or whatever you'd like. I think there's a coffee shop a couple of blocks away."

"Sure," Cam agreed before she could take the time to decide if it was a good idea or not. It probably wasn't, but something inside her rebelled at the idea of saying goodbye.

8

Now what am I doing?

Jackie stood beside Cam and tilted her head back to read the menu board at the coffee shop, but her brain wasn't processing the words. Part of her mind was preoccupied with wondering what in the world it was about Camryn Durant that made her act on sheer impulse every time she saw her. The other part was still reeling from the fact that she'd run into Cam again. It was the absolute last thing she'd expected when she'd left her house this morning. But here they were.

Long, warm fingers suddenly came to rest on Jackie's arm, and her skin prickled even though she was wearing a coat. She looked into Cam's dark eyes. No glasses today. Maybe she only wore those at home. They'd been cute on her, but now Jackie could see her rich, brown irises better.

"Do you know what you want?" Cam asked.

I have no clue.

Jackie blinked. Oh, her coffee order! She'd been stuck in her distracted state so long, she hadn't even noticed that Cam had already ordered. Tearing her gaze away from Cam, she noticed the barista was patiently waiting for her to get with the program. "I'm sorry."

She approached the counter and gave a sheepish smile. The barista, who wore a nametag that read "Shiloh Toole, Owner" along with a "They/Them" pronoun pin, appeared amused by Jackie's obvious distracted state. "Looks like someone could use a late afternoon caffeine fix!"

"Indeed," Jackie said with a chuckle. "I'll take a French vanilla latte, please."

"Coming right up," they said, accepting Jackie's payment then hurrying away.

While Jackie waited for the drinks, Cam excused herself to go to the restroom. She watched Cam walk away. Her stride was poised and relaxed, but Jackie still couldn't help worrying she'd made Cam uncomfortable by suggesting they get coffee.

She had surprised herself by asking, but when Cam agreed, she'd been relieved. The afternoon had taken such a strange turn. Her interactions with Cam after the first shock had worn off had been painfully awkward. All she'd been able to think about was how badly she wanted to run out of the museum and never look back. Judging by Cam's nervous energy, Jackie was certain Cam had been every bit as uncomfortable as she was. She probably would have been relieved to see Jackie go. But Jackie had stayed put. Running away would have been rude and immature.

Then something had shifted as they toured the museum.

As they'd talked about the Hilda Spaulding letters, they'd started to regain the ease of conversation that had been present when they'd first met at the bar and again at breakfast the next morning.

There was no denying it now; when she stepped back from the embarrassment and confusion over sleeping with her, Jackie found talking to Cam relaxing and enjoyable. She had an aura of tranquility and kindness that appealed to Jackie. And today, Jackie had gotten a good look at Cam's intelligence and passion for the subjects that interested her.

Jackie had been captivated watching and listening while Cam discussed the Pueblo pottery exhibit. She suspected the topic was personal for Cam because she herself was Indigenous, but she hadn't wanted to be insensitive by asking too many personal questions. It hadn't stopped Jackie from being curious, though. She wanted to know more about Cam.

Shiloh called out Jackie's name, and she took the drinks with thanks before finding a small table in the corner of the shop. As she set the drinks down, she frowned. Cam had been gone for several minutes now. Was she sick? Or had she escaped out the back door?

As Jackie looked around the coffee shop, she started to really examine it for the first time since coming in. The furniture was simple but cozy, and the walls were adorned with colorful abstract paintings with tags that suggested they were created by local artists and were for sale.

Oh.

No wonder Cam was taking so long coming back. She'd probably spotted an interesting painting in the bathroom and was analyzing the artist's bold use of color or something.

Jackie was taking her first sip of latte when Cam appeared and sat down opposite her. "Sorry to keep you waiting. There was some cool local art on display back there, and I got distracted."

Jackie grinned into her cup.

"What's so funny?" Cam asked.

"Nothing." Jackie slid Cam's herbal tea across the table to her. She accepted it and took a sip.

She watched as Cam closed her eyes to savor the drink. She had an earnest, unaffected way of enjoying things: food, art, and…other pleasures.

Jackie gave herself a slight shake and sat up straighter. "Thank you again for showing me around the museum. I know it must have been unexpected and awkward for you."

Cam took another sip of her drink without answering. She appeared thoughtful. Finally, she set the cup down. "Definitely unexpected. Okay, and awkward too, at first. But honestly, as we got to talking, the discomfort went away. At least for me."

Relief rushed through Jackie. "For me too," she said. "In fact, it was really nice exploring the art and talking with you."

"It was," Cam agreed.

They continued enjoying their beverages in companionable silence, but Jackie wasn't completely at ease. An inexplicable longing had begun churning inside her chest as they'd walked and talked together in the museum. Although she didn't fully understand it, it had been pressing enough to prompt her to ask Cam to have coffee. Now that they were here, that vague longing had solidified into a question.

"Do you want to exchange numbers?" Jackie blurted out.

Cam blinked twice before a confused frown crossed her face. "You're asking for my number? I don't think that's how one-night stands work."

"No, not to sleep together again!" Jackie said. Then she flinched at how loudly it had come out. She glanced around the coffee shop and lowered her voice. "I'm asking if you want to stay in touch, but I don't mean it *like that*."

Gosh, she was making a mess of this. Why couldn't she have left well enough alone? A one-night stand and an unexpected but pleasant afternoon at a museum. Why did she have to drag Cam to this coffee shop and send her all these mixed signals? What was wrong with her?

"I'm sorry." Jackie stared down at the table.

"Jackie." Cam's low, soothing voice disrupted the downward spiral of her thoughts. "It's okay. Why don't you explain how you did mean it?"

Jackie looked up. Cam's expression was frank and inviting. Was it that simple? She sat up in her chair.

"Last Friday night was a one-time thing for obvious reasons. I was upset and you were right there, and I wanted to forget everything for the night. But that's not who I really am. I'm sorry if I made you feel used because of that."

"Hey, it's okay. I knew the score before and after," Cam assured her in a gentle tone. "And I was a very willing participant. I certainly don't feel used."

"Good. That's good." The tension in Jackie's shoulders receded. Then she drew in a breath. *Okay, on to the next part.* "But today was nice, as I said, and it got me to thinking, well…would you be interested in being friends?"

Cam brought her elbows to rest on the table and studied her, but she didn't say anything.

"Maybe that's a weird question," Jackie admitted. Of course it was. Her highschoolers all based their friendships around shared interests and activities. While she, a supposedly mature adult, was struggling to make friends with someone she'd slept with.

She hurried on. "It's just that I don't have that many friends that I really connect with. I don't really relate to a lot of the people I grew up with because we chose different paths. I have a few friends who are fellow teachers, but most of them are married with children, so we don't get together often."

Wow. Can I sound any more pathetic? Is that all I care about? Meeting a friendship quota?

"I don't want it to be one-sided, though," Jackie rambled on. She sent Cam a nervous smile. "If we hung out, I could encourage you to keep pursuing your interests, like the museum, and I think I'm a fairly decent listener. Also, I enjoy baking now and then, so if you like—"

"Whoa, whoa, wait a minute!" Cam held up her palm in a stop gesture. "You don't need to fill out a friendship application, Jackie. The fact that we enjoy hanging out is good enough."

"Is it?" Jackie asked with a hard swallow.

"Sure," Cam said. "But do you really think we can be friends after...what happened? Are you able to do that?"

Jackie chewed her lip. "I think so. That is, it might take a little time to get into the friendship rhythm. A little time and distance, so I can forget we saw each other naked."

Cam nearly spit out the tea she'd just sipped. Her cheeks went red.

Jackie fought to hide a smile. It was fun to see Cam get flustered. *Fun.*

It was fun for Jackie, but probably not for Cam. In all likelihood, none of this sounded fun to Cam. Jackie sobered. "I don't want to be a nuisance, though. If this won't work for you, or if you're not interested in being friends, I completely understand."

Cam shook her head. "You're not a nuisance, Jackie. As it happens, I think we'd make great friends. Queer women can be friends with straight ones, you know."

"I know that!" Jackie said with a laugh, before giving Cam's arm a playful slap.

Cam grinned and pressed on. "We're also good at staying friends with women we once slept with. There usually isn't an overlap between those friends and the straight ones but..."

Jackie snorted. *Why do I keep doing that?* "Yeah. I suppose I'm sort of chaotic right now."

"Maybe a tad, but it's understandable." After a moment, Cam flashed a smile whose warmth filtered through Jackie better than Shiloh's coffee. "I don't see why we can't try."

Jackie returned the smile. This was refreshing. There was an openness and honesty in this conversation that she'd rarely experienced in the past, not with boyfriends, friends, or family most especially.

"So...friends?" Cam held out her hand, and she accepted it. The solid gentleness of Cam's hand felt nice as it enveloped hers.

"Friends," Jackie agreed. As she shook Cam's hand, their eyes met. Somewhere deep in her belly, that heat that had sparked to life between her and Cam a week ago was still present. But it was bound to dissipate in a few weeks.

9

Cam watched the chaos unfolding on her computer screen with a fond chuckle. She was in her apartment on a Sunday afternoon on a video call with her mom. Every few minutes, her seven-year-old nephew Cody would appear behind her mom as he chased her five-year-old niece Jo around the sofa where her mom was sitting. Then, a few minutes later, Cam's sister Mari would appear, chasing them both as she tried to get their shoes and coats on them so they could go home. Occasionally, Grandma's firm but gentle voice would trickle through the background as she called out commentary from her place in the kitchen.

Mari and her family were at Mama's house as much as they were at their own. Since Cam lived too far away to visit that often, it was soothing to watch and listen to the bustle of activity from the four generations of the Durant family, even if it was only on video.

Although Cam called her mom every Sunday and sometimes in between Sundays, she was especially craving the steady, familiar presence of her family today. With the lost promotion and the unexpected turn of events with Jackie the week before, Cam's life felt haphazard and confusing. As she sat and listened to Mama talk about her week, her mind settled a bit.

"But enough of that!" Mama declared. "How are you, my heart?"

Cam swallowed at the conversation's abrupt shift back to her. "I'm great," she said quickly. Too quickly. Mama would see through that.

Sure enough. Her mother didn't respond. She merely folded her arms and sent Cam a soft, knowing smile. Silence built around them for a few moments. The kids continued their sprints in the background, but Mama's wordless focus remained on Cam.

Finally, Cam gave in and blurted out everything about her lost promotion. She'd thought she was starting to get over it, but now that there was an opportunity to vent again, all the frustration and disappointment came flooding back.

Mama sighed. "I know that's not how you wanted things to go, but it'll be okay. You're young. You have plenty of time ahead of you to get what you want. What's the rush? You don't have to be reaching and struggling and climbing ladders all the time."

"It's not like I'm trying to take over the world or even the company, Mama! All I want is recognition for my hard work. Is that asking too much?" Cam demanded.

Mama's tone remained even and smooth. "I know you're upset, Camryn, but I promise your time will come if you're patient. I hate to see you so worked up. It's not good for you. There is more to life than work. Why don't you find some of the things that feed your soul and focus on those for now, hmm?"

"Well, believe it or not, I'm trying," Cam said. "I started volunteering at the museum again."

"Ah, you used to enjoy that so much. I don't know why you ever quit. But I'm glad you're back at it now. That was very wise of you."

"To be fair, I wanted to stew in my irritation some more," Cam admitted, "but a friend gave me similar advice."

"Was it Britt from your work? I like her."

Cam smiled. Mama had met Britt once when she'd visited Cam, and they'd gotten along well despite the fact that Mama was from a small town in Oklahoma and Britt had grown up in Long Island, New York in a successful family of Indian immigrants. "No, it wasn't Britt. It was…a new friend. I met her a couple of weeks ago."

"A fast friendship if she's already giving life advice!"

A nervous chuckle slipped from Cam. "Yeah. She's nice."

Mama went silent again, but this time, Cam didn't give into the subtle pressure to elaborate. Instead, she wiggled out of it with Mama's favorite distraction. "Are Cody and Jo almost ready for their Christmas break?"

Mama laughed. "It's all they talk about!"

Then she launched into a story about Jo's latest kindergarten antics. When Cam's mom ended the call so she could help Grandma in the kitchen, Cam drew in a deep breath and sank deeper into her sofa cushions. It had been nice to talk to Mama, as always, but it was also a relief to get off the call before the conversation had returned to the tricky topic of her new friendship.

Cam definitely hadn't been prepared to explain Jackie to her mom. Not that she completely understood everything herself. In the week since she and Jackie had talked at the coffee shop, Cam hadn't had much time to process the fact that they had agreed to be friends.

Cam shook her head then stood and shuffled to the kitchen to put on a kettle of water for tea.

Friends

If someone had told her a few weeks ago that she would become friends with a woman she'd had a one-night stand with, she would have called them a world-class joker. Although, to be fair, her credulity probably would have stopped at the one-night stand part. It so wasn't her style. But putting that aside, even in the abstract, she wouldn't think a friendship in these circumstances would be a great idea. It was one thing to be friends with an ex. That wasn't so unusual, but befriending someone when the extent of your interaction had been getting naked together was strange and implausible.

The tea kettle water started bubbling up right along with her churning emotions.

Why had she agreed to the friendship thing? This would never work! She and Jackie barely knew each other beyond the circumstances that had led them to hook up in the first place. And she had a feeling they didn't have much in common.

Once the kettle whistled, she took it off the stove and poured the steaming water over her favorite herbal tea blend. She inhaled deeply. The rich, floral fragrance of the tea was already having a calming effect.

As she sipped her tea, she admitted to herself that the short conversations with Jackie since their night together had been nice. They'd even talked openly about their lives.

"A fast friendship if she's already giving life advice," Mama had said. And Cam agreed. It was odd how Mama and Jackie had given similar advice about pursuing her passion instead of agonizing over her stagnant career.

She rubbed her chin. Maybe the friendship was doable after all.

It was only a friendship.

Contrary to what Mama thought, Cam wasn't in the habit of

reaching and struggling for the unattainable all the time.

She knew Jackie had just been having a bad time of things that night when they'd slept together, and there was no way in hell anything of a serious, romantic nature could come of it. But friendship? It was a possibility.

The more she thought of it, the more she began to look forward to getting to know Jackie better. Sure, she was attracted to Jackie. How couldn't she be? But that didn't matter. She had been attracted to female friends before. She'd dealt with it then, and she'd do it now. With any luck, the more she and Jackie got acquainted, the more the attraction would fade away.

10

The heels of Jackie's shoes clacked on the marble floor as she stepped inside the broad, sweeping foyer of her father's house on Thanksgiving Day. Even as an adult, the room, with its tall ceiling, enormous chandelier, and spiral staircase framed by an ornate wrought iron banister, made her feel tiny and insignificant. Part of her felt like shrinking inward the way she had when she'd been eight or nine right before Ms. Braxton, her nanny, would scold her for slouching.

On instinct, as if she could still hear the austere woman's harsh voice, Jackie straightened her shoulders and stood taller. In this house, she was Jacqueline Webster, the polished and pretty only daughter of former state senator Clive Webster.

Since he was the reason she'd arrived two hours early for the holiday dinner, she quickly put her overnight case in the guestroom that had once been her childhood bedroom then sought out her father in his study.

Unlike the rest of the house, which was well-luminated thanks to numerous windows and decorated in light colors—Jackie's mother's influence—her father's study was windowless with dark wood paneling. When she knocked and entered, he was seated at his wide cherry-wood desk studying a newspaper.

"Hi, Dad." She walked closer and bent to kiss his cheek. The strong, woodsy smell of the aftershave he'd worn for the last thirty years flooded her senses.

Like his scent, her father's clothing choices hadn't changed much with time. He wore dark jeans, a tailored Western-cut sport coat and an open-collared shirt. However, he didn't fill out his clothes the way he once had. Since being diagnosed with pancreatic cancer, he was much thinner. His complexion was paler than it used to be too.

He accepted her kiss before pulling away as he usually did. Jackie had long ago learned to chalk that response up to his determination to never show softness or vulnerability.

"Hello, Jacqueline. Why are you here so early? You know we always have dinner at six."

Jackie backed away and took a seat on the brown leather sofa across from his desk. "I thought we could visit for a few minutes. I'm sorry I haven't been by since the school year started. They've given me more classes this year since I'm becoming more experienced."

His eyes were back on his paper, but she wondered if he'd caught the mention of her experience. Years ago, as a college freshman, when she'd stated her intention to become a teacher, he'd said it was a silly whim she'd never carry through. Now she was on her seventh year.

When he didn't respond, she barely suppressed a sigh. "I'm sorry for rambling. In any case, I've been meaning to come visit to see how you are, but I've been busy."

"So you keep saying." He finally looked at her and removed his reading glasses. "In fact, that's all you ever tell me."

She fought the urge to squirm beneath his stern regard. Sitting up straighter, she said, "My work makes me happy, Dad. I like sharing that with you."

His brows furrowed in confusion, as if she'd spoken to him in Old English instead of modern.

"Yes, well, there's more to life, especially for a woman in your position. You're thirty-one, Jacqueline. Thirty-one with no sign of a husband or children. Do you know how that looks?" he demanded. "I can't understand your arrogant disregard for all the values I taught you like family and decency and tradition. Don't you care how lucky you are? After all the advantages and privileges I gave you, this is how you repay me?"

Jackie's thoughts swarmed in confusion the way they always did when her father confronted her like this. It always came back to an issue of gratitude. The life she chose and her priorities were somehow an affront to him, and consequently, she was failing to show him proper appreciation. "D-dad, I've never meant to disrespect you."

Surprisingly, he didn't argue, but maybe that was because he was breathing heavier now. She leaned forward in concern. "Maybe we should continue this later so you can—"

A quick rap on the doorframe interrupted her, as her older brother Conrad walked in. "Dad, hi, I just got in. Lisa and Riley will be here in a few minutes."

Conrad came to a stop when he spotted Jackie on the sofa. "Jackie, hey. I didn't see you."

She stood to greet him, and he leaned over to give her a brief side hug. He stood back and looked at her, hands in his pockets, as if he was searching for something to say. With their fifteen-year age difference, they'd never had much in common.

"How are things with Rob?" he finally asked.

Inwardly, Jackie cringed. Of course that would be the one topic he could come up with. "We broke up."

"Oh." He tugged on his shirt collar, the way she'd seen him do on TV when he was on the campaign trail and a reporter asked him an unexpected question. "I'm sorry about that."

"It's okay. It was the best thing for both of us."

Their dad made a "humph" sound. Clearly, he'd caught his breath. She slid away from the sofa. "You two probably want to chat. I'll go see if Lisa and Riley are here yet."

Ordinarily, she might have chafed at her own willingness to play the dutiful daughter who meekly excused herself to let the menfolk talk business, but right now, she was relieved to escape. Her dad's voice carried into the hallway after her, but his ire was no longer directed at her. Now, he was criticizing Conrad for some stance he'd taken at the most recent legislative session.

She shook her head. As frustrating as her father's lack of respect for her life and career was, at least he didn't interfere with her job, the way he'd always done with Conrad. Despite her grim mood, she chuckled at the thought of her father coming to her classroom and critiquing her lesson on Jane Austen or F. Scott Fitzgerald.

When she got downstairs, her sister-in-law and nephew still hadn't arrived, so she made her way to the less formal of the house's two living rooms, which served as a family room for holiday gatherings.

She was still too tense from the interaction with her dad to sit and relax, so she circled the room and looked at the smattering of photos on display. Most of them were pictures of her dad with other politicians and peers during his career. The few family photos felt more like publicity shots than genuine representations of affection or togetherness.

She picked up one of her dad, Conrad, and her teenage self. They were all dressed in formal clothes and posed at a fundraiser of some kind. All three of them wore their *public* smiles. Maybe the rest of the world thought they were genuine, but they looked artificial to her eyes.

A chill slivered through her.

Then, a surprising image entered her mind. An image of Cam's face lighting up with unaffected joy when she first saw the Pueblo pottery exhibit. Then she pictured Cam's sincere smile when she accepted Jackie's muddled offer of friendship.

Maybe it was that sincerity that had drawn her in and made her want to stay friends with Cam despite the way they'd met.

Putting that thought aside for later, she returned her focus to the photo in her hand. Not for the first time, she noticed how little she resembled her father. In hair and eye color, build, facial features—they were completely different. With Conrad, she could see a few traits they'd gotten from their mother, but there were no such similarities between her and her dad.

She'd never admit it to anyone, but some part of her was glad she didn't look like him because she never wanted to be like him. The life of advantages he always bragged about giving her with its rules and expectations had stifled her for as long as she could remember. It was impossible to live up to the standards of the great Clive Webster.

He had still been every bit the great Clive Webster when the photo in her hand had been taken. He stood tall, handsome, and confident. She hadn't really resented him back then. Back then, she'd been in awe of her father.

She squeezed her eyes shut. She'd loved her father. She still did. And despite everything, she *was* grateful for the life he'd provided for her. And, yes, some of her goals really were in line with his. She wanted to be married and to have a family of her own.

They could agree on that, couldn't they? Couldn't she make him see that she was grateful and loyal to what he wanted for her in her own way?

Sudden guilt gnawed at her. She wasn't doing much for her goals right now, was she? She'd chased off her partner and had a one-night stand. Thank heavens her father didn't know anything about that last part.

No. She would show her dad that, in all the ways that mattered, the two of them were on the same page.

That was yet another of many reasons that the sincere and intriguing Camryn Durant would only remain a friend.

11

Cam leaned against the Woller information desk. Her breath released in a heavy *whoosh* of exhaustion.

Apparently, the Saturday after Thanksgiving was when every family with small children in the tri-state area decided to soak up some culture.

Her entire volunteer shift had been a nonstop stream of answering questions, giving directions, helping the custodian clean up apple juice and peanut butter cracker mishaps, and even searching for a four-year-old who'd temporarily been separated from his parents. Fortunately, they'd found the boy just as he was crawling beneath the velvet exhibit ropes that surrounded a priceless crystal vase.

"Are weekends during the holiday season always this wild?" she asked Wendy, who was picking up a display of brochures that had been knocked over at some point. "I don't remember it being that way before."

"Why do you think I was so eager to accept your offer to help out?" Wendy asked with a mischievous grin.

Cam playfully rubbed her temples. "I think I walked into a trap!"

They continued organizing the information pamphlets in silence for a few minutes until Wendy said, "What are your plans for the rest of the weekend? Hanging out with your pretty ginger girlfriend, maybe?"

"It's not like that, Wen-deeee," Cam groaned. "Jackie and I are new friends. Barely past the casual acquaintance stage, really."

Wendy tilted her head. "Is that so? Then why is she coming over here?"

"What?" Cam looked up so fast she nearly gave herself whiplash. Sure enough, Jackie was strolling up to the information counter. She wore dark jeans and a simple green blouse that complimented her fair skin. Her hair hung down around her shoulders and bounced with her stride.

Cam swallowed. Moving past her attraction to Jackie would be a lot easier if the woman didn't keep popping up unannounced like this. Still, Cam couldn't manage to muster any real annoyance about it. She put on a smile that was friendly but hopefully not *too* friendly.

Jackie leaned one elbow on the counter across from Cam, managing to appear relaxed and graceful at the same time. "Hey, Stranger. How are things at Wolly today?"

"Thanks to an influx of families with young kids, I'd say it's been wild and woolly today," Cam quipped.

Jackie snorted then quickly touched her lips, as if hoping to contain any other unladylike noises. *Why must she be so cute?* "I'm sure that was quite a headache."

"It's fine. I'm glad they're learning to appreciate art at such a young age." She waved a dismissive hand. "So, what are you up to?"

"I came to return my class trip paperwork to Ms. Suarez."

At the mention of her name, Wendy appeared beside Cam, or maybe she'd stayed there all along. In her distracted state, it was hard to say.

"Please, call me Wendy, and thank you. You could have mailed it back, but I can see why you didn't." There was a teasing tone in Wendy's voice, and Cam barely resisted the urge to elbow her.

"I'll go and file this right away before it gets lost." Wendy took the papers from Jackie then turned her back so that only Cam could see her. She winked at her before bustling away.

She tried not to scowl at Wendy's retreating back. *Enough with the winking, Wendy!*

"Have you gotten any new exhibits since last time I was here?" Jackie asked, reclaiming her attention.

A gust of excitement swept through her as she thought of the newest exhibit. "I'm glad you asked. You'll like this one."

She hurried around the desk and started pulling on Jackie's hand without thinking. Jackie's warm fingers flexed beneath hers, and Cam realized what she was doing. "Oh! I'm sorry."

Embarrassment prickled over her skin, and she loosened her grip on Jackie's hand. But Jackie held on and sent her an amused grin. "It's all right. Lead the way!"

Cam nodded and started down the hall with Jackie in tow. *Don't make a big deal out of it!* It wasn't weird for two women who were friends to hold hands now and then, was it? Only a week ago, Britt had grabbed Cam by the hand at work and hauled her to the breakroom to discuss some juicy tidbit of office gossip. It was nothing.

Of course, holding Britt's hand had been a completely different experience. That truly had been friendly. She and Britt didn't have the brief but intimate history Cam had with Jackie. And her palm hadn't tingled at the contact the way it did now.

Before her musings could completely swirl down the drain of the Overthink Sink, they arrived at the exhibit hall.

"This," she said, taking advantage of the need to gesture at the ceiling to release Jackie's hand, "is a display created entirely by grade school kids."

"Wow!" Jackie gazed up at the ceiling where hundreds of colorful paper butterflies dangled from wire so thin that the butterflies appeared to be floating in midair.

Jackie moved to the center of the room and continued to look up. She raised her hands in the air and gave a little twirl. "They're wonderful! School kids did this, you say?"

"Yes. I thought you'd like that," Cam said. "The museum had a contest for fourth and fifth grade students all over the state to submit ideas for an art installment and then help create it. This is called *Butterfly Dream Garden*. Three fourth grade classes from Wise County collaborated on this idea. The students designed and cut out the butterflies and wrote one of their dreams for the future on each one."

"That's such a great idea!" Jackie said. "Let's see if we can read some of them."

Cam looked up at a blue butterfly and read the words written on it in white crayon. "My dream is that my little league team will win all the games next season."

"That's quite an ambition," Jackie observed, and they both laughed.

Jackie pointed at a yellow butterfly that had been cut with scalloped edges. "My dream is to have a home and garden show on TV."

"I feel like that kid spends a lot of time with a grandparent, what do you think?" Cam asked.

"Most definitely," Jackie said with a nod. Then her face sobered as she looked at a dark green butterfly above her. "My dream is that the Army won't send Mommy abroad anymore."

"God love them," Jackie murmured.

They continued walking around the room and kept reading the messages, some sad, some funny, and some downright profound.

After a few moments, Jackie faced her. "What kind of dream would nine-year-old Cam have put up here?"

"Hmm. That's a good question." Cam reflected back on her childhood hopes. "I remember when adults would ask me about the future, I'd always say I wanted to be an artist who lived in a big city. I guess my butterfly dream would have been some kind of nonsense like that."

She laughed at her own silly juvenile aspirations.

"Why is that nonsense?" Jackie asked, her face looking genuinely puzzled. "You did that. You live here, *and* you're a graphic designer."

"I-I'd never really thought about it that way," Cam admitted. She spent a disturbing amount of time dwelling on how things hadn't gone the way she'd thought they would but had never given much consideration to the ways they *had* worked out.

"Well, you should. You had an idea of who you were and what you wanted when you were still a child, and then you grew up and found a practical way to make it happen. That's quite remarkable, if you ask me."

Cam stared at her surprising new friend. How did she always manage to be so encouraging with a few simple but thoughtful words? She had a feeling the skill made Jackie a phenomenal teacher, maybe even better than her beloved Mrs. Donovan.

"Thank you for saying that."

Jackie's eyes searched hers. Was she mistaken, or had Jackie stepped a tiny bit closer? She must have because a hint of her floral scent reached Cam's nostrils. That fragrance had lingered in her room for days after—Cam mentally elbowed herself. *Stop it!*

She took a subtle step back. "Okay, your turn. What wild hope or dream would little Jackie have?"

"Now *that* would have been actual nonsense, I'm sure." Jackie said, pursing her lips. "I probably would have wished for straight As or a coveted part in the school play or something."

She'd answered so flippantly that Cam suspected she wasn't being forthright. Instead of responding right away, Cam put her hands in her pockets and simply looked at her, giving her the silence and space to say more.

Jackie met her steady gaze. "You don't believe that, do you?" Her shoulders lifted and fell in a sigh. "Okay, if you want to know the truth, I probably would have said that my dream was for my mom to still be alive. She died when I was a week old, and so many times when I was young, I'd desperately wish for her, even though I'd never really known her."

Jackie folded her arms over her chest as if she were hugging herself. "I used to imagine so many things about her, that she was funny, patient, and understanding. I guess all kids who don't know a parent do that. It was comforting because she was such a blank slate to me."

Cam's heart clenched, and she gently placed her hand on Jackie's arm, this time not caring if it was too familiar a gesture or not. "I'm so sorry. Did your father ever talk to you about her?"

"No, never. Sometimes my older brother would talk about her, but if Dad ever heard, he'd shut Conrad down."

"Wow. I guess it upset him too much to discuss her."

Jackie's lips formed a firm line. "Yeah, maybe."

She sounded unconvinced, but Cam didn't want to press any more than she already had. "Thank you for telling me. And I truly am sorry."

"It's okay. I worked through it, but those childhood years were hard."

"I'm sure they were. I can relate. Not completely, that is. I can't imagine what life would have been like without my mom. But we lost my dad when I was five and my older sister Mari was eight. So many of our memories have faded over the years, but we still have photos with him."

"Goodness," Jackie said softly. "I'm sorry too."

After a lengthy pause, Jackie continued. "What an odd and lonely thing for us to have in common."

Cam nodded. She was about to say more when Wendy appeared in the doorway of the exhibit hall.

"Cam? Are you still here? Your shift ended an hour ago. The museum is closing!"

She disappeared without waiting for a reply, leaving Cam and Jackie to watch her retreating back.

Turning to Jackie, Cam shrugged. "Wanna grab a coffee at Shiloh's?"

12

Jackie picked up her latte and inhaled the rich cinnamon scent before taking a careful sip. *Mmm.* Shiloh's cinnamon latte was even better than the vanilla one.

"Trying new flavors again?" Cam said as she took a seat and set her tea on their table.

Jackie's eyebrows went up as she looked at Cam. There was a twinkle in her mellow brown eyes. She chuckled. "Yes, in coffee, at least."

Cam's answering laugh was hearty and bright.

It was nice to see her comfortable enough to joke about the way they'd met. At first, Jackie worried she'd made things awkward for Cam and had all but forced friendship on her when she really wanted to move on and leave their encounter in the past. But now she'd seemed to relax into the situation.

"You mentioned your mom and sister a minute ago. Do they live close enough for you to go see them for the holiday?" Jackie asked.

"In Oklahoma, yes. My family doesn't really do the whole Thanksgiving thing, as such, but Mari and I both get the day off, so we spend it with our mom, grandma, and great aunt. Plus, Mari has a husband and two kids."

"That's quite a crowd!"

Cam took her phone from her jacket pocket and opened the photo application to show her. "Those last few pictures are from Thursday."

Jackie eagerly accepted the phone and looked at the photos. A middle-aged woman with long dark hair streaked with a few strands of silver stood in a kitchen and smiled at the camera. She was flanked by two older women with salt and pepper hair pulled back in matching buns. All three women had Cam's kind brown eyes.

The next photo was of a bulky thirty-something man who was laughing at something off camera. His arm was around a woman who looked like a shorter, more feminine version of Cam.

The final photo showed Cam sprawled out on the floor wrestling with two adorable dark-headed little kids. Cam's broad face was flushed with laughter and exertion, giving it a radiant quality.

Jackie had found something intriguing about Cam's appearance from that first night, but seeing her like this with an expression of pure, uninhibited joy was something entirely different. The only word Jackie could come up with was *beautiful*.

Jackie swallowed. What was that? *Beautiful!?*

She studied the photo a while longer. Well, so what? She did think Cam looked beautiful laughing and happy like that. Jackie had thought and even told female friends they looked beautiful before. It was no big deal.

Shaking off her confusion, she swiped to the final photo.

This one captured the entire family. As with the previous photos, everyone was smiling or laughing. The obvious affection and happiness in the image warmed Jackie, but at the same time, it sent a sliver of loneliness through her. There was a jarring contrast between this gathering and the cool, stilted conversation around her family dinner table on Thanksgiving.

"Thank you for showing me those," Jackie said, as she slid the phone back across the table.

"Tell me about your holiday," Cam said.

"I have a feeling it was quieter than your family dinner. My dad is in poor health, so we kept the meal small and brief."

"I'm sorry about that." Cam's expression was sympathetic.

"Thanks."

"Did you take advantage of the quiet to relax, then? I'm sure it's a shift from the classroom."

"I can't say I find my father's house particularly relaxing, even though I grew up there. It feels less like a home and more like a museum."

She sipped her coffee. "Not an entertaining museum like Wolly, of course."

"Of course not!" Cam said with a laugh before pointing to herself. "Unless the house has a fun, nerdy tour guide, how could it be?"

Jackie giggled. "Precisely. I have to admit, though, my family has collected some nice things over the years."

Now it was Jackie's turn to pull up the photos on her phone. On a whim, she'd taken a few shots of her dad's art with the idea of showing Cam later. "This has been my dad's favorite for the last several years."

Cam took the phone and studied the bronze statue of a cowboy on a bucking horse. Her eyes widened. "A Frederick Remington? This looks like one of the famous ones that sold at auction about a decade ago. I remember reading about it at the time."

"Yeah, I believe that's when he got it, now that you mention it." She took the phone back then finished her coffee. "I could use one more cup. Do you want anything?"

Cam stared at her.

"What?" Jackie glanced down at her blouse. Had she spilled coffee on herself without realizing it?

"Jackie…" Cam stopped and took a quick swallow of her own tea, as if needing fortification. "If that's the sculpture I'm thinking of, it sold for something like nine hundred thousand dollars. The winning bid went to some wealthy…"

Unease began to churn in Jackie's stomach as Cam's gaze snapped to hers. "Wait a minute, are you part of *that* Webster family? As in the oil tycoons-turned-state-politicians Websters?"

Cam was gaping at her now, and Jackie's palms began to sweat.

Not again.

People always treated her differently when they knew who her family was, even the ones who were in her "social circle." When she'd been a teenager and in her early twenties, other young people vied for her attention because of how influential her family was.

Now that she was older, she never lied about her upbringing, but she'd learned to keep quiet about it. Most of the people she worked with didn't even know.

Her boyfriends had known, of course. She'd gotten the idea that a couple of them thought it would be fun to date a rich man's daughter, like her life was full of sports cars and exotic vacations. Then they'd been disappointed when they realized she preferred a quiet life and her teaching career.

Rob had been drawn to her family connections and wealth initially too, but after two years, she'd thought he had settled down and accepted her for who she was. Obviously, she'd been wrong.

Would Cam now be more enthralled with her family money than interested in getting to know Jackie? *Why did I show her that picture?*

She released a heavy sigh. "Yes, I'm part of *that* Webster family. Clive Webster is my dad."

Cam scowled. "The one that lobbied, voted, and who knows what else to keep the nature reserve from happening a few years ago?"

"I suppose he did. I don't really follow—"

"I guess protecting plants and wildlife so the next generation doesn't grow up in a barren wasteland is bad for business," Cam pressed on, ignoring Jackie's reply. "Your family grew rich off this land, and then they couldn't be bothered to protect it. Typical billionaire mentality."

Wait a minute. Cam wasn't enthralled with her family wealth. She sounded…irritated about it. As inappropriate as it would have been, Jackie almost laughed in relief. Cam was different from most people Jackie knew, and she was starting to suspect that, if they stayed friends, it would be in spite of Jackie's family and not because of it.

"Listen, Cam." Jackie scooted closer to the table. "I know I should be better informed about what my family does, but that's not *me.*"

"You're not an oil princess?" Cam asked with more than a trace of sarcasm.

"No! That's where I came from, but it's not my life."

"You didn't go to expensive private schools with all the right people and the freedom to do whatever you want or use whomever you want as long as the newspapers didn't get a hold of it?"

Jackie flinched at the question and Cam's harsh tone. "Well, maybe, yes. But that's not who I've chosen to be now."

Her pulse picked up as she continued. "You're not too far off the mark with that newspapers remark. It's true. My dad cared more about what I looked like and how I acted as it affected his and my brother's image than he did about loving his family. Everything my father has ever given me is leverage for him to get me to do what he wants and care about what he wants me to care about, but I never did!"

Jackie shoved her coffee cup away in frustration. "I hated growing up around politics, and I hated his business. It was all so fake and suffocating. And lonely. All I wanted was to become an adult and have a halfway normal life. To try to raise a real family that cared about each other. And I wanted to work in an ordinary job where I could maybe do some good. That's why I chose to become a public-school teacher."

Jackie sank back into her chair, breathing hard after the outburst. She wasn't used to even talking about her background, let alone laying bare her thoughts and feelings about her life and why she'd made the choices she'd made.

Her shoulders sagged. "Look, I'm sure I sound like the 'poor little rich girl' to you. I get it. I've lived a very privileged existence. But I want to believe there's more to me than that. When I'm in the classroom, I feel like there is. And I was starting to feel that way being with you: becoming friends, and getting to know each other. But maybe that's not possible..."

She looked down at her empty coffee cup. Silence settled around them.

When Cam shifted in her seat, Jackie winced. Was she going to get up and leave?

"Jackie," Cam said, her tone surprisingly gentle.

When Jackie looked up, the irritation was gone from Cam's face.

"I'm sorry for being so judgmental." Cam leaned her elbows on the table and pinned her with a serious gaze. "I had no right to be that way, especially when I didn't really know your story. And I certainly didn't mean to hurt you. Finding out about your family caught me off guard, but that's no excuse to be rude."

Now Jackie leaned forward. "You mean that?"

"Yes, I mean it. Can you forgive me?"

A tangled ball of emotions rolled through Jackie's stomach. She wasn't sure she could ever remember anyone in her life asking for her forgiveness.

"Of course, I can. And I understand your being overwhelmed. Me...my family. That's a lot to take in."

"It is," Cam acknowledged, "but I have to say, the fact that you've chosen such a different path is impressive. I'm sure it hasn't been easy."

"No, but finding your own way never is. I mean, have you always done exactly what your family and friends expected of you?"

Cam scoffed. "Lord, no. They all thought I'd stay put, get married, and live my whole life in the exact same place I was born. But growing up queer and artistic in a small rural town is about as much fun as it sounds."

"Does your family have a problem with your sexuality?" she asked. Concern tugged on her heart.

"No, my mom and grandma figured it out pretty quickly and learned to accept it, but they still couldn't understand my restlessness. Families like ours tend to stay and go as a unit, but I wanted other things."

"But you still visit them."

"Oh, yes. All the time. And I send Mama and Grandma money to help out despite their protests and occasional death threats over it."

Jackie chuckled. "Then I'm sure, deep down, they appreciate you for being a good daughter."

"I hope so." Cam colored slightly.

"So this…" Jackie took a deep breath and gestured between them. "Our differences, my background—those things aren't dealbreakers for friendship?"

Cam reached over and brushed her fingers over Jackie's hand, making it tingle the way it had when she'd grabbed it at the museum earlier. "I don't have a lot of dealbreakers for my friendships, Jackie. I try to accept my friends for who they are, and ask that they do the same."

When Cam smiled, Jackie's heart felt lighter than it had in weeks. "That sounds fair to me."

13

Cam sat down at the metal picnic table in the courtyard of her office building and stretched out her legs so the sun could warm them through her slacks.

The afternoon temperature was mild for early December, but still too cool for most people to be outside. She didn't mind, though. The town where she'd grown up in northern Oklahoma got much colder than this in the fall and winter, and she and Mari had fun playing outside in the cold and the snow.

Settling onto her seat with an insulated cup of hot tea, she opened her laptop to get back to work. Being able to sit in the courtyard to work was one of her favorite things about this job. Her company hadn't kept up with the times as far as remote work options were concerned, but at least she could enjoy a change of scenery now and then. Only one other person was out there, a man sitting with his back to her at a table on the opposite side of the courtyard. The lack of people was an added bonus. Maybe the quiet would help her be productive.

Her thoughts had still been jumbled all morning from Jackie's revelation about her family. She had known Jackie was classy and probably from a wealthy family. The effortless elegance of her dress and manners gave that much away. Plus, she vaguely remembered Jackie mentioning a politician brother, but she would have never made the connection that Jackie was practically Texas royalty. Not that anyone could blame her for her lack of imagination. After all, she never would have expected to see Texas royalty dumped at a mid-tier downtown bar.

She kicked at a dry leaf that rustled across the ground in front of her feet. If she *had* realized who Jackie was, she wouldn't have gotten within a football field's length of her, not for chit chat, not for friendship, and definitely not for a fling.

It would have been like getting mixed up with her ex-girlfriend all over again.

When she had met Tina during their sophomore year of college, Tina had been curious, vibrant, and eager to explore her sexuality. Her desire for freedom had led her to attend school in Texas instead of South Carolina where she'd grown up as the daughter of a wealthy and influential businessman. Cam had been her first girlfriend, and they had been inseparable for the two remaining years of college.

The year after college, they'd maintained a long-distance relationship with the intent of finding jobs in the same place and moving in together. But that year back home around her powerful family and well-to-do friends had changed Tina's mind, it seemed, although Cam had been oblivious to the changes until it was too late.

The breakup had been ten years ago, and Cam could still picture Tina's face in that moment Cam finally realized it was truly over.

"You knew this wasn't going to work out," Tina said.

"No, I didn't! I only KNEW that I wanted to spend the rest of my life with you."

Tina had turned away. "I didn't realize it was that serious to you."

Then with a halfhearted "Sorry," Tina went back to her big, important life, leaving Cam all alone.

Cam's temples began to throb and her skin heated the longer she thought of it.

If her experience had taught her anything, it was to stay miles away from pampered, "curious" girls with rich families. They could talk a good game, but in the end, all they cared about was appearances and holding onto their precious positions in the world.

A sudden breeze wafted through the courtyard, chilling her but also soothing the feverish ball of hurt and resentment that had started to whirl in her stomach.

It rustled the pages of her sketchbook and blew pieces of paper from the other side of the courtyard onto her table. She hurried to gather the wayward sheets up before they got dirty.

When she spotted the logo of a locally-based chain of sporting outfitters on the first page she grabbed, her pulse jumped.

Open Air Hill!

Her firm was so keen to secure the company as a client that Cam's boss's boss, Mr. Bolton, was working on it himself even though he rarely rolled up his sleeves to work on individual accounts anymore.

Cam looked up and searched the other side of the courtyard.

Sure enough, a few yards away, Charles Bolton was crouched over a pile of papers that had blown to the ground. He scrambled to put the papers in order.

Gathering the sheets that had landed on her table, Cam headed across the courtyard and gave the logo another wistful glance. The project looked like a fun one. As soon as she'd heard about it, she'd started dreaming up ideas for Open Air's branding update. She'd even started on a simple mood board.

But it was a pointless exercise. If she'd gotten the promotion, she would have had the opportunity to work on it, but not now.

"I think you lost these, Mr. Bolton," Cam said as she approached.

He stood quickly, as if she'd startled him. The middle-aged black man was a few inches shorter than her, so they weren't quite eye-to-eye when he sent her a faint smile. "Thank you, Ms. Camryn. I don't have the energy for chasing those all over kingdom-come today."

"I don't blame you," she said with a chuckle. She started to turn and go back to her table, but she hesitated. "Is the Open Air proposal zapping your energy?"

Mr. Bolton rubbed his neck. "Is it ever! They have the potential to be one of our biggest clients, but all the ideas we've generated are as stale as a gas station sandwich."

Cam's pulse picked up. The team was struggling? Was there a chance they'd want help, even from someone who wasn't in a senior position?

Half her mind stayed with Mr. Bolton as he complained, but the other half was vibrating with possibility. Did she dare offer? Would that be risky to her job?

Ugh! Risky? What's happened to me?

As Jackie had pointed out, Cam had once been good at following through with her dreams. Maybe that strategy hadn't paid off in her love life, but it had with her career. She pictured the honest admiration on Jackie's face when she'd talked about Cam knowing what she'd wanted at a young age and then going after it. The warmth that had filled her chest at the compliment returned, spurring her into action.

She took a deep breath and, when Mr. Bolton paused his mini-tirade to catch his breath, she said, "I'd be glad to offer some extra help, if you think it would benefit the team."

Mr. Bolton's mouth snapped shut and formed a firm line. He studied her for a while, and she forced herself not to squirm. "That's kind of you to offer, Camryn, but based on what I've heard from Logan, you have enough challenges with your own workload."

Cam ground her teeth. That sounded like a polite way of saying Logan had told Bolton she was behind on her work, which absolutely wasn't true. She always met her deadlines. Hell, she usually finished projects a day or two *before* the deadline. Did Logan misrepresent her work to justify not giving her the promotion? Why would he do that?

Some deeply irritated side of her wanted to press Mr. Bolton for more details, but she didn't want to come across as argumentative or whiny. Swallowing, she carefully chose her next words. "I find that I'm generally more productive when I have a variety of projects. It's the blessing or curse of a creative mind, I suppose. I'm sure you understand that better than me."

Mr. Bolton nodded sympathetically.

"For the last couple of years, I've been working on the same types of projects, which I enjoy, but sometimes I worry I'm getting in a bit of a rut. If you let me help with Open Air, I think it could help both of us. And, I promise, I'll put in the extra hours to ensure I stay on top of all my other projects too."

Stroking his chin, Mr. Bolton hummed tonelessly for several seconds, which felt more like an hour. At last, he clapped his hands once. "All right, Camryn. What you say makes sense. And I'm sorry if you've gotten into a rut. I think it's important for all of our skills if we include some variety in the projects we work on. We could definitely use a fresh perspective for Open Air. I'll make sure Jody shares all the project files with you."

"Thanks, Mr. Bolton!"

As she strolled back to her table, Cam couldn't help beaming. For the first time since she'd been passed over for the promotion, she was excited about her work. She'd surprised herself with her assertiveness and confidence. Both of those things had been dormant for such a long time. And what was equally surprising is that it had partly been inspired by Jackie's encouraging words.

Maybe their friendship really would work.

When Jackie had revealed who her family was, Cam's nervous system had gone into overdrive as memories of Tina had flooded her mind. She'd been snarky and harsh with Jackie as a result. But that wasn't fair. Jackie hadn't done anything to deserve that, and Cam had no right to judge her life. From everything she had seen so far, Jackie was a truly kind woman who worked in a job that was probably thankless more often than not.

She wasn't Tina.

And more importantly, she wasn't a girlfriend or even a potential one. Jackie had made her intentions clear. She wanted friendship and only friendship. As long as that friendship boundary line remained firmly in place, she had a feeling everything would work out fine.

14

Jackie's eyes squeezed shut, and she released a faint moan as Cam's strong arms wrapped around her from behind. Jackie was lying on her side, and Cam was pressed against her back, her breath hot on Jackie's ear as she nibbled at it. Liquid hot desire trickled through her body.

Cam's gentle hand slid across Jackie's middle and underneath her shirt. She palmed Jackie's breast, making her pant.

"Cam," she sighed.

Cam responded by kissing her neck then stroking her stomach before slowly dragging her hand down lower and lower and lower until she reached the waistband of Jackie's panties. She pushed one finger beneath the band and traced the sensitive skin there.

Yessss.

She tilted her head back so she could seek out Cam's lips over her shoulder, but there was only cold, empty air.

Jackie's eyes flew open and she sat up in bed.

Her empty bed.

Of course it was empty! She'd been dreaming.

And what a dream!

Her body was damp from sweat, and not only that…she slid her hand beneath her panties and found moisture of a different kind down there.

Dear God.

She'd gotten hot and aroused dreaming about Cam. What was wrong with her? Yes, she'd had wet dreams a time or two in the past, but they were never about anyone in particular, not even the men she'd been in relationships with. What brought this on?

She had tried to shove her reckless night with Cam out of her memory and ignore the flashes of energy that occasionally coursed through her when she looked at or thought about Cam. She had zero intention of letting her mind dwell on that ill-advised night, which was most certainly a fluke. Or on the possibility that she still felt a physical pull toward Cam.

The dream had probably been the result of exhaustion from work, a few stubbornly clinging memories from *that night*, and the fact that she'd talked to Cam on the phone shortly before going to sleep.

Jackie had called Cam after dinner and asked if she'd wanted to go with her to a Christmas street fair that was happening in a small town around 50 miles away. It had been short notice, and she hadn't wanted to imply she thought Cam didn't have enough of a life to have weekend plans already, but she'd put her misgivings aside to ask.

She hadn't known about the fair until a former student had messaged her on social media with a flyer about it and an explanation that he would be selling his own original artwork there. He'd been one of her favorite students a couple of years before, and she was happy to support him.

The more she read about the street fair, with artist booths and other activities, the more it sounded like something Cam might enjoy, so she had called.

Cam had agreed to accompany her, and then they'd kept on chatting. Before Jackie knew it, it was eleven o'clock and they'd been talking for hours.

She was relieved that Cam had recovered from her apparent shock and dismay over learning who Jackie's family was, allowing them to build on their friendship connection. The last thing she wanted was to interrupt that progress simply because her brain and body were confused.

"I'm downstairs when you're ready," Jackie texted Cam.

They'd decided she would drive them to the small town where the festival was taking place.

She found an empty parking place in the apartment building's lot and watched for Cam to come out, trying not to think about the last time she was here. Fortunately, that wasn't as difficult as she thought it would be since it was daytime now, and she could take in her surroundings better.

The brick apartment building was modest but neat and modern-looking. Small dogwood plants flanked the side door nearest the parking lot, giving it a bright, welcoming appearance. People of various ethnicities and ages went in and out as she watched, including families with small children, twenty-somethings with a dog or two, and a few retirees.

Before long, Cam emerged through the door, and Jackie swallowed. She wore a light olive button-up shirt under a tan leather jacket and blue jeans that accentuated the outline of her long legs. A pair of aviator sunglasses completed the outfit. She looked confident, relaxed…and hot.

Jackie squeezed her eyes shut. *No, not hot. Shut up!*

Then she opened her eyes again. Well, what was wrong with that? Cam *did* look hot…in a friendly way.

Before she could dwell on the matter any longer, she got out of the car and waved so Cam could see her in the crowded parking lot. Cam waved back before coming over.

"Morning," Cam greeted her with a smile. Her gaze shifted to Jackie's Ford Taurus, and her eyes widened.

"Is something wrong?"

Cam quickly returned her attention to Jackie. "No. Not at all. I just thought…"

Jackie turned to study her car. *Oh.*

"You thought I drove a fancy sports car? Or maybe I'd show up with a limousine and chauffeur?"

"No. I mean, maybe." Cam lowered her eyes. "Sorry."

She bit back a smile. It was impossible to be annoyed or to keep needling Cam when she looked so sheepish. "It's okay. I suppose I can see why you thought that. Ready to go?"

The car discussion was quickly forgotten by the time they had stopped for drive-through coffee and set off on their way to the festival.

Even with the nightmarish Dallas traffic, it took less than an hour for them to reach their destination. The streets of the small town were only beginning to get crowded with festival-goers as they searched for a parking spot.

Cam craned her neck to stare at the massive brick courthouse with a clock tower that reigned over the town square. "Why does a town this size need a giant courthouse like that?"

"Well, it's a county seat for one thing and, well, this is Texas, after all," Jackie replied.

Cam nodded, eyes still on the building. "Impressive."

"I suppose it is."

She pulled into an empty space on a side street a few blocks from the town square. "I don't think about it much because I grew up coming to all of these towns when my dad was on the campaign trail. I think the courthouse in Granbury in Hood County is my favorite."

"So, you'd go to these towns and your dad would make speeches or something?"

"If he got the chance," Jackie said with a bitter chuckle. "Mostly, he'd mix and mingle at big events like the summer and holiday festivals. Work the crowd. My brother and I would follow around to show what a great family man he was."

"It sounds like you grew up under a microscope." Cam shuddered. "Did you at least get to have fun at the festivals once the speeches were over?"

"Fun?" Jackie said. She clutched an imaginary strand of pearls. "Fun wrinkles dresses!"

Cam didn't react to her attempt to laugh off her childhood experiences. Instead, she watched Jackie in silence and waited. It was a habit of hers that Jackie was beginning to notice. When Cam detected bullshit, she neither accepted nor contradicted, she simply sat back and waited for the truth.

Jackie's shoulders dropped. "No. There wasn't much room for fun. I was always too scared of embarrassing my dad or being a distraction, so I stayed in my place."

"It must have been rough having your childhood so closely regulated like that," Cam said with a shake of her head. "I never had to worry about that. Mama and Grandma kind of let me run wild when I was little, even when my sister was competing."

Jackie shifted in her seat to see Cam better. "Competing?"

"Yeah. Mari did competitive fancy dress dancing at pow wows and other festivals when she was younger."

"Oh, wow! That's so cool."

Cam smiled. "I was the proud if annoying little sister. We went to events all over the state and region. Mari was always serious when she was competing, but afterwards, we'd run all around the fairgrounds, looking at the jewelry and craft tables. Then we'd stuff ourselves with fry bread. It was great."

Happiness and affection played across Cam's face as she talked.

"That does sound great," Jackie agreed, not realizing how wistful she felt until she heard it in her own voice.

"Hey!"

Jackie jumped at the exclamation. "What?"

Cam tapped her knee and sent her a broad grin. "You're not on the campaign trail today. So let's have some fun!"

Her energy was irresistible. "Okay!"

They exited the car and strolled toward the town square. The main thoroughfare that wrapped around the courthouse was barricaded to traffic so the vendors could set up their tables on the street. Large wreaths with red ribbons hung from the street lamps, and the storefronts surrounding the area were adorned with garland and bows. A guitarist stood on one of the street corners and serenaded the shoppers with Christmas carols.

At the first vendor table they reached, a woman and her adult daughter were selling silk flower crowns of all colors and sizes. Jackie marveled at the lush and vibrant combinations of flowers in each crown.

Moments later, Cam walked toward her with a crown made of pale pink roses and daisies. "Cam, what are you—"

Cam promptly set the crown on Jackie's head then stood back to study her.

Jackie blinked in surprise.

"Well, don't just stand there," Cam said. "Give us a twirl, so we can get the whole effect."

Jackie rolled her eyes, but she complied. She lifted the hem of an imaginary ballgown skirt and gave a twirl. She even threw in a curtsy for good measure.

"Stylish! But I'm not sure that's the right crown. What do you guys think?" Cam asked the women behind the table.

The younger woman shook her head then picked up another crown. "No, not quite. Try this one."

Cam accepted the crown, which had an exquisite arrangement of sunflowers, greenery, berries, and orange roses. She placed it on

Jackie's head. This time, she didn't back away, and Jackie's skin prickled at the closeness.

Cam's gaze swept over her. "Magical. You look like a woodland fairy queen."

Jackie's cheeks heated. Was Cam flirting with her?

When the women behind the table murmured their admiration, Cam looked away. "Y'all do such lovely work. We'll take this one."

"Cam!" Jackie protested. "You're right. It is lovely, but what am I going to do with a flower crown?"

"Anything you want," Cam answered with a shrug. "That's the great part about doing fun things. It doesn't always have to be practical."

Jackie gave a resigned sigh as she took off the crown and handed it over to be boxed up. "Maybe I can wear it the day I teach *A Midsummer Night's Dream*."

Cam snorted. "See? You already found a way to make it practical."

"Very funny," Jackie retorted. "I think it's time we found some fun for you."

They walked for a few minutes until Jackie spotted a covered booth with contents that glittered in the sun.

"There!" Jackie exclaimed. "A sword booth. You should like that."

"Wow! Stereotype much?" Cam stopped and put her hands on her hips, but the smirk that played across her lips belied her combative stance.

"Are you saying you don't want to look at the swords?" Jackie asked.

"Of course I want to look at the swords. I'm a lesbian for crying out loud! Come on!"

Laughter burst from Jackie's chest as she allowed herself to be dragged to the booth.

Once Cam had admired every single blade the vendor had and purchased a letter opener replica of the *Wonder Woman* film sword, they moved on.

Finally, Jackie spotted a familiar face behind a booth. "Max!"

The tall, skinny twenty-year-old looked up at the sound of his name, and his pale face lit up. "Ms. Webster! You're here!"

"It's good to see you, and look at all this!" She gestured at the dozens of sketches and paintings arranged on the table.

"Yeah, I've been working for months to get enough pieces to sell on the holiday fair circuit."

"Max, this is my friend Cam." Jackie stepped aside so Cam could approach the table. "Cam, this is Max, one of my former students and soon to be bestselling artist."

He playfully covered his face with his hand. "Oh gosh, don't make me blush!"

He shook Cam's hand. "Ms. W was my favorite teacher. High school sucked. But she was the only one who cared what a bullied queer kid thought. She encouraged me to write about my feelings and find other ways to express them instead of turning all that negativity inward."

A lump formed in Jackie's throat. She'd never realized her words had impacted him that much.

Cam smiled at Jackie. "I can't say that surprises me."

Then she picked up one of the paintings, which appeared to be painted with acrylic greens and bronzes to form a snake skin pattern. "Ooh, you used a swipe and swirl-technique to make scaly patterns. Very nice. And excellent choice of color."

Cam tilted the painting back and forth. "It has a three-dimensional quality. Clever."

"Thanks!" Max beamed.

"Cam is an artist too," Jackie explained.

"Well, a graphic artist. But I draw and occasionally paint for the job," she said.

When he heard that, Max unleashed a barrage of questions at Cam, and she graciously answered them all, sharing stories and inside jokes about her career as she went.

Jackie left them to their discussion while she examined the rest of the art. Most of it was abstract like the piece Cam had first picked up, but there were also a few sketches of flowers and animals. The sketches included short poems as well.

Good. He's keeping up with his poetry.

Max's table began to attract other people, so Cam and Jackie each selected a piece to buy—Jackie chose one of the poetry sketches, and Cam got a striking rainbow-colored acrylic abstract painting—before saying goodbye.

By that point, the temperature had climbed a good fifteen degrees from when they'd arrived, so they took their jackets to the car and continued exploring the festival.

Cam insisted on getting nachos, corn dogs, and candy apples for lunch. Jackie raised her eyebrows when Cam set the feast on the picnic table they'd claimed, but Cam showed no remorse at the extravagance.

She picked up a corn dog and took a big bite before pointing it at Jackie. "You still have a lot of missed fun to make up for. That includes fair food."

Chuckling, Jackie picked up a nacho and popped it in her mouth. The melty cheese and crispy chip were decadent and delicious. Almost as delicious as Cam looked in her olive-green shirt with the sleeves pushed back from her strong forearms. The arms Jackie had felt wrapped around her in her dream.

Oh no you don't. She chastised her brain with the internal version of the stern teacher voice she occasionally broke out for misbehaving students.

She cleared her throat. "Thanks for talking with Max about his art and career. That was sweet of you."

"It was nice chatting with him. He seems like a good kid."

"He is," Jackie agreed.

Cam regarded her with a serious expression that pulled her in. "You were clearly a positive influence on his life, and I could tell it meant a lot to him that you were here to see his work today."

Tingly warmth filled her chest. "Well, it meant a lot to *me* that you came with me and encouraged him too."

As they ate their lunch, she pondered how sincerely she'd meant that last statement. She couldn't picture Rob, any of her other exes, or any of her friends, for that matter, giving up their Saturday to come help her support a former student.

Either Cam was special or Jackie needed to keep better company. Probably both.

After a few minutes, Jackie pushed away her food containers. "Whoa. I think that's enough. All this 'fun' is going to give me major indigestion, if I'm not careful."

Cam sat back and rubbed her belly. "Yeah. This was easier when I was a kid and had an iron stomach. I think I'm going to need to take a walk after that."

"Definitely." Jackie surveyed the booths and tents around them to see if they'd missed anything interesting.

A sign caught her eye, and she pointed. "Hey, that looks neat. There's someone at that booth who will sketch your portrait while you wait. We can do one together to commemorate my first non-campaign-trail festival."

Cam agreed and they made their way to the tent.

While the silver-haired artist set up a fresh sheet of sketching paper and arranged her pencils, Cam and Jackie settled into two chairs facing her.

"Closer, please," the artist said without looking up from her pencils. Jackie scooted closer to Cam until their arms brushed. Jackie barely managed to suppress a shiver. She really needed to get a hold of herself.

"I've never sat for a portrait before," Cam said. She gave Jackie a sidelong glance. "I'll bet your family has."

"Ugh, yes. My dad commissioned a painting with him, me, and my brother when I was still in high school. It felt so pretentious, and on top of that, we all three looked constipated in it."

Cam coughed then doubled over in laughter. "Come on. I don't believe that for a minute."

Jackie shrugged one shoulder and bit back a laugh of her own. "It's how it looked to me."

Glancing at the artist, Jackie said, "Sylvia, no constipation in this sketch, please."

Cam's laughter intensified, and Sylvia shook her head disapprovingly. "Okay, ladies, relax. We're ready to start now."

They settled down so Sylvia could get to work.

Cam remained still, but she continued talking. "I saw another booth where they do silhouettes. We could get one of those too, if you want."

"Not of me, thanks, but you can if you want," Jackie said firmly.

"What? Why?"

"My chin is too pointy."

"Is not," Cam scoffed. "Your chin is…uh…just the right amount of pointy."

Jackie snickered. "I'll bet you say that to all the girls."

"Not if their chins are too pointy," Cam said without missing a beat.

"Ooh, are you a *chin* woman?"

Cam's eyes squeezed shut, and her shoulders shook with barely contained laughter. It was fun watching her fight for control.

"Quit joking around," Cam chided. "I'm trying to be a good model here. This sitting still business is harder than it looks. I don't know if I can last much longer."

"Stop complaining." Jackie lowered her tone suggestively. "I happen to know you can last *much* longer than this."

Cam sputtered. "You really went there, didn't you?"

Yep. Apparently, she had.

"All finished!" Sylvia proclaimed.

Thank goodness. Jackie had been heading into dangerous territory.

Cam insisted on paying for the sketch and, while she did, Jackie studied it.

It was a surprisingly lifelike sketch, considering how quickly it had been done. Even though they had both faced forward most of the time, Sylvia had chosen to capture a brief point when they'd looked at each other while trying not to laugh. Something about the way they were sitting so close together or the secret smile they appeared to be exchanging conveyed the energy that had pulsed between them since the moment they'd met at that bar weeks ago.

Jackie's hand shook the tiniest bit as she held the sketch.

15

Cam couldn't remember when she'd had a better day. Exploring the festival with Jackie, sharing stories, seeing her interact with Max, laughing and joking around—it had all been unbelievably fun.

Any residual awkwardness over the way they'd met faded the more time they spent together. Cam's attraction hadn't faded, of course, but she was learning to manage it. Jackie hadn't helped with her occasional flirty jokes, but Cam didn't hold it against her. It proved Jackie had moved past the awkwardness better and faster than Cam, but why wouldn't she? She was a straight woman who'd had a fling with another woman. Cam was a lesbian trying to be friends with a stunning, intelligent, and funny woman.

Because of the disparity in their feelings, wisdom probably would have directed Cam to put some space between Jackie and herself after spending the whole day together, but Cam didn't feel like listening to wisdom. Instead, she wracked her brain for ways to extend their time at the festival.

But Nature had other ideas.

As soon as Cam and Jackie exited the tent where they'd had their picture sketched, a loud clap of thunder cracked through the air, making them both jump. Cam stared up at the sky, where dark gray clouds hung low. "When did that happen?"

Jackie looked up too, but her answer was drowned out by exclamations from other festival goers as the sky unleashed a torrent of rain.

"Let's get back to the car!" Cam shouted over the chaos.

They consolidated their purchases into one plastic bag to protect them from the downpour then hurried toward the car. Since it was parked several blocks away, they were both soaked and shivering by the time they sloshed up to the vehicle.

Once they were inside, Jackie cranked up the heater which, combined with the conversation and laughter as they drove, went a long way in warming Cam inside and out.

All too soon, they pulled into the parking lot of Cam's apartment building.

Jackie rubbed the sleeve of her blouse. "Ugh. My clothes are still damp."

"Mine too," Cam said. "Do you want to come up?"

Jackie bit her lip and stared straight ahead without answering. Only then did Cam realize how her offer may have sounded. "I-I mean to dry off. I'll turn on the fireplace. It's only gas, but it gives off some heat, and I can make us some coffee or tea."

"Yeah," Jackie nodded slowly. "Yeah, that sounds nice."

They waded through a second, shorter downpour on the way to the building, and got on the elevator. Cam hadn't yet turned around to press the button for her floor when Mrs. Crowley, one of her neighbors, hurried on behind them with her three Labrador retrievers on leashes.

One of the dogs hurled himself into the back of Cam's legs, making her knees buckle. She pitched forward right at Jackie, making her fall back against the elevator wall. Cam braced her hands on the wall on either side of Jackie to get her balance.

Mrs. Crowley apologized and fussed at her hyperactive dogs, but Cam barely heard because her focus was on Jackie. They were pressed together, and Cam could feel the moisture and heat from Jackie's body against her own. Her scent tickled Cam's senses: a sweet mixture of her floral perfume and the rain.

Cam swallowed. "You okay?"

Jackie's soft hazel eyes were wide as she looked at Cam. "I think so," she murmured. Her breath seemed unsteady, or maybe that was Cam's. They were standing so close; it was hard to tell.

Cam pushed off the wall and backed away as far as she could with the dogs still trotting around the elevator.

Jackie straightened and pulled on her white blouse to smooth it, causing the top button right above her cleavage to loosen and come undone. Cam's pulse skittered, and her gaze fixated on the newly revealed skin before she could stop herself.

Jackie looked down at her blouse then back up at Cam, her expression intense. Quickly, Cam looked away.

Finally, the elevator stopped and the doors opened, allowing Mrs. Crowley and her dogs to spill out.

Cam gestured for Jackie to exit ahead of her and tried to take the opportunity to get her wandering eye and elevated heartrate in check.

When they reached her apartment, she busied herself turning on the lights. "Feel free to go dry off. You can grab one of my sweatshirts, if you want, and hang up your blouse. You probably remember where the closet and fresh towels are."

"I remember," Jackie said, her tone husky.

Their eyes met, and Cam's throat went dry.

Great! Now we're thinking about the last time she was here.

"All righty, then," Cam said, aiming for a cheerful, nonchalant tone, but it sounded forced even to her own ears. "Why don't you go take care of that, and I'll turn on the fireplace and get some coffee brewing."

Jackie nodded and left the room. She'd been so quiet ever since they'd entered the building. Was she uncomfortable being here again? Had Cam made it worse with that little mishap in the elevator?

She went to the fireplace and started it up. As she watched the orange flames dance to life, she mulled over the situation. If Jackie truly was uncomfortable, she might not say so for fear of being rude. After all, smiling and being polite in difficult situations was probably second nature to her, given how she'd grown up. But Cam didn't want Jackie to feel the need to pretend with her.

She gave a determined nod and took a step back from the fireplace. When Jackie came back, Cam would clear the air, and let Jackie know she wouldn't be offended if she wanted to leave.

A rustling sound behind Cam made her turn around. "Hey, Jackie, if you w—"

Cam froze mid-sentence, and her jaw went slack.

Jackie had indeed changed out of her damp blouse, but she hadn't borrowed a sweatshirt. Instead, she was standing in the middle of

Cam's living room wearing only a beige silk bra and matching panties. Her hair was still damp and slicked back, and her expression held that same intensity it had when they'd been in the elevator.

Cam's insides started humming. "Uh...am I out of clean laundry?"

"No." Jackie's gaze was fixed on Cam as she took a step closer.

Cam's fingers ached to reach for Jackie, but she kept her arms at her sides and clutched the fabric of her jeans. "Then w-what do you need?"

"You." Jackie closed the distance between them. "Can I kiss you?"

A dozen questions flooded Cam's brain. *Aren't you supposed to be straight? What happened to only being friends? Is this another fluke?*

But instead of voicing them, Cam nodded. Then Jackie was on her, planting a hot, breathy kiss on Cam's lips.

Cam's arms came up around Jackie's slender frame on instinct, and she kissed her back. When Jackie pressed even closer and brought her hands up to tangle in Cam's hair, her rational brain vanished. Her arms tightened around Jackie as they continued kissing.

Jackie's tongue brushed the seam of Cam's lips until Cam opened her mouth, allowing Jackie's tongue to slip inside. Cam's body ignited with desire. She slid her hands up and down the smooth, damp skin of Jackie's back.

Jackie broke the kiss with a gasp, and Cam panted for breath.

Is this where Jackie's common regret kicks in? No, not common regret. Common sense. Or regret. Cam's mind was too jumbled for proper vocabulary right now.

Jackie didn't step back, however. She tugged at the buttons of Cam's shirt. "May I?"

Okay. Guess we're really doing this.

Cam gave a shaky nod, and Jackie's nimble fingers trembled as they undid each button, pulled the shirt off, and let it drop to the floor. Slowly, she ran her hands up Cam's bare arms and over her shoulders. Her touch was feather soft, but the contact, combined with the intense look of concentration on Jackie's face, set Cam's skin on fire.

Jackie wrapped her hands over Cam's shoulders and pulled her in for another kiss. Cam groaned as their bare skin touched, and the kiss turned frantic. This time, Cam was the one to break it. "Do you want to take this to the bedroom now?"

"No," Jackie said breathlessly, and Cam's heart dropped.

"No?"

Jackie shook her head. "No, I want to do it by the fireplace."

She took Cam's hand and pulled her toward the carpet by the fireplace while Cam's pulse went haywire. Jackie taking the lead and telling her what she wanted was sexier than Cam could have ever imagined.

They removed the rest of their clothes in a flurry then sank onto the carpet together with Jackie on top. Her weight felt like heaven to Cam's feverish body. They kissed and kissed until Jackie slowly pulled away and sat up to straddle Cam. She traced graceful, curious fingers all over Cam's upper body, from her face to her neck and down to her breasts. "Cam?"

Cam's eyes closed as Jackie massaged her breasts and nipples. "Y-yes?"

Before responding, Jackie leaned down and kissed one of Cam's breasts. When Cam's breath hitched, Jackie hummed in satisfaction and repeated the sweet and tantalizing gesture. She slowly ran her tongue over Cam's nipple, and her hips jerked beneath Jackie.

Finally, Jackie sat up again and searched her face. "Can I taste you? Down lower, I mean?"

Cam stared up at her. They hadn't done *that* the first night. Cam enjoyed oral, but she'd usually been on the giving side in past relationships. The past didn't matter, though, because all she could focus on now was the magnificent sight of Jackie looking down at her, that luscious red hair a wild tangle around her lovely face and her eyes full of passion and need. In that moment, Cam would have let Jackie do anything she wanted to her.

Unable to speak, Cam could only nod.

Jackie smiled and slid down Cam's body, trailing her lips along Cam's stomach and making every single muscle twitch along the way. When she settled between Cam's legs, Cam exhaled a shaky breath and opened her legs wider.

The first touch of Jackie's tongue was tentative and light, but Cam's entire body gave a jolt at the contact.

"Is that okay?" Jackie murmured. Her breath tickled Cam's wet center as she spoke, and Cam shuddered. She couldn't remember being so sensitive in the past.

"Y-yeah, it's great," Cam whispered.

"Good." With no further preamble, Jackie dove in: kissing, licking, and sucking at Cam with reckless hunger.

"Jackie!" Cam moaned as her arms flew to her side and her fingers clutched the carpet. "God, Jackie, what are you doing to me?"

Cam's hips bucked against Jackie uncontrollably, but Jackie held onto Cam's thighs with a tight grasp and continued to devour her. Cam raised up on trembling elbows to watch and moaned again. Seeing this gorgeous woman between her legs was more breathtaking than the wildest and boldest of Cam's dreams.

Jackie slid a hand around and thrust her fingers inside Cam, making her cry out. Her head dropped back against the carpet, and her body turned into a quivering mass of pleasure.

When Cam finally stilled and regained her senses, Jackie was once again lying on top of her. She nibbled and licked at the sweat on Cam's neck and pressed against her until Cam felt the moisture of Jackie's center on her leg.

New desire awakened in Cam, and she shifted so that Jackie's core aligned with her own. Jackie lifted her head and her eyes bore into Cam's. She rolled her hips, and they both groaned. They moved together faster and faster until Jackie's eyes squeezed shut and her mouth widened in a silent cry.

Breathlessly, she collapsed against Cam's sweaty body.

16

Jackie couldn't remember ever feeling quieter or more still inside than she did in those moments when she lay in Cam's arms by the fireplace. The rise and fall of Cam's chest beneath her cheek was so rhythmic that she wondered if Cam had dozed off.

Slowly, she lifted her head to study Cam's face, but she was taken aback to see Cam staring at the ceiling with her brow knit in a grave expression.

Unease replaced Jackie's serenity. Cam looked like she might be upset. Was she angry at Jackie? Was she about to tell her to get out?

Cam looked at her then, as if only now noticing Jackie's stare. Her expression softened. "Do you want a snack?"

Jackie's heart gave a relieved *thump,* and she nodded. Cam had made her work up an appetite, yet again.

They got dressed in t-shirts and shorts Cam provided then raided her refrigerator for cold cuts, cheese, fruit, and water. Instead of sitting at the kitchen table, they took their snacks to the sofa. Cam didn't seem overly concerned about crumbs, but maybe that's because she was still quiet.

After they'd eaten in silence for a few minutes, Cam set her plate on the coffee table and gestured toward the fireplace. "What was that?"

Jackie swallowed hard and sent a nervous glance to Cam's face. She didn't appear angry, per se, but she did look agitated. Jackie bit her lip. "I'm sorry."

Cam frowned. "You're sorry?"

"No, no. Not sorry about *that,*" she rushed to explain. "I'm sorry for being so mixed up. I-I really thought this would be a one-time thing that first night and that it was only because I was so upset and wanted to forget my messy life for a while, as I said. But today…"

Jackie set her plate down, picked up her glass, and took a big gulp of water. Cam, being Cam, didn't press her to continue until she was ready. But Jackie wasn't sure if she'd ever be fully ready to say this.

She drew in a deep breath. "Today, I realized or maybe I let myself realize that I'm truly attracted to you, Cam."

Jackie's heart started to race as she said it aloud, well, in a whisper: "I'm attracted to a woman."

Her thoughts spun like a tilt-a-whirl. *Oh, God. I like women.*

She set her water glass down with a thud. "I can't believe this is happening. What's wrong with me? I'm thirty-one years old, and I'm only figuring this out now!"

"There's no set timeline for figuring yourself out, Jackie," Cam murmured. "This is a big discovery. Don't make it more complicated by beating yourself up."

Jackie shook her head. "I wasn't even mature enough to try to figure things out. That first night. The way it felt. I must have known I couldn't be completely straight, but I pretended that was the case instead of facing it. Then today… I'm so sorry, Cam. I shouldn't have dragged you into my confusion."

"I wasn't exactly an unwilling participant," Cam said with a mischievous glint in her eye. "Those sounds I was making weren't protests."

"Cam!" Jackie's face overheated even as laughter threatened to bubble up in her chest. She squelched it, though, because this was serious. "You're missing the point. I shouldn't have handled things this way. When I realized I was attracted to you, I should have gone home and dealt with the feelings on my own instead of just…just jumping you like I did."

"Look, you're new to this," Cam said firmly. "I knew I was gay in high school. I've had almost twenty years to learn how to keep my attractions in check around friends I liked in locker rooms and at sleepovers and…you get the idea. You don't have that history, so you should show yourself some grace. For my part, I wasn't bothered or hurt. This doesn't have to be stressful, if you don't make it. You can relax and enjoy figuring yourself out. It's a good thing."

"A good thing," Jackie murmured.

So why did her stomach feel like she'd swallowed an entire hill of fire ants? She slowly shook her head. "But I can't come out, Cam. I *can't*. You know who my family is. My father would have a complete meltdown, which is the last thing he needs with his health right now."

Questions about what her mother would have thought briefly flitted through Jackie's mind. Was she as stodgy and set in her ways as her husband, or would she have tried to be understanding? Jackie squeezed her eyes shut at the speculation. It wouldn't do any good.

Opening her eyes again, she rambled on. "Then there's my brother. Sometimes he's just a younger, milder version of Dad. I'm sure he'd see it as a blight on his sterling reputation. And then—"

"Hey, hey. It's all right," Cam soothed. She scooted closer to Jackie and gave her a quick side hug. The warmth of the gesture along with Cam's now familiar scent settled Jackie a bit. "One step at a time, okay? You don't have to decide or even think about coming out right away. You only just came out to yourself! You're allowed to sit with that for a while."

Jackie scoffed. "What are you, a coming out coach?"

Cam folded her arms and regarded her with a stern expression. "I'm a friend. I'm *your* friend, and I'll be glad to support you through this in whatever way you need."

The assurance was comforting, but questions nagged her brain. "But what about…?"

She gestured toward the fireplace. "What about this physical thing between us?"

"What about it?" Cam said with a shrug. "We could explore that too, if you want."

"But Cam, I can't get into a relationship with you!" Only after she'd practically shouted that did she realize how unkind it must have sounded. As if she were repulsed by the idea of being Cam's girlfriend.

Girlfriend. The word felt strange, mysterious, maybe even exciting, but that was beside the point.

"Who said anything about a relationship?" Cam replied. "I just took on a project at work with the potential to double my workload, that's on top of a half dozen old emotional hangups I clearly need to work through. The last thing I need is a relationship."

Jackie wondered about the hangups she was alluding to and if she'd ever get to hear about them.

"I wasn't talking about us getting into a romantic relationship,"

Cam continued.

"What were you talking about, then?"

Cam shifted to face her better. "Have you ever had a friends-with-benefits type thing?"

"Goodness no." The thought was laughable. "I think I've been looking for serious and long term since high school."

Her mind skated over her relationship history, giving her pause. "Maybe that's the problem. I've put all the weight of mine and my family's expectations on every single romantic connection. I get so invested so quickly that I end up putting up with a lot of crap from the men I date. That's probably why I'm in the situation I am now with my sexuality. I never gave myself time and space to see what I like. I never gave myself time for…"

"Fun?" Cam prompted.

Jackie turned to face her better and their gazes held. "Yeah. Fun."

A small smile danced on the corners of Cam's mouth. "We could be fun."

"We *are* fun, Cam," Jackie assured her. "With or without sex, it's fun being around you."

"I feel the same." Cam nodded. "So…what if we keep having fun? If we want to sleep together now and then, we can. If that's not working out, then we stop."

"And we can keep hanging out?" Jackie asked with a hint of pleading in her tone.

"Sure." Cam pointed at the fireplace, which seemed to represent their sexual connection. "This can be casual. It can be whatever we want it to be."

The tension in Jackie's muscles began to ease. "And when one or both of us meet someone we want to be serious about, we'll be honest and move on with no hard feelings?"

"Absolutely!"

Cam's tone and expression exuded a confidence that Jackie couldn't yet emulate, but she was beginning to relax more fully now.

Jackie's eyes swept over Cam's long, lithe body casually reclined against the back of the sofa, her white t-shirt clinging to her firm breasts.

No, *relax* wasn't the right word for the way her insides pulsed and her imagination sparked as she thought of all the ways she and Cam could be casual together.

17

As Cam suggested, Jackie did allow herself to explore her sexuality, or she made an effort to, anyway.

It was confusing at first. The internet provided a plethora of resources and, for the first few days after her time with Cam, she tried to consume them all whenever she had free time. She read articles, watched videos, and even read a few sapphic romance novels. The books were her favorite part of the research process. Some of them were exceptionally good and tugged at her heartstrings in ways no straight romance ever had.

On social media, she found groups for people who realized they were queer later in life. It was both eye-opening and inspiring to read about people who came out as gay or finally embraced the fact that they were transgender in their forties or fifties. These people were brave in ways she couldn't begin to comprehend, but she found their stories comforting nonetheless. Like her, most of them had grown up and lived their adult lives in environments where the possibility of being gay or trans was either discouraged or ignored altogether.

When she got overwhelmed by all the information, she took online quizzes, which felt adolescent, but also kind of fun. Most of the results placed her in the bisexual category. It seemed to fit her feelings and experiences better than any other label.

One evening, after spending three or four hours online when she'd gotten off work, she decided that much screentime was unhealthy and went for a walk. The cool air refreshed her, and it was fun to people-watch in the park near her apartment.

A few children bundled up in little coats played on a swing set while their parents chatted off to the side. A man played fetch with his dog, and an older man and woman sat on a bench laughing.

Jackie watched the couple for a while and smiled at the affection and happiness they seemed to share after who knows how many years together.

For so long, *this* is what she'd wanted: to find a good husband, raise kids in a happy, loving home completely different from the one she'd grown up in, and grow old with the man she loved. Besides her teaching career, that dream mattered to her more than anything. Did that really need to change because she had this new information about herself?

Okay. She was bisexual. It didn't mean she needed to date women or come out. Certainly not to her family. She could explore and have fun with Cam for a little while until she met the right man. Her goals could remain intact and this other part of her life could eventually fade into the background.

Just then, an image of Cam at the Christmas festival, smiling and laughing filled her mind, and guilt twisted her insides. She had to remember, even though Cam had agreed to casual sex, she was so much more than a means to an end. She was a friend. A kind, funny, interesting, and talented friend.

Jackie got to see how artistically talented Cam was one evening when they were lying in bed after a steamy *exploration* session. They had spent several nights together since agreeing to the friends-with-benefits relationship.

Sometimes they only hung out and watched TV after one of them cooked dinner, but more often than not, they ended up in each other's arms. Jackie never would have believed she could be so insatiable. She hadn't been that way with the guys she'd dated, but maybe the novelty of discovering this new side of herself was to blame for that. Whatever the case, Cam didn't seem to mind. She was a generous and enthusiastic lover.

As Jackie lay sated in Cam's bed, waiting for her to return with some cool drinks, her attention fell on Cam's desk, where a large flat zippered case she'd never seen before was sitting. When Cam returned dressed in a robe and carrying two glasses of water, Jackie pointed at the case and said, "What's that?"

Cam glanced at the case. "That's my personal portfolio. I don't get it out much, but there was a piece in there I painted years ago that I wanted to reference for the Open Air campaign at work."

She sat on the bed and offered Jackie a water, but Jackie's curiosity was more pressing than her thirst. "May I look at it?"

Cam's eyebrows furrowed in confusion as if Jackie had asked to see something boring like her refrigerator instructions. "It's only a few pieces I've painted and sketched in my spare time and a couple from my college days. Nothing interesting."

"I doubt that," Jackie said as Cam picked up the case from her desk and handed it to her.

Jackie pulled up the covers and sat with her back against the headboard as she opened the portfolio. The first piece of sketch paper showed a black and white pencil drawing of a little black-haired boy with big dark eyes. She remembered that face from the photos Cam had shown her after Thanksgiving break. Looking up at Cam, she said, "Your nephew?"

Cam smiled fondly. "Yeah. That's Cody. He's the sweetest little terror."

Laughing, Jackie brushed a finger over the page. "The detail on this is remarkable. I feel like he could jump off the paper and start talking."

"And there's his mom," Cam said when Jackie turned the page. Jackie gasped at the drawing of a woman in Native American fancy dance regalia. "Wow. This is stunning."

The next paper was a small watercolor. It was a simple but pretty landscape.

"That one was from college. I was still experimenting with watercolors then, so it's kind of basic," Cam explained.

"It's lovely," Jackie said before turning to the next sheet and the next. There were more black and white sketches, abstract paintings in vibrant colors, and a few more watercolors. "Cam, these are amazing!"

"Thanks." The tan of Cam's skin deepened a few shades from her face all the way down her chest, and Jackie struggled not to let herself get distracted by the sight.

She bit her lip. "Can I ask you something?"

"Sure." Cam settled against the headboard beside her.

Jackie's thoughts drifted to that day at the butterfly exhibit of childhood dreams at Wolly, "Was this the kind of art you envisioned doing when you were young? Like with gallery showings and the whole scene?"

"Yeah. That's what I wanted to do," Cam answered in a quiet voice.

"Did you change your mind?"

"I guess you could say that."

She shifted to study Cam's face. Deep lines crinkled her normally smooth forehead, and her mouth was set in a tight line.

"We don't have to talk about it, if you don't want," Jackie said.

Cam searched her eyes for a moment, maybe looking for signs that she could trust Jackie with the explanation. Jackie made a point to keep her own expression open and patient.

Finally, Cam took a deep breath then exhaled it. "I changed my mind because of my ex-girlfriend, Tina. We were together for two years in college, but I thought we'd be a couple for a lot longer than that."

A bitter chuckle escaped Cam's throat. "I was so young. I had no idea how the world worked back then. Tina said she loved me and wanted to be with me, and I believed her even though I knew she came from a completely different world from mine. Her family were old-fashioned, traditional-values types in South Carolina and very privileged.

"I knew enough to realize they probably wouldn't be pleased with the idea of their daughter being with a woman, but Tina said she didn't care. The plan was for us to spend the year after graduation apart. She'd take the time to come out to her parents and look for a job, and I'd get work too. There was no way we could build the kind of life she was used to, of course, but I wanted her to be comfortable. I didn't see how I could make that happen as the stereotypical starving artist, so I shifted to the corporate world with graphic design. It doesn't pay a fortune, but it's steady work."

Cam paused her narrative to take a drink of water and, perhaps, collect her thoughts. "That year we were apart, Tina started pulling away, although I didn't recognize it as that. Not until she sent me a breakup text."

"A text?!" Jackie interjected before she could think better of it.

"Yeah." Cam clenched the folds of the bedsheet until her knuckles turned white. "She said we weren't going to work out, and that I should move on...if I hadn't already."

If she hadn't already? A flame of ire rose up in Jackie's chest. She hadn't known Cam for that long, but every instinct told her Cam was loyal and faithful. Hell, she'd changed her whole career path for Tina!

"I was in shock," Cam continued. "No, scratch that. I didn't believe her. I thought for sure she was having a hard time with the separation and distance and that we needed to meet and talk it out. That's when I drove all day to where she lived and showed up on her front porch with flowers."

The mental image of a younger Cam, exhausted but hopeful, standing on the porch of a fancy house with flowers made Jackie's heart ache. She probably understood Tina's family situation better than most, so she knew where this story was going.

"When Tina answered the door, she looked horrified that I was there," Cam said. "She grabbed my arm and pulled me around to the back of the house where no one could see us and asked why I'd come. I tried to reason with her, tried to get her to change her mind or at least promise to think things over, but she shut me down. She acted like we'd never been anything serious in the first place. And that was that."

Cam rested her head against the headboard and stared up at the ceiling. "A few months later, I found out on social media that she was engaged to some guy from her high school class."

They sat in silence for a while. Jackie was emotionally wrung out from the story, so she could only imagine how Cam must be feeling. So many things made sense now, like Cam's reaction when she'd learned who Jackie's family was. The parallels between Tina's background and Jackie's were striking. Not to mention the fact that Cam had once again been swept up in a confused woman's experimentation.

That painful history, more than anything, proved that Jackie was the last person on earth Cam would ever want a serious romantic relationship with.

On some levels, that should have been a relief to Jackie, but it mostly made her sad. Not for herself, of course. That wouldn't make sense. No, it was most certainly sadness for Cam. It was deeply unfair that a woman like her had gotten her heart broken so badly that the repercussions still weighed on her some ten years later.

"Cam…" What could she say? *I'm sorry?* That was so trite. "I can't imagine how hard that must have been. Thank you for telling me. I'm sorry for dredging up painful memories, though."

"Don't feel bad. You didn't know," Cam reassured her. She gave her head a sharp shake, as if to clear out the bad thoughts. "Long story short: I wasn't feeling too adventurous after the breakup, so I stuck with graphic design. I've been doing it ever since."

Jackie accepted the change of topic. "It seems like a good field. But I hate that your employers don't appreciate you enough to promote you like you deserve."

"I don't know." Cam's shoulders sagged. "Maybe I wasn't even ready for the promotion."

Cam's insecure, downtrodden demeanor tugged on Jackie's heart. "That's unlikely. What was the job, anyway?"

"A senior designer role. I would have been working on one or two large projects for the high dollar clients instead of a dozen small ones like I do now."

Jackie mulled over that for a minute. "Do those projects still fall under your current manager's supervision? That is, would you still be doing work *for him*?"

"No, Logan was the one who chose which one of us got the job, but he's not in charge of the senor designers' projects. That falls under his boss, Mr. Bolton."

Something clicked in Jackie's brain. "Didn't you tell me once that Logan uses your design ideas more than the others?"

Cam nodded.

"That's it, then! I imagine your work made him look good. Maybe you were even doing some of his job for him. If you moved on to another role, it might reveal how subpar his own work really is. My guess is he couldn't afford for you to get promoted."

"You really think that was the problem?" Cam asked, her eyes wide.

Jackie scoffed. "I grew up around politicians, darling. I know a thing or two about egotistical men."

Cam ran her hand through her hair as if deep in thought. Fortunately, she hadn't seemed to notice the term of endearment that had slipped out. *Darling?* Where had that come from?

Jackie refocused on the matter at hand and tapped the portfolio. "I'm no expert, but I know artistic talent when I see it. If what you do for your job is anywhere near as good as this, I imagine you're one of the best designers at your firm."

When Cam didn't respond, Jackie added, "I suppose that doesn't help much, though. You still didn't get the promotion."

"No, it does help," Cam said. "I was beginning to wonder if maybe my work wasn't good enough and Logan had been right not to give me the promotion. It's good to have another perspective."

Cam's brown eyes were soft and sincere as she looked at Jackie. "I like the way your mind works."

A fluttering sensation danced in Jackie's chest, and she looked away. "And here I thought it was my body you liked."

"That too." Cam's voice lowered to a near-growl. "But you have very nice insights, Jackie Webster."

When Jackie looked at Cam again, Cam's gaze was sweeping over her body.

"Why does 'insights' sound like a euphemism the way you say it?" Jackie asked with a husky chuckle.

"No idea." Cam leaned in until their faces were almost touching. "I was only talking about your beautiful insights."

"Hmm. In that case, I have another one for you."

"What's that?" Cam brushed her lips against Jackie's, but instead of staying there, she placed a whisper soft kiss on Jackie's jaw.

Jackie's breath grew shallow. "For entirely selfish reasons, I'm glad your boss was such a jerk about the promotion. If he hadn't been, you wouldn't have gotten so angry that you decided to seduce a supposed straight woman."

She could feel Cam smile against the skin of her neck where she was currently kissing and nibbling. Jackie's heartbeat stuttered when Cam slowly began to trail her lips down her chest. Cam shoved the bedsheet aside and started down her ribs and stomach next. "Hey, Jackie?"

"Yes?" Jackie gasped, as Cam slid even lower.

"I think I'm feeling angry again."

18

She's an extraordinary teacher.

Under the pretense of checking the velvet ropes in front of one of Wolly's displays, Cam watched Jackie lead her class through the Hilda Spaulding exhibit.

She effortlessly kept up with her students' random chatter. Sometimes she'd joke around with them, and sometimes she'd encourage a student to expand on a comment, which she would then turn into a group discussion. When things got off-subject, she'd redirect everyone with calm authority. It was clear the young people liked and respected her. Their behavior with Jackie was better than that of some college students and older adults that Cam had seen pass through the museum's halls.

Cam was so caught up in pondering Jackie's interactions with her students that she didn't realize the group was exiting the exhibit hall until it was too late. Two dozen highschoolers shuffled past Cam followed by a young woman in her twenties—maybe a teacher's aide—and Jackie.

Immediately, Jackie spotted her, and her eyes widened. "Cam! Hi. I thought you only volunteered on the weekends."

It was true. Cam had never volunteered at the museum on a weekday because of her work schedule, but she'd made special arrangements today because she'd wanted to see Jackie in her element.

As Jackie stood facing her, brows knit in an adorably quizzical expression, Cam almost admitted to checking the schedule and ensuring she would be at the museum on the day Jackie's class visited.

But she chickened out at the last minute. Was that something a friend and casual lover would do? Rearrange her whole day so she could watch her *friend* from afar? Cam had no idea, so she took the cautious route.

"You're right," Cam said. "I'm usually only here on the weekend, but my office was being painted today, and we couldn't stay because of the fumes. So, I thought I'd come here for a while."

The office really was being painted, but management was willing to bend their normally rigid rules against working from home for the day. However, Cam had chosen to take the day off instead, even though it meant she'd be working late for the rest of the week. Seeing Jackie had been worth it.

Cam rolled her eyes at herself. *Yeah, super casual.*

Jackie sent her a broad smile, and Cam forgot whatever she'd been thinking about. "The kids loved the exhibit!"

"I'm glad," Cam replied, returning the smile. "It was a great idea bringing them here."

"Thanks, I thought—" The sound of Jackie's cellphone buzzing with an incoming text cut her off, and she frowned and pulled it from her pocket. "I'm sorry. I need to check this. It's from my brother. He doesn't usually contact me during the school day…or at all, really."

Before reading the text, Jackie glanced down the hall, and called to her teacher's aide. "Kay, could you take everyone outside to wait for the bus, please?"

When Kay nodded, Jackie returned her attention to her phone. "Conrad says my father's health has taken a turn, and they've called in hospice. They don't think he has much time left, so Conrad thinks I should come."

Concern filled Cam as she took in Jackie's grave expression. "Oh, I'm sorry. Are you going to go?"

Jackie nodded and chewed on her bottom lip. "I'll need to see if I can get another teacher to cover for me for a couple of days."

She looked so stressed and overwhelmed that Cam longed to wrap her in a hug, but she knew that wouldn't be a good idea. Not here in public with Jackie's students nearby. She settled on a brief touch to Jackie's arm. "Are you going to be okay?"

"I'll be fine," Jackie said. "My dad's been declining quickly. I guess we were all sort of expecting this."

"Still, I'm sure it's not easy. Give me a call if you need anything, okay?"

"I will, Cam. Thank you."

Jackie started to turn to leave but hesitated. Her gaze met Cam's then dropped to Cam's lips for a second.

Cam's heartbeat sped up. *She's not going to…*

Jackie stepped forward, but she only gave Cam a hug and lightly brushed her lips over Cam's cheek. All too soon, she pulled away. "I'll call you later."

"Please do. Let me know how your dad…and you are doing."

Jackie nodded once then walked away.

Cam watched her go, her feelings and thoughts as layered and tangled up as the colorful lines of the abstract painting she was standing beside. It had only been a couple of weeks since she'd taken it into her head to suggest being friends with benefits, and in some ways, she was already starting to regret it.

She'd been in exactly four relationships, including her high school girlfriend, and had considered them all fairly serious. She had no idea how to be casual.

Or maybe she had no idea how to be casual with *Jackie*.

It was like trying to do a complicated dance without knowing the steps. She frequently found herself wondering how much was too much. Was she being too affectionate? Too clingy? And where did their casual intimacy leave off and their growing friendship begin?

The whole thing made her head spin, and as much as she hated the prospect of Jackie's absence and the reason for it, Cam couldn't help but think that maybe a little distance was a good thing.

19

The moment Jackie entered her dad's house, she realized this visit would be different from all the others.

Conrad, Lisa, and Riley were in the family room, as were her dad's Aunt Constance and his sister Joan. Jackie only saw her great aunt and aunt once a year at most. If they were here, things must be very serious.

Once she entered the room, she approached her brother. "Conrad, how's Dad?"

He stood and gave her a quick hug then stepped back. "He's basically unconscious now."

Jackie's heart dropped to her stomach. "What?"

"Yeah. It was very sudden." Conrad ran his hand through his thinning brown hair. "The doctor says he's not in pain, though. It's just like he's taking a long nap in his room."

For a moment, Conrad's tone and description made Jackie think of the way he used to talk to her when she was a child: patiently and gently, like he was trying to word things in a way she could understand. She wondered if he was reverting back to help soften the shock for her, or if it was because Riley, her six-year-old nephew was listening. Maybe both.

"Why isn't he in a hospital?" Jackie asked.

"He made me promise to keep him here at home, if something like this came up, so I'm trying to honor his wishes."

Jackie nodded. That sounded like their dad. He hated the helpless feeling of being in a hospital and would avoid it at any cost. Being here in his own house probably gave him some sense of autonomy, however limited. "Can I see him?"

"Yeah, sure. The nurse is in there with him, but he'll step into the hall for a minute, if you want him to."

"Thanks."

Before leaving the room, Jackie hugged Lisa and Riley then greeted Aunt Constance and Joan. Both women exuded her dad's sternness, and their greetings were as cool and distant as usual. Ever since she was a child, she'd been convinced they disliked her. Conrad had insisted it was only their personalities that made it seem that way, but Jackie was unconvinced. While they weren't exactly doting with him, Aunt Constance and Joan were much warmer with Conrad. Maybe it was because he was more like their dad than she was.

When she said hello to Joan, the older woman's thin lips set in a firm line. "Nice of you to finally join us. It's been two days since Clive started to decline."

"Now, Joan," Conrad protested, "I didn't call Jackie right away. I knew she was working."

Joan's scowl lines deepened when Conrad mentioned Jackie's work, but she didn't comment.

She didn't apologize either.

"Well, I better get in there to see him, if you'll excuse me," Jackie said, hurrying from the room as quickly as decorum allowed.

Despite the undercurrent of unease she felt at the prospect of facing her dad, Jackie was relieved to escape her aunts. She made her way to the master bedroom, taking several deep, steadying breaths as she walked.

When she got to the room, the door was ajar, so she pushed it open the rest of the way and entered.

Tom, the professional nurse who had visited her father weekly for the last several months and who was now assuming the role of fulltime caregiver, was seated in a chair near her dad's bed. He rose when she entered.

"Hi, Tom," she murmured. "I'm glad you could be here with my dad. How is he?"

"I don't think it will be much longer, Ms. Webster." He patted her arm then slipped past her toward the door. "I'll give you a few minutes."

Jackie thanked Tom and sat in the chair he'd vacated. When she scooted closer to the bed and studied her father's face, her breath caught in her chest.

Although she'd been used to seeing her dad get paler and thinner over the past year, the difference in his appearance now was shocking. His complexion had lost most of its color, and he somehow looked even smaller than he had before. The large, four-poster bed practically swallowed him. He was very still except for his breathing.

Conrad had been right. He appeared to be sleeping. In fact, she didn't know when she'd seen him so quiet. It was more than simple unconsciousness. It was as if all the vigor, all the strength, and the fight had drained out of him.

For the first time in her whole life, Jackie didn't feel tense sitting beside him. There was no more apprehension about what he'd say or do or ask of her. No guilt over not measuring up. Not even hurt or resentment for all the ways she'd lived with those feelings for so long. Those emotions might come back later, but at the moment, she felt as quiet as her dad was. There was a sobering heaviness in the room, a force bigger than either one of them.

As she studied his relaxed features, she wondered if he was aware of his situation. Did he know he didn't have much time left? How did he feel about it? Was he afraid?

She hoped not. She reached over and brushed his arm. If he knew what was happening, she hoped he had peace about it.

Her dad had insisted the whole family attend church when she was growing up, but she'd never seen much indication that he took his religion personally. Jackie always felt there was a disconnect between the lessons about compassion and love she heard in Sunday school and the way her dad conducted his business, but she had no idea what he truly thought or believed, at least not enough to speculate if his faith brought him comfort now or not. Did he believe in an afterlife? Did he hope to be reunited with her mom, perhaps?

If that's how things worked, Jackie almost envied him that. He would get to see her mom again, but Jackie didn't even have memories of her.

It struck her, then, that she and Conrad would soon be without both parents. That was a lot to process. What would the future look like now with only the two of them?

Well, there was Aunt Constance and Joan, of course. A flash of guilt swept through her at the thought of them. Maybe she should have made more of an effort to get along with them over the years.

20

Cam's phone buzzed on the desk beside her. She picked it up and read the text.

Jackie: I think my aunts hate me.

Cam: Come on! No one could hate you.

As soon as she sent the message, Cam gulped. *Ugh. Was that too sappy?* She hadn't put her usual forethought into the message since she and Jackie had been rapidly messaging back and forth for the last thirty minutes.

Cam was in the office late, as usual. Since Jackie had been at her dad's house, Cam's workdays had gotten even longer. The Open Air Hill campaign was almost finished and, on top of that, Logan had been loading her up with more assignments than usual. Most days, she stayed at her desk until eight or later.

She wouldn't let that stop her from checking in with Jackie, though. She and her family were in a painful waiting period, knowing Jackie's dad would pass but not knowing when.

Cam's heart ached for her, and she did her best to be supportive through texts. Jackie didn't call because her family was around. She tried not to let that bother her, though, given the challenging circumstances Jackie was facing.

Her phone buzzed again, and Cam realized she'd missed two messages in her distracted state.

Jackie: Aww. That's sweet. Thanks.

Jackie: Maybe hate is a strong word, but they definitely disapprove of me. Part of it is because I'm so focused on my job and not producing a family of my own.

Cam: They sound like your dad.

Jackie: They're definitely cut from the same old-fashioned cloth. But I feel like there's something else with them, and I can't figure it out. Especially after what I overheard Aunt Constance say this morning when she thought I'd gone out.

Cam: What'd she say?

Jackie: She and Joan were criticizing the fact that I haven't visited Dad more often, and then Aunt Constance said, "It shouldn't surprise us in the least, given her background." What do you think that means?

Cam ran her fingers through her hair and scowled out the window. *Background?* Jackie had the same background as the rest of her family, didn't she?

Cam: I have no idea. That's bizarre. Why don't you just ask her about it?

Jackie: Ha! You don't know my family. We don't have open conversations like that. This house has big rooms so it can accommodate all the elephants we ignore.

Cam: That sounds kind of awful. It makes me appreciate my family, even if we do tend to get up in each other's business a little too much sometimes.

Jackie: Does your mom pry into your affairs?

Cam: Well, sort of. She seems to sense when I'm having a rough time and won't rest until she finds out what's going on. She calls me up, but she doesn't pressure me, exactly.

Jackie: She just waits quietly until you tell her yourself? Sounds familiar.

Cam: Wait…do I do that too?

Jackie: lol. Now and then.

Cam: Sorry.

Jackie: Don't be. It's nice.

It's nice. The simple statement filled Cam with a glow of delight, as did the mental image of Jackie smiling at her phone while she texted.

Cam: Back to your family. I get why you don't plan to ask your great aunt what she meant, but does it really matter so much what she thinks about you?

Cam held her breath as she awaited the response, although she didn't understand why.

Jackie: Maybe it shouldn't. But when Dad isn't here anymore, she and Joan will be the only older family members we have left. I know I didn't always make a success of my relationship with Dad, so I guess I don't want to alienate them too.

Cam: It sounds like they are the ones doing the alienating, but I get it. Family is important. I'd hate for you to lose that.

Cam released a heavy sigh. She *would* hate to see that. Truly. But this conversation was reinforcing the point that Jackie definitely wouldn't come out and choose to have a relationship with a woman, at least not for a long time.

But so what? Cam had known that from the start. There was no point in feeling disappointed about it.

Cam: Maybe this time you have to spend with your aunts is a

good thing. When they're around you more, they're bound to love you.

Cam started to send the message then groaned. *Bound to love you?* That was too much. She deleted the last sentence and typed, "When they're around you more, they're bound to change their minds about you."

> Jackie: Thank you. I'm not so sure, but it's kind of you to say that. And I'm sorry to take up half your evening whining about my family.

> Cam: Don't apologize. You're going through a lot right now. And talking to you is giving me a nice break.

> Jackie: Break from what?

Before Cam could respond, another message popped up.

> Jackie: Wait a minute. You're not still at the office again, are you?

> Cam: Maybe.

> Jackie: Cam! It's after nine. You can't keep doing this.

Cam wasn't about to admit it, but she kind of liked to see Jackie fussing over her. It had been a long time since she'd let anyone close enough to do that.

> Cam: I won't be doing it for long. The big project is almost finished.

> Jackie: I hope so. But project or not, I wish I were in town right now. I think I could persuade you to leave work and relax for a while.

A swarm of tingles buzzed through Cam, and her pulse kicked into high gear.

Cam: Oh really? And how would you do that?

Jackie: Well, I know you're a visual person, so I might send you a photo or two to inspire you about what you could be doing instead of working. Or should I say, what *we* could be doing.

Cam: Geez, Jackie! Don't even talk about it. I don't want to disgrace myself right here in my office!

Jackie: Okay, okay. I'll take pity on you. But promise me you won't overdo it. Please?

Cam: I promise. And you get some rest too.

Jackie: I will. Goodnight.

Cam: Goodnight.

Cam tapped the icon next to Jackie's name on her screen and gazed at the profile photo. It was a candid shot Cam had taken the day of the Christmas festival. Jackie's pretty face was lit up in a smile that was on the verge of turning into a laugh.

As Cam studied the photo, she replayed the text conversation in her mind. It had felt so *real*. So close to a genuine romantic relationship better than any Cam had ever experienced in the past.

But it would never be any closer than this, and she couldn't let herself forget that.

The sound of her office door creaking made Cam jump. When she looked up, Mr. Bolton was standing in the doorway. "Camryn? How can you still be here working late again?"

She sent him a small grin. "You're still here too, Mr. Bolton."

He chuckled. "Touché. But I'm an old widower with no life. You're not."

He looked at the cellphone on Cam's desk. "Isn't your partner upset about all these late evenings?"

Cam looked at the phone. No way in hell was she going to try explaining her friends-with-benefits situation to the boss. It was best to keep it simple. "She's out of town visiting family."

"Ah. I guess that worked out nicely then." He turned to leave then stopped and faced her again. "Camryn, I really appreciate the extra work you've put in to help with the Open Air campaign on top of your regular projects. You've done some great work."

He paused for a second and, in a surprised tone, repeated, "Really great work."

Cam sat up taller in her desk chair. "Thanks, Mr. Bolton."

He looked around her office for a second, as if searching for something. His gaze finally fell on an open sketchpad on her desk, and his eyebrows dipped in a frown. "Is that the logo from the Play Smart campaign?"

"Yes. Well, it's one of the earlier drafts I did before we finalized it."

Cam smiled at the logo for the children's sporting goods company startup that had hired them a few months ago. Several cartoon children's hands in different skin tones linked together to form the letters of the company. She was proud of her work on that campaign, enough so that she had been referencing some of it for inspiration for her current work right before Jackie texted her.

Mr. Bolton stepped closer to Cam's desk, his focus still on the sketchpad. "You keep all your drafts from your projects in that?"

Cam flipped through the pages. "Pretty much everything from the past eighteen months up to today. The older stuff is in other sketchpads."

"Do you think I could borrow it?" Mr. Bolton asked.

His expression was suddenly grave, but Cam didn't get the sense that he was upset with her. It was confusing, though.

"Uh, sure. If you want. That one is almost full, and I was going to get out a new one anyway." She closed the sketchpad and handed it over.

"Thanks." He tucked it under his arm then nodded to her. "Have a good evening, Camryn. And when your lady gets back in town, try not to work so much, hmm? Don't do like I did and waste the time you have together."

"Okay," Cam said.

As she watched him leave, half of her mind was still puzzling over his sudden interest in her sketches, but the other half was already back on Jackie. Mr. Bolton didn't know the details of her relationship, but he had a point. Maybe it was best to appreciate her time with Jackie for what it was instead of wasting it wishing for something more.

21

Jackie followed Cam's advice to spend more time around her aunts. Since they were all in a difficult waiting game with her father, she tried to make their days more comfortable. She ran errands for them and volunteered to navigate the stressful Dallas-Fort Worth traffic to drive them to appointments and shopping excursions.

By the third or fourth day of playing taxi and delivery service for them, Jackie was as exhausted as she was after a week of teaching. Cam had picked up on that fact during one of their text conversations and had gently suggested her aunts might very well like her without her working so hard to ingratiate herself with them, but Jackie was unconvinced.

Naturally, Cam would think that because that was the kind of person she was. Jackie had never felt the pressure to earn anything with Cam. She'd been completely willing to be friends with Jackie and nothing else simply because she liked being around her. And even if Jackie put a stop to the physical aspects of their relationship tomorrow, she trusted that Cam would still be her friend.

But Jackie's family wasn't like Cam. Jackie had always felt driven to perform her loyalty, love, and respect for it to be accepted, and most days, she fell ridiculously short. It was messed up. She knew that, but she played the game anyway. This was the only family she had, and it was shrinking.

Although Constance and Joan hadn't exactly warmed up to her yet, they were accepting her help and thinking of other things for her to do, so Jackie took it as an encouraging sign right up until the moment she once again overheard one of Constance's tirades.

Jackie had left the house one Saturday evening to go fetch Constance's dry cleaning when she realized she'd left her wallet in her room. She hurried back in the door and past the living room. Then her foot nearly slipped on the bottom step of the staircase when Constance's raised voice reached her ears.

"Can you believe that girl, Joan? Look at the way she's trying to insinuate herself into our good graces! I'm sure she knows she won't get much from Clive's will, but trying to make us her meal ticket? That's beneath even her."

Jackie's heart started pounding as she stared at the living room doorway. For a moment, she remained frozen at the bottom of the stairs. Her thoughts were spinning, but a memory of Cam's words overrode them. *Why don't you just ask her about it?*

Suddenly, she couldn't stand the questions or confusion a moment longer. Squaring her shoulders, she spun around and marched to the living room.

"Aunt Constance, I have no idea what you're talking about, but I'm not trying to make anyone my meal ticket," Jackie proclaimed as she strode through the living room doorway.

Both women faced her with matching shocked expressions, but Constance recovered first. "Jackie! What are you still doing here? Are you eavesdropping now?"

Jackie's jaw hardened, but she forced herself to keep her tone calm. "I don't know why that should surprise you, given your obvious low opinion of me. Now, do you mind telling me what you mean with all this talk about meal tickets and my dad's will?"

Constance sat up straighter and pinned Jackie with a glare. "Don't think we can't see through you, Jacqueline. We know you're only being sweet and helpful to us because Clive is dying. It won't do you any good."

"What do you want from me?" Jackie snapped. "Okay, yeah. I probably should have made more of an effort in our relationship in the past. But I've really been trying to rectify that now, and I wish you'd both meet me halfway. Knowing we'll lose Dad soon has reminded me how important family is."

"And this family's money too, no doubt," Joan interjected. "You figure you'd best play nice with us in case Clive leaves more to us than to you."

"I don't care about that!" Jackie huffed, her head beginning to throb. "I have no idea what the terms of Dad's will are, but it doesn't matter. I have a career, and I haven't even spent the trust Mom left. I'm better off than so many people. I don't need to play silly games over money."

Neither of her aunts responded, but they continued to appraise her with unconcealed cynicism.

Jackie rubbed her forehead. There was still so much about this conversation that flummoxed her. "Dad had the right to do whatever he wanted with his assets, but why are you so convinced he didn't make provisions for me?"

A dull ache pulsed through her chest. "D-does he disapprove of me and my choices that much?"

"Don't play dumb, Jacqueline," Constance chided. "Clive did what he needed to do to keep it from the public, but the whole family knows the truth about you."

For a fraction of a second, a thought of her relationship with Cam flashed through Jackie's mind, but she dismissed it. There was no way they could have all heard about that. "What truth are you talking about?"

Constance scowled and shook her head in disgust. "The truth about Clive not being your real father, of course. What else?"

Jackie's breath exhaled in a sharp gasp, and her heart felt like it stopped for a second. Surely, she hadn't heard that correctly. "What did you say?"

"For heaven's sakes, Jacqueline. This act is really getting tired. We all know your mom had an affair with Doug McCurdy, Clive's campaign manager, and had his baby. You do a fine job of putting on the manners and clothes of a real Webster—well enough to fool the public—but the family has always known."

Jackie shook her head, even as tears stung the corners of her eyes. "I don't believe you! Why are you saying this? I know who my mom was, and I know Clive Webster is my father. I grew up in this house. He raised me!"

"Of course he did," Constance said in a caustic tone. "What choice did he have? He found out about the affair and that you weren't his right after you were born. When he confronted your mom, she ran off to cry to her lover about it, and they both died in that car crash. Clive was running for office. He couldn't afford to let that humiliating scandal go public, so he covered it up."

Joan smirked. "It was a stroke of genius, really. When people saw the grieving widower left to take care of his new baby girl all alone, his public approval went through the roof. He won by a larger margin than any candidate in the history of the district."

I was a prop.

Jackie's legs grew too shaky to hold her up any longer. She sank into the nearest chair. There was an odd buzzing sound in her ears that prevented her from hearing any more of Constance or Joan's ramblings for several minutes.

Finally, Constance's harsh voice broke through. "I fail to see the point in your pretending you didn't know any of this, Jacqueline."

Joan had gone quiet, and Jackie could feel her curious stare without needing to look up. Joan's tone was incredulous as she said, "Constance, I'm not so sure she *did* know."

"I didn't. I swear," Jackie rasped over the tightness in her throat.

Constance made an exaggerated huffing noise. "That's impossible! Clive must have told you."

Jackie looked the older woman in the eye. "He never said a word."

Constance put a hand to her chest, and she and Joan exchanged tense glances. The room went awkwardly silent.

After several minutes, Constance burst out, "Well, wasn't it obvious to you? You look nothing like Clive, and you certainly don't share the same priorities."

That was it? After unloading this enormous revelation in Jackie's lap, they were going to go right back to criticizing her life choices?

The contents of her lunch began to roil in her stomach. If she didn't get out of here now, she might lose it completely. With a muffled half-sob, Jackie climbed to her feet and ran out of the house.

She stumbled her way to the car before getting in and starting the engine. Her thoughts scattered in every direction like the gravel spewing from underneath her tires as she sped away.

Clive Webster wasn't her father! She'd been lied to for her entire life. It was impossible, wasn't it? Maybe it was only a hateful rumor Constance and Joan held onto because they disliked her or her mom.

For a moment, she clung to the theory with a grip as tight as the one she had on her steering wheel, but it was already slipping away. Too many things were starting to fall into place.

No, she didn't resemble the man she'd thought to be her dad, not in looks, personality, or habits. A deep, inexplicable antagonism had always underscored their relationship, or it had been inexplicable up until today. Had he ever loved her, or had he resented her all these years for being the product of his wife's betrayal?

Jackie shook her head so hard that it made her vision swim for a second.

No! He'd chosen to keep her and raise her! That had to mean something. Didn't it mean he'd loved his wife enough to provide for her child and had enough compassion for Jackie to give her his name?

His public approval went through the roof.

Joan's words rattled through Jackie's brain, making her insides seize up all over again.

Of course he'd kept her! What else could he have done? Given her up for adoption and have the media ask questions until they discovered the truth and broadcasted it to all his would-be constituents? The scandal would have ruined his campaign, possibly even his career.

Instead, he and his campaign had spun the tragedy of her mom's death to garner sympathy, and the infant Jackie had become a prop in the theater of Clive Webster's public image.

A prop!

And she'd been expected to be a prop ever since.

She always had to dress the right way, say the right things, date the right men. And when she didn't, she was accused of being ungrateful.

Ungrateful!

Sometimes her…dad would talk to her like she was a spoiled brat for not appreciating what she had, even though she'd always thought she'd had a healthy sense of gratitude for her privileged life. Now she realized no amount of gratitude would have been enough in his eyes. Nothing she could do would be sufficient recompense for being an interloper.

She was an outsider in her own family.

Shadows lengthened and darkness closed in around her as she sped down the highway. Her mind was in turmoil, and her heart was ripping apart at the seams. And there was only one place she could think to go.

22

A loud, rapid knock on Cam's apartment door startled her awake. She'd dozed off while sitting on the sofa with her e-reader.

Typical. It had been the first opportunity she'd had to relax after working all week and volunteering all Saturday, and she'd fallen asleep.

The knock sounded again—louder and faster this time—and Cam's heartrate picked up. Her apartment building had keypad codes on all the outside entrances, so she doubted this was an attempted home invasion. But the urgency of the knocking unnerved her.

She stood, stretched her stiff muscles, and went to the door. When she looked out the peephole, her jaw dropped.

Jackie was standing outside the door. Her hair was uncharacteristically messy, and she looked paler than usual.

Cam scrambled to unlock the door and open it. "Jackie? What are you doing here? Are you ok—"

Jackie threw herself at Cam and pressed their lips together. Cam staggered backwards at the impact but managed not to fall over. On instinct, her lips responded to Jackie's, but she forced herself to pull away.

"Jackie, what's going on?"

Cam moved to close her apartment door and lock it. When she turned around, Jackie was on her again, pushing her back against the hard door and kissing her with a ferocity Cam had never seen from her before.

Cam moaned and her eyes closed as Jackie's tongue stroked her bottom lip then slipped into her mouth. But Jackie tasted more of desperation than passion. Somehow, Cam found the strength to pull back and break the kiss.

"Jackie…"

"Please, Cam. Not now." Jackie kissed her again. This time, she slid her arms under Cam's t-shirt and began to stroke her back. Cam's skin burned at the contact, and her arms automatically closed around Jackie's slender frame…which was shaking.

"Jackie, stop it!" Cam leaned her head back and stared into Jackie's eyes. She ran her hands over Jackie's shoulders and arms. "You're trembling. Talk to me!"

When Jackie only stared back, Cam blurted out. "I'm not going to let you use me like this without telling me what's going on first!"

Jackie's eyes widened and so did Cam's. She'd surprised herself with the outburst.

They continued their odd little standoff for a moment, both breathing heavily.

Suddenly, Jackie began to sob uncontrollably.

"I'm sorry," she whimpered. "I never meant to make you feel that way."

A lump formed in Cam's throat at the sight of Jackie in tears. "Come sit down and talk to me."

She guided her to the sofa. Jackie was still shaking, so Cam grabbed the throw from the back of the sofa and covered her with it. She scooted closer, and Cam wrapped an arm around her shoulder. "What is it? Has your father passed?"

"No," she murmured. "Or I don't think so. That's not it."

Cam rubbed Jackie's arm slowly and waited.

When Jackie began to talk, Cam listened intently, but she also focused on remaining still. Still and calm for Jackie as she told this shocking, painful story. Despite the shock, Cam was careful not to react too much. Jackie needed this time and space to air all the heavy thoughts and emotions she was going through.

"There you have it," Jackie concluded in a grim tone. She had shed many angry and heartrending tears while talking, but now her pale face was impassive, as if she were going numb. "I'm the product of a scandalous affair, and a family embarrassment. What a mess."

She leaned back to look at Cam better. "I'll bet you're regretting opening your door tonight, aren't you?"

"No, but I'm thinking I probably should have just let you fuck me after all," Cam replied dryly.

"Cam!" A sharp laugh burst from Jackie, and she buried her face against Cam's shoulder.

Cam held her and ran her fingers through Jackie's long, soft hair. "I know this has been a lot to absorb today, and you probably won't fully absorb it for some time. And that's okay. Just work through it and feel whatever you need to feel."

"I don't even know what to feel right now," Jackie's muffled voice admitted. "Except lost. Like I don't know who I am anymore."

Gently, Cam guided Jackie back into a sitting position so they could face one another. "That's understandable, but you're still a lot of things outside of your family. You're an excellent teacher who cares and makes a difference in her students' lives. You're also a kind and supportive friend."

Jackie gave a shaky smile, but she didn't look up. She appeared to be struggling to accept Cam's words.

"Oh, and you're hot as hell too," Cam finished.

Jackie's head snapped up then her eyes squeezed shut as she laughed. "Cam, I'm trying to have a meltdown here. You can't keep making me laugh like this."

"I know, babe. I'm sorry," Cam said. She didn't regret the affectionate term that had slipped out, but she worried for a second that she could have made Jackie uncomfortable.

Jackie put those worries to rest, though, when she snuggled back against Cam. "I forgive you."

They sat in silence for a while until Jackie's rhythmic breathing suggested she'd gone to sleep.

Cam's heart swelled, and she longed to stay like this all night, but it wasn't the most comfortable sleeping arrangement for either of them.

"Jackie," Cam whispered, carefully shaking her awake. "Why don't you lie down now?"

Jackie nodded and allowed Cam to help her to her feet. Then she washed her face, changed into the t-shirt and shorts Cam provided, and climbed into bed.

She turned on her side with her back to Cam and peeked over her shoulder. In a small, sleepy voice, she said, "Cam? Will you hold me for a while?"

Everything inside Cam went squishy and warm. "Of course."

Cam lay down beside Jackie, scooting up against her soft, graceful back and encircling her waist. Jackie settled Cam's arm around her more securely until her hand rested against Jackie's thumping heart.

It only took a few moments for the thumping to slow to a calmer rhythm as Jackie drifted off to the dream world. Cam hoped they were gentle dreams. Not unpleasant memories and reflections of this nightmarish day.

Jackie had faced a terrible blow. Cam couldn't fathom the depths of hurt and betrayal she must be feeling after finding out her whole history was based on a lie, and the people she should have been able to trust had perpetuated that lie, mostly for their own benefit.

Cam's heart ached for Jackie. She longed to absorb Jackie's pain. She wanted to hold her for however long it took for healing and wholeness to return to her spirit. And most importantly, she wanted to be the person Jackie brought all of her hurts too. She wanted to be the one to listen and comfort and cheer up and kiss away Jackie's pain…forever.

Oh God. I'm in love with her.

Cam swallowed hard and tried to steady her breath, which had gone shallow with anxiety.

I can't believe this is happening again.

In some corner of her heart, she was grateful and relieved. After Tina, she hadn't been sure she was capable of this kind of love again. She'd held back in the few relationships she'd had since then, and she suspected her girlfriends could sense that fact. That was probably why things hadn't worked out with them.

But now? Now all the love she'd kept stuffed away for more than ten years had broken loose, desperate to pour into this unexpected connection she'd found with the woman in her arms.

That was the problem, though. Cam had no right to give her heart to Jackie. That wasn't what they were. All they had ever agreed to was a friendship with occasional intimacy. Jackie had so much happening in her life right now, from a recent breakup to discovering a new aspect of her sexuality to all these family complications. Cam had a feeling if she pushed too far, if she tested the tenuous terms of their casual relationship too much, she might push Jackie away completely.

The thought of that was unbearable.

Jackie awoke in a surprisingly peaceful state, considering the turmoil from the evening before. That turmoil still swarmed inside her, but it was partly allayed by the feel of being in Cam's arms.

Although she couldn't remember precisely when and how she'd gone to sleep, Jackie was fairly certain she and Cam had been spooning. Then sometime during the night, they had shifted until Cam was on her back and Jackie was lying on her with her cheek on Cam's chest. Cam's firm, steady arm was curled around her shoulders.

It was heavenly.

When Jackie had barreled into Cam's apartment the night before and threw herself at Cam—her cheeks overheated at the memory—she'd convinced herself she was in desperate need of human touch, maybe even release. Anything to help her forget the feeling of her life falling apart.

But when Cam had stopped her advances and, in her patient way, persuaded Jackie to explain what was upsetting her, she quickly realized she'd actually needed to talk. Not only that, she'd needed *Cam*.

Cam had listened, offered comfort, and even managed to make her laugh. Then she'd taken care of her. She'd held her all night.

Now, in the clear morning light, as she rested on the still sleeping Cam, Jackie realized it wasn't any human touch she'd craved. It was Cam's. She'd wanted Cam's arms to hold her. Wanted to hear her low, soothing voice. She'd wanted to rest, surrounded by her scent and warmth and serene presence. Cam was the realest thing in Jackie's whole life right now.

Jackie drew on the comfort of Cam's body beneath hers for a few minutes longer then sat up in bed, careful not to disturb Cam. Locating her phone on the nightstand beside her, she picked it up and checked for notifications.

There were no texts or calls from Conrad, so that probably meant there hadn't been any changes overnight.

Had he spoken to Constance or Joan? Did they talk about last night's drama? How much did Conrad know about her situation? She couldn't believe for a second that he'd been left in the dark the same way she had.

She stewed over the questions for a while before opening her web browser and typing "Douglas McCurdy" into the search bar. It was a strange sensation needing to rely on the internet to learn about her own father.

Even though he'd died in 1992, she found his obituary on a website with archived newspaper articles. As she tapped the link to the article, a rustling sound beside her made her turn her head.

Cam was beginning to stir. It struck Jackie then that this was the first time she'd seen Cam wake up beside her. The times they'd slept together, Jackie had either left before staying the whole night or, if she did stay, Cam had gotten out of bed before Jackie had awakened.

Cam's short hair was adorably tousled as she stretched. Then her eyes opened, and she gazed up at Jackie. There was a soft, maybe even tender expression in those soulful brown eyes that made Jackie's breath catch. "Hey."

"Hey," Jackie replied in a raspy voice.

With a slight groan, Cam sat up beside her. "How do you feel this morning?"

"My head is still spinning."

Cam gave a sympathetic nod, but didn't respond, as if she sensed Jackie would elaborate.

"I'm doing some research on the man who was my biological father."

Jackie tilted the phone toward Cam, showing her the photo at the top of the obituary.

Cam's eyes widened as she studied the image. "My gosh. You look like him!"

"Yeah, I do." Jackie looked at the picture again. "This is so surreal."

She skimmed the obituary until she got to the part about surviving relatives. "It says he had a sister and a couple of nieces."

Jackie chewed on her lip. "I wonder if she's still alive. Do you think she knew about the affair? About me?"

"It might be a good idea to find out, if and when you're ready to keep digging into this. I mean, you've had a lot to process in only a day or so." Cam brushed her fingers over Jackie's arm. Her touch steadied and excited Jackie in equal parts.

Clearing her throat, Jackie returned her attention to the topic at hand. "Dad probably bribed the McCurdy family to keep quiet about whatever they knew. No one was supposed to find out the truth and mess up his perfect life. Not even me."

Bitterness and hurt tinged Jackie's voice, even to her own ears.

Cam slid back down into bed and propped herself up on her elbow. "You know the situation better than me, of course, but I wonder if your dad was also trying to protect you."

"Protect me?"

"Yeah. I'm sure it was more expedient for him to keep all this a secret, but I also think learning the truth would have been a lot for you to handle when you were younger. Maybe he thought you were better off not knowing."

Jackie pondered that for a while. Was it possible her dad considered her feelings like that? The idea was a surprising yet comforting one.

"You may be right. I hadn't thought of it that way."

She slid down into bed so she was at Cam's eye level and mirrored the conversation they'd had only a couple of weeks ago. "You have very nice insights, Camryn Durant."

A slow grin spread over Cam's face before she leaned in and softly kissed Jackie's lips.

Jackie's eyelids closed and she returned the kiss. Then another and another. It was heady and so, so sweet. Heart beating fast, she pulled away and groaned. "I have to go back and face the family soon."

Cam closed the gap between them again and kissed the tip of Jackie's ear, making her shiver. She whispered, "Why don't you stay with me here where it's safe just a while longer?"

When Cam's lips slid down to Jackie's neck, she gasped and rolled onto her back, tugging on Cam until she lay on top of her. "Yesss..."

She would savor this sanctuary of comfort and passion just a while longer.

23

After spending a good part of her Sunday in bed with Cam, Jackie didn't arrive back at the family home until dinnertime. Constance, Joan, and Conrad were still there, but Lisa and Riley had gone home.

The conversation around the dinner table was stilted and impersonal, but no more than usual. At least Jackie finally knew why Constance and Joan were so distant. As the evening wore on, it became evident neither woman had any plans of introducing the subject of Jackie's background again. Apparently, their plan was to pretend their big revelation and Jackie's reaction had never happened.

Why was she even surprised?

After dinner, Conrad pulled her aside to talk in the library, away from the aunts. If they'd talked to him about the previous night's discussion, he didn't show it.

He sat down on the library sofa with her and said, "Dad took another bad turn last night. He probably won't make it to the morning."

Even though they'd all been expecting it for over a week now, the news still gave her a jolt. She nodded slowly. "Is he in pain?"

Conrad's mouth set in a grim line. "Tom doesn't think so."

"I'm glad for that."

"I am too." He turned to face her more fully. "Do you want to go up and talk to Dad before...that is, you certainly don't have to, if you aren't comfortable with it. But, if you want to, this would probably be the time to do it. I'm not sure that he can hear us, but you never know."

Jackie appreciated that he was being so considerate with her. For all their differences, not only in age but in personality and priorities too, he'd always tended to be patient and kind to her.

"Yes, I'll go see him."

When she entered the master bedroom, she immediately sensed the change, even from the day before. Nearly all of her dad's color was gone and his breathing came in short spasms.

After Tom left the room, Jackie approached the bed once again and stood over it. She'd half-expected to be angry as she stared down at the man lying there, now that she knew about his long deception. But she wasn't.

Jackie had no idea if he'd kept the truth from her all these years partly to protect her, as Cam had suggested, or if it had entirely been to safeguard his reputation. By this point, though, it didn't matter.

His decisions had shaped her life, just like knowing the truth would likely shape it from here on out.

She swallowed hard then leaned over to kiss his pale, sunken cheek: the last time she'd do her customary dutiful daughter gesture.

"Dad," she whispered. "I don't know if you can hear me, but I want to tell you I appreciate the things you did for me."

Her own breath grew shaky as she inhaled and exhaled slowly. "And I am choosing to believe you did what you thought was best. I'm going to try to make peace with that. I hope you find peace too."

As she left the room, there was an unexpected lightness in her step, despite the gravity of the moment. She had a long, emotional road ahead now that she knew the truth about her parents, but she felt the importance of choosing to begin the journey with compassion and forgiveness.

Her resentment couldn't hurt her dad at this point. *She* would be the one to suffer from carrying it around. Starting now, she would do her best to put it down and move forward.

As expected, Jackie's dad died in the middle of the night. The following morning brought business and confirmation of the funeral arrangements made in the previous week.

The mood was understandably solemn when Jackie joined Conrad, Joan, and Constance for a late breakfast that morning. Apart from talk of arrangements, though, no one directly discussed the death. If

Constance and Joan were upset, they didn't show it. Everyone behaved with the stiff and stilted formality that always characterized their interactions.

It was so stifling that Jackie finally had to make a quick escape and take a walk in the garden.

As she breathed in the chilly, late morning air, Jackie found herself missing Cam, the way she had several times since coming back to this house. Cam was so genuine and sweet; as different from this family as she could possibly be.

She sank into a wrought iron garden chair, wincing at the feel of the cold, hard metal beneath her. Right now, she longed to be back in Cam's arms more than she'd ever longed for anything.

She couldn't keep lying to herself. It was hypocritical for her to call out her family's insincerity when she was hiding from her own truth.

The truth was that she wanted Cam. Really *wanted* her. Not only for friendship and sex but for…everything. What would it be like? Being together every day, eating breakfast in the mornings after long, passionate nights, going out on dates, coming home from work to each other.

A future.

Goosebumps formed on her skin. She could picture it all. But would Cam ever want that with Jackie? She believed Cam cared for her. It was there every time they talked or touched, but were those feelings deep enough? Would she be willing to take that risk—and it would be a risk, Jackie knew that—or was she still too wounded after Tina?

"There you are."

Jackie jumped at the sound of her brother's voice as he approached her garden hiding place.

"Aren't you cold?" he asked.

"I don't mind," she said. "I needed some air."

"Mind if I join you for a minute?"

"Not at all." The polite response fell from her lips before she could even pause to consider if it was true or not. Honestly, she'd preferred to be left alone with her thoughts of Cam, but she wasn't about to say that to Conrad.

He sat in the chair facing her. "You've probably been wondering about the division of Dad's estate."

Jackie heaved a tired sigh. Why did everyone think that? "No,

Conrad. To be one hundred percent frank with you, I *haven't* been wondering about that. If he decided to leave it all to you, his aunt, and his sister since you're his only real blood relations, that's perfectly fine with me."

Conrad's eyes widened. "Wait, you know about that?"

Jackie nodded.

"For how long?"

"For about two days. Constance and Joan alluded to it, and I insisted they tell me the whole story."

He rubbed his forehead. A scowl deepened the wrinkles that had begun to form on his face in recent years. "Dammit. I never wanted you to find out like that."

Curious, Jackie leaned forward. "How long have you known?"

"Dad told me around the time I graduated college," he said with a weary shake of his head.

Jackie frowned. She would have been around seven years old then. So Conrad had known he was only her half-brother for almost twenty-five years?

"We already knew I'd be going into politics," he continued. "And Dad said it was important I know about something that could be…."

"A liability? An embarrassment?" Jackie supplied, not quite keeping the edge from her tone.

"He probably said something like that. You know how he was. But I don't think of you that way, Jackie. Truly." His expression was serious and uncharacteristically open. "To this day, I may not understand why things happened the way they did with Mom and Doug McCurdy, but it doesn't matter. You're my younger sister, and I never wanted you to feel bad about any of that."

"I see," she murmured. She might never know her dad's motivations, but for Conrad's part, it sounded like he'd really been trying to protect her.

He leaned his elbows on his knees and stared at the ground. "I know Dad was…hard on you sometimes."

"On both of us," she corrected. Were they actually having an honest conversation about their family dynamics?

"Yeah, on both of us. But it's different for you."

"Because I'm a delicate female?" she asked with a smile.

He met her eyes and chuckled. "I was going to say sensitive or feeling, but I guess you've always been a delicate little flower. In fact, I remember when you were five and played a tulip in your kindergarten play and—"

"Stop right there!" she demanded before he could rehash the whole story of how she'd done one of her dance spins too enthusiastically and knocked over the boy next to her.

They shared a laugh for a few moments, but he soon sobered. "What I meant was I think Dad was harder on you because of your past, things you had absolutely no control over. And I'm sorry about that."

She reached over and squeezed his hand. "Thank you, Conrad. It means a lot that you'd say that."

They didn't speak for a while. Only the chirp of a distant bird interrupted the silence.

Finally, Conrad said, "You think I'm exactly like him, don't you?"

The past few days had reminded her of all the ways he was milder, kinder, and more considerate than his father, despite their parallel ambitions. Today's conversation reinforced the disparity. "Maybe not exactly."

"He rallied a little and talked to me, you know?" Conrad said. "Right before he got bad. But he knew he was going to die soon. And you know what he talked about?"

Jackie shook her head.

"A mistake he thought I'd made in my re-election campaign and what I needed to do to fix it." Conrad squeezed then opened his fists. "It was the last conversation we'd ever have, and he wanted to talk politics."

A pang of sympathy shot through Jackie. "I'm sorry."

"Well, it got me thinking. What if I'm doing that with Riley? He's only six, but I already have all these plans and expectations for him about school and sports and all of that. Am I setting us up to be like Dad and me one day when I'm older? If he doesn't get sick of it and cut me off before then."

Jackie shook her head. "Don't say that. You have time, Conrad. Time to find balance and be a loving dad to Riley but still want what's best for him. I think you're off to a better start than you think."

He searched her face. "What do you mean?"

"I'll show you." She reached in her sweater pocket and pulled out her phone. After scrolling through her photo application, she found what she was looking for. It was a picture she'd taken on Thanksgiving.

Conrad had been at the family house first, and Lisa and Riley arrived later because they had been visiting Lisa's parents. Just before she'd snapped the photo, Riley had run up to the front porch to greet Conrad. She'd captured the moment when Conrad had swooped the boy up in his arms and hugged him.

Jackie had taken the photo on a whim because it had been such a sweet moment. Now she was glad that she'd kept it, since it highlighted the contrast between her brother and his dad.

She handed the phone to Conrad so he could see the photo. As he studied it, a smile spread over his face. "I didn't know you took this."

"I'll send it to you, if you want." She gestured at the phone. "Anyone can see you love that boy to pieces. And Lisa too. Despite never really having it modeled for you, you're a loving husband and dad. And a decent brother too, for that matter."

Conrad grinned. "Thank you, Jackie. I needed that. Turns out you're a more than decent sister."

Jackie laughed. She couldn't remember when she'd smiled or talked this much with Conrad. Maybe never. It felt like a potential new beginning for them.

Their laughter was interrupted by the buzz of Jackie's phone, which was still in Conrad's hand. He glanced down and handed it over.

Jackie's cheeks heated when she spotted a text from Cam on the screen.

Conrad smirked. "New boyfriend?"

"Uh…" Her entire face felt feverish now. "No, not really."

A longing to tell her brother about Cam stirred inside her. But it frightened her too. She and Conrad were finally connecting after so many years, but she had a feeling her situation with Cam was something he wouldn't understand or condone.

What would she be telling him anyway? Despite how Jackie felt and what she might want, she and Cam had never agreed to anything serious.

24

"Camryn, could you come to my office, please?"

When Mr. Bolton's message through the company chat application popped up on Cam's computer, it startled her from her deep concentration on the layout she was revising, but it didn't send her into a tailspin of anxiety like it once might have.

After two weeks of working closely with Mr. Bolton on the Open Air campaign, she no longer expected a random summons to his office to portend doom for her career. He probably wanted to discuss the latest design iteration she'd sent him the evening before.

But when she arrived in Mr. Bolton's office, her vacation from job anxiety came to an abrupt end. In addition to Mr. Bolton, her supervisor Logan was there as well as Regina Stewart, one of their vice presidents.

Cam's palms started to sweat.

This can't be good.

"Please sit down, Camryn," Mr. Bolton said, his tone serious.

Once Cam was seated, Mr. Bolton produced the sketchpad he'd borrowed from her the week before. "I need to return this to you, but first, would you mind opening it and giving us a brief overview of the first three or four sketches?"

It was an odd request, but Cam nodded. As she opened the book, Ms. Stewart leaned in, but Logan didn't look.

Cam named the campaign for each drawing, summarized the clients' requests and her thought process when sketching out the designs. When she got to the fourth one, Mr. Bolton raised a hand to stop her. "That's fine. Thank you."

He turned to Ms. Stewart. "I asked Camryn to discuss these sketches to verify what I told you earlier. These rough drafts clearly show Camryn did the lion's share of the concept work for most of the campaigns this department completed in the last eighteen months."

Mr. Bolton scowled at Logan. "However, Logan has been claiming that he did these designs himself with little or no input from this team."

Cam's jaw dropped. Logan had said they were his designs? Jackie had been right! Cam had basically been doing Logan's work for him. Not only that, he'd been deceiving management about it.

She looked at Logan. He was half slumped in his chair, eyes refusing to meet those of anyone else in the room.

Mr. Bolton continued speaking. His voice held a hard edge. "Now, I'd demand Logan apologize to you, Camryn, but I don't have the right to demand anything because he is no longer an employee, effective immediately."

Logan sunk even further into his chair, and Cam couldn't help but feel sorry for him. She turned to the others. "Mr. Bolton, Ms. Stewart, I know what Logan did was wrong, but I'd like to ask you to reconsider. I think he did what he did because he felt overwhelmed by the requirements of his particular role, but he's good at other things like coordinating teams and organizing projects. Maybe this is a sign of a skills mismatch."

Ms. Stewart spoke up for the first time since Cam arrived. "Your kindness is admirable, Camryn, and you're not entirely wrong. As managers, we should have recognized this mismatch sooner or, at the very least, been more vigilant to create a work culture where Logan and everyone else feels safe to admit when their roles aren't working out. We'd always prefer to shift team members around and retain them than lose them altogether."

She folded her arms and sent Logan a stern look. "That being said, the level of dishonesty and abuse of power Logan showed by misrepresenting your designs as his own and mischaracterizing the quality of your work to justify denying you a well-deserved promotion cannot be allowed to stand here at the Propagate Agency."

Cam knew better than to protest again after a speech like that, so she merely watched in silence as Mr. Bolton dismissed Logan from his office and sent him to Human Resources.

Once Logan was gone, Mr. Bolton said, "Camryn, I need to

apologize to you for not realizing what was going on with Logan earlier. It took working with you one-on-one to figure it out. Also, since we now have a vacant senior designer position, Regina and I would like to offer it to you. No one in this department is more deserving."

Cam was still shocked but elated by the time she got home that afternoon. The first thing she wanted to do was call Jackie, but she knew this was the worst possible time since her dad's funeral had been the day before, and Jackie was probably surrounded by relatives.

But as soon as Cam sat down to eat dinner, her phone rang and Jackie's photo appeared on the screen. She scrambled to answer it. "Hey, Jackie."

"Hi." Her voice sounded small and tired, but it still zapped a current of excitement through Cam. "Shoot. I just saw the time. Did I interrupt your dinner?"

Cam smiled at her concern. "I don't mind."

"What are you having?"

"A sandwich," Cam said, glancing down at the turkey and Swiss on her coffee table.

"Oh, Cam. A sandwich? You're such a wonderful cook. You can make something more substantial than that."

It's no fun cooking for one. "Don't worry about that now. How are things with you?"

Jackie's heavy sigh rustled through the phone's speaker. "Exhausting. There's been paperwork and discussions with attorneys and all kinds of other nonsense."

She was quiet for a moment, and Cam waited.

Finally, Jackie continued in a low tone. "My dad left the house to Conrad and Lisa, but the rest of his assets were divided equally between Conrad and me, except for a modest trust for Constance and Joan."

When Jackie fell silent again, Cam asked, "How do you feel about that?"

"I don't know," she admitted with a groan. "I mean, the money was never a concern for me. I didn't want it. I didn't look forward to having an inheritance. It felt like it would only tie me to my dad's world when all I've ever wanted is to live my own life apart from that."

"I know," Cam murmured.

"But now I have all these questions. Did he leave his estate this way because he really cared about me and wanted to keep providing for me, or was he afraid of what it would look like if he didn't leave me anything?"

The hurt and confusion in Jackie's voice weighed heavy on Cam, and she wished she could reach through the phone and hold Jackie's hand. She deserved so much more than those questions. Jackie deserved to have people in her life who adored her unambiguously.

Jackie heaved another sigh. "I guess I have no choice but to learn to make peace with never having the answers."

"I'm afraid so," Cam agreed. "But no matter what your parents did or didn't do, it's not a reflection on you. They had their issues, but you still turned out great."

Cam bit the inside of her cheek. 'Great.' What a trite and inadequate word to describe all the things Jacqueline Webster was. But she wasn't sure it would be a good idea to say anymore.

"Thanks," Jackie said quickly. Then she cleared her throat, and her tone brightened. "Enough of that. Tell me about your day."

Cam hesitated. "It can wait. I'm sure you're tired."

"Yeah. I'm tired of talking about my family drama. I'd like to escape it for a while. So, please, Cam. How was your day?"

She wasn't budging, so Cam gave in and spilled the whole story about what had happened at work.

Jackie listened with rapt attention, apart from exclaiming, "That dirtbag!" when Cam got to the part about Logan passing off her designs as his own.

When Cam finished by talking about her promotion, Jackie said, "Oh my gosh, that's amazing! Congratulations!"

Her words warmed Cam through and through. "Thanks."

"Seriously, I'm in awe."

Cam felt her cheeks go hot. "I didn't really do anything. Mr. Bolton was the one who figured out what Logan was up to."

"But you're finally getting the recognition you deserve. And you wouldn't be in this situation now if you hadn't been willing to put yourself out there and volunteer to help with the Open Air project. That's huge!"

"Yeah, but I think I have you to thank for that," Cam murmured.

"Me?"

"Yes, you." Cam swallowed and chose her words carefully, trying to say what was on her mind and heart without sharing too much. "Since meeting you—what I mean is—there's something about being around you that…it's made me bolder, more alive, and confident again. Right from that first night we met. My approaching Mr. Bolton was the result of that. So…that's why I need to thank you."

Jackie went very quiet. Cam couldn't even hear her breathing. She squeezed her eyes shut. She'd said too much. She should have known—

"Cam." Jackie's voice was soft and low. "I think that's the sweetest thing anyone has ever said to me."

Cam's fingers tightened around her phone, relief and happiness coursing through her. "Well, I mean it."

There were so many other things she could say and mean just as much. *I miss you. I need you. I want you here in my arms for a long, long time.*

But Cam was smart enough to quit while she was ahead.

25

"I really appreciate the ride, Britt," Cam said, as they entered Shiloh's. "I hate that I took up part of your Saturday over a silly dead battery."

Britt waved away her statement. "It's no big deal. Besides, we haven't hung out in ages."

Cam dipped her head. "Yeah. I'm sorry about that. I've been so busy."

"I know you have, but it paid off, Ms. Senior Designer." Britt thumped her shoulder. "Now you can afford to buy me one of these fancy coffees you're always going on about."

Cam chuckled. "You got it."

As they approached the counter, a shadow of guilt still hung over Cam, despite Britt's reassurances. She'd gotten so wrapped up in work…and Jackie, that she hadn't spent as much time as she should with friends or family.

Ordinarily, she and Britt got together on a weekend or evening for a movie or dinner every other week. But that hadn't happened in a while. Cam hated that she'd only broken the friendship slump by asking for a favor when her car had refused to start after her volunteer shift. Still, she was trying to rectify the situation by buying Britt coffee now that the car was safely on its way to the mechanic.

Britt pushed Cam ahead of her in line to give herself time to decide on a beverage, so Cam walked up to the register and greeted Shiloh.

Shiloh smiled. "Hi! Where's your girlfriend today?"

"Uh…" Cam's ears felt suddenly hot.

Britt jostled her way to the counter. "What girlfriend?"

Shiloh's brown eyes widened as they shifted from Cam to Britt. They mumbled something under their breath that sounded like, "Crap. I've done it now."

Their dismay made Cam chuckle, easing her embarrassment in the process. "Relax, Shiloh. You didn't stir up anything. This is my friend Britt. The woman I usually come in with, Jackie, she's just a friend too."

The last words stuck in her throat, but she managed to get them out.

"Oh, sorry to assume," Shiloh said, looking sheepish. "The vibe between you and Jackie is always so intense. I figured you were a couple."

Britt elbowed Cam and grinned. "Vibe, huh? I want to hear more about this mysterious Jackie."

Cam swallowed. She couldn't say too much about Jackie. She was in the closet and from a high-profile family.

"Come on, Shiloh, give it a rest," another voice piped in.

Cam turned to see two women—the only other customers at the moment—approach the counter. One was tall with short, dark hair and the other was slightly shorter with long, auburn hair in a ponytail. Cam had seen them here before. They were usually both using laptops.

"Give what a rest, Becca?" Shiloh said with an innocent shrug.

Becca, the auburn-haired woman, shook her head disapprovingly. "Your meddling is going to get you in trouble one of these days."

"What meddling? All I said was that they had a vibe."

"You said the same thing about me and Carmen," Becca said, gesturing to the woman beside her.

Shiloh flashed a toothy grin. "And was I wrong?"

Carmen snickered and put an arm around Becca. "They have a point, baby."

Cam raised a hand to interrupt the banter. "I don't think Shiloh was meddling, in my case, but for the sake of clarity: Jackie and I are friends. That's really all there is to it."

Britt heaved a sigh. "Too bad."

Everyone chuckled, and Becca said, "Shiloh, when you finish with their order, can I get another one of those yummy cranberry scones?"

"Of course," Shiloh said before turning to Cam. "What can I get you today?"

Cam stared at the display case of baked goods. "You have cranberry scones?"

"Sure do. You want one?"

"Yes. But I'll get it to go," Cam said.

Cranberry scones were Jackie's favorite. Cam remembered that from the morning after their first night together.

Was that strange?

Cam probably remembered everything Jackie had ever said. But did she really want Jackie to know that? Cam was in constant danger of saying too much. The night before, she had almost gotten carried away with her little speech about Jackie making her more confident. How much further could she push?

"No, never mind!" Cam said a bit too loudly. Britt gave her a strange look, and Becca and Carmen's attention was back on her.

"You don't want the scone?" Shiloh said.

Cam released a frustrated growl. "I do…but I don't."

Shiloh frowned. "Are you watching your carbs?"

"No. It's not that."

Cam's head began to throb. How long could she keep up this emotional balancing act?

"I can't keep doing it!" she blurted out, heedless of everyone watching. "I'm tired of trying to control my feelings around Jackie. I'm tired of pretending I don't think she's the loveliest woman I've ever laid eyes on. I'm tired of pretending I don't think she's incredible. Because she is! Why do I have to keep playing this game?"

Cam started pacing in front of the counter. "She wanted a one-time thing, so I went along with it. Then she wanted to be friends, so I agreed to that. She wanted to be fuck buddies next! Okay, fine. That one was my idea. But only because I figured that's all I could ever ask for, but it's wrong! I want more. I deserve more, and so does Jackie. She deserves better. She could move on and find some guy to marry and build the picture-perfect life with, but it won't be better because I'm the one who really loves her."

Cam was breathing heavily after her outburst, but as her pulse returned to normal, reality set in.

She glanced around at Britt, Shiloh, Carmen, and Becca, who were all staring at her like she was the newest exotic creature in the zoo.

She winced. "I'm sorry for making a scene, guys. I…uh…I've been under a lot of stress lately."

A new thought struck her, sending her pulse into panic levels. "I shouldn't have said any of that. Jackie, my…um friend, isn't out yet. I mean, it's not like any of you know who she is but—"

"I do!" Carmen said, raising her hand. "I know who she is."

Cam stared, and Carmen shrugged. "I've seen you two in here before, and I recognized her. Probably because I'm a journalist."

"Oh shit." Cam bit her lip hard.

"Don't worry," Carmen said. "Contrary to what people may say about journalists, I'm not a complete asshole. I wouldn't out your friend. I was in the closet once."

Carmen looked at Becca and Shiloh. "We've all been in the closet at some point, I think. We wouldn't give away Jackie's secret."

Cam lowered her eyes. "Thanks."

Britt put an arm around Cam's shoulders. "And you know I have your back. I wouldn't tell either, but I have a lot of questions. Are you saying this Jackie is the same woman you had that fling with over a month ago?"

Cam nodded. Then—why not? —she told an abbreviated version of the whole story. She left out most of the parts about Jackie's family, though, to protect her privacy.

When Cam finished, Britt shook her head. "You've been busier than I thought."

"Yeah. I'm sorry. I would have told you. But it didn't feel like there was anything to tell. Not really. We were casual, but now…"

"Now you're in love," Britt finished.

"Yeah."

Britt smiled. "Well, it's obvious to me what you should do."

"It is?" Cam gaped at her friend.

"Perfectly." Britt looked around at the others. "Isn't it obvious?"

Three heads nodded in unison.

"You need to get your woman," Carmen said.

Cam swallowed. "I don't know about that."

"Faint heart never won fair lady," Shiloh declared, placing a hand over their heart.

Becca rolled her eyes. "So cheesy, Shiloh." Then she turned her focus on Cam. "But seriously, as you already said: Jackie deserves to know how you feel, and you deserve to be able to say it."

Cam wasn't sure that was *exactly* what she'd said, but deep inside, she knew Becca was right. She needed Jackie to know this wasn't a casual thing for her anymore and find out if maybe, just maybe, Jackie might be willing to try for something more.

26

"I'm outside your apartment," Jackie texted Cam. It was her first day back in town, and they'd agreed to meet for dinner.

"Come on up. The door's unlocked. I'm still finishing dinner," Cam texted back.

As Jackie slid her phone back into her purse, she realized her hands were shaking. She squeezed them closed to steady them.

Why was she nervous? She was only going to hang out with Cam like she had dozens of times before.

Yet something felt different now.

First of all, there was the urgent longing she'd felt to see Cam as soon as she was back. She'd only returned to her apartment a few hours ago, feeling impossibly tired. It would have made sense to wait until the next day to see Cam, but she couldn't stand to wait that long. She missed Cam that much.

Then there was a change with Cam too. When they'd talked a few nights before, after Cam had told her about her promotion, there had been a tenderness in her voice that Jackie hadn't heard before.

Maybe neither of them wanted to admit it, but something had shifted for both of them that night Jackie had come running to Cam after learning the truth about her family.

But Jackie wasn't sure what, if anything, that shift meant for the future.

When she got to Cam's apartment, she knocked twice then opened the door. Cam was busy in the kitchen, but at the sound of the door opening, she turned.

A smile formed on Cam's soft lips. "Hi."

"Hi," Jackie answered in a raspy voice.

As she looked into those deep brown eyes, all those pesky nerves went still. Everything inside her felt bright, peaceful, and excited at the same time. She crossed the few steps to Cam in half a second and threw her arms around her.

Without hesitation, Cam's arms enfolded her in a full, satisfying embrace. Jackie buried her face in Cam's shirt and closed her eyes, savoring the scent that mingled sandalwood body wash and Cam's own unique essence.

After a long while, Cam leaned back to study her face, but she didn't let go. "Are you okay?"

Jackie nodded.

I am now.

She smiled at Cam then sniffed the air. "Mmm. Except for being hungry."

Cam grinned. "You're in luck. The stew is almost ready."

Reluctantly, Jackie released her. "Great. I'll set the table."

They set about their separate tasks in companionable silence, and it all felt so natural and…right.

Once they sat down and started eating the savory beef stew, Jackie asked, "What does your schedule look like the next few days?"

"I have tomorrow off since it's the day before Christmas Eve, so I'm going to volunteer," Cam explained.

"But it's Friday."

Cam nodded. "Yeah, but Wolly is closed on Christmas Eve, and I still wanted to get my weekly hours in. I'll probably do the same thing next week: volunteer the Friday before New Year's Eve."

"Spending all your free time volunteering? Wow! That's dedication," Jackie said.

"Well, not *all* my free time. I also get the Monday after Christmas and the Monday after New Year's Day off."

Excitement stirred in Jackie. Since she was still on winter break and Cam had several days off work, did that mean they'd get to spend more time together? She didn't quite know how to ask, so she kept on topic. "Do your new job responsibilities start next week?"

"First thing Tuesday morning," Cam said. "I'm excited but nervous too."

"That's understandable, but I know for a fact you can't be any worse than your predecessor."

"I should hope not." Cam laughed.

"What part makes you nervous?"

"I don't know." Cam tore off a piece of the cornbread she'd made to accompany the stew and chewed it slowly. "Getting to work on the larger projects is exciting, and my head is spinning with ideas already. But this isn't just a designer role. There's an element of project management to it as well. I'll need to organize teams and coordinate efforts from all kinds of different personalities. I've never done anything like that before."

"That does sound challenging," Jackie admitted. "But I wouldn't worry. You're great with people."

Cam's eyebrows went up. "What are you talking about? I don't even like people!"

"That may be," she said with a chuckle before brushing her fingers over Cam's hand. "But I've seen you in action at the museum. You're patient and wonderful with visitors of all ages. Who knows? Maybe your volunteer work has even helped prepare you for this new role."

"Another one of your beautiful insights?" Cam asked. A hint of passion sparked in her eyes as she swept her gaze over Jackie.

Jackie's body heated under her perusal. "Something like that. And if you're lucky, I'll show you a few more of my insights later tonight."

"Hmm. I certainly hope so," Cam said in a husky tone.

A short giggle escaped Jackie before she went back to eating. This ease between them—the conversation, the laughing, the flirting—it was such a welcome relief after all the tense hours she'd spent around her family. The pressure of assuming her gracious and genteel Jacqueline Webster façade for the public eye, all while carrying around the burdens of the family secrets had been draining. But now? Now it felt like she could finally breathe again.

Her face must have sobered during her reflections, because Cam reached over and squeezed her hand. "Hey. Are you sure you're okay?"

"I'm sure." She returned the hand squeeze. "All this family stuff has really taken it out of me, though."

"I'm sorry."

"It's okay. Or it will be," Jackie assured her. "In fact, one positive thing that happened is I managed to clear the air with Conrad."

"Really?"

"Yeah. We had a little heart-to-heart the morning after Dad passed away, and it felt like a new beginning."

Cam's face lit up. "That's great! I'm happy for you."

"Thanks. I still don't know what to do with everything I found out about my parents, but maybe some good can come of it."

Cam wiped her mouth and pushed her bowl aside so she could lean on the table. "Have you thought anymore about contacting your biological father's family?"

"I looked up his sister's contact information," she said with a sigh. "I don't know if I want to use it, though. What am I supposed to do? Call her up and say, 'Hi. I think I'm your long-lost niece'?"

"That would be a shock," Cam acknowledged. "Maybe writing a letter would be better."

"Maybe. I'll think it over."

Jackie finished her stew then picked up the two bowls. "I should wash these before everything sets in. It was really good, Cam."

Cam reached out to stop her. "Hang on a second. There was something I wanted to talk to you about."

Uh-oh. That sounds serious.

Jackie eased back into her chair. "What is it?"

"I heard at the museum that The Majestic is going to be showing a production of *The Sapphire Hourglass.*"

"You mean the musical adaptation of Hilda Spaulding's last novel?" Jackie scooted closer to the table.

"That's right. Opening night is tomorrow."

"Oh wow!" Jackie bounced in her chair. "I've been a fan of Spaulding's writing ever since I was an angsty adolescent. You probably guessed that from my interest in her letters. I've been wanting to see this musical for ages, but I didn't think it would be showing down this way for a long time."

Cam grabbed her water glass and took a long swallow. "Yeah, uh, I had a feeling you'd be interested. So I went ahead and bought a couple of tickets."

"You did?" Jackie's pulse skipped.

"Yeah. Figured they'd sell out quickly, you know." Cam's grip on her glass was so tight that her knuckles were changing color.

Why is she so nervous?

"I was wondering if you'd want to go." Cam quickly added, "I mean together."

144

She set her glass down with a thud and rubbed her forehead before meeting Jackie's eyes. "I mean with me."

Jackie blinked. Apart from the Christmas festival and a few coffees at Shiloh's, she and Cam had never really gone out together anywhere before. And while the musical could easily be another simple outing between friends, Jackie knew it wouldn't be. Cam's sudden bashfulness in asking told her that. So did her own thudding heartbeat.

Would it be a date? Did Jackie want it to be? Was she ready for that? Would she ever be?

She didn't have anything resembling an answer to these questions, but as she looked into Cam's dark eyes, which shone with their usual warmth and sincerity despite her nerves, Jackie knew she would agree to go to Neptune with Cam, if she asked. What was a little excursion to the theatre?

"I'd love to."

\

\

27

On Thursday afternoon, Jackie stared at the outfits strewn all over her bedroom and groaned. For the first time she could remember in her thirty-one years, she had no idea what to wear.

As the child of a public figure, she'd been brought up to know exactly what type of ensemble to wear to every occasion. But that usually depended on understanding the nature of the event she was attending, and this time, she wasn't sure.

Is this a date?

The question had played on repeat in her brain throughout the day the way radio stations had been replaying Mariah Carey's "All I Want for Christmas is You" all month, but she was no closer to an answer.

Or maybe she did know the answer but wasn't ready to face it yet. If she were being honest with herself, she'd admit that every outing with Cam had felt like a date. From the museum and that first coffee at Shiloh's to the Christmas festival. If Jackie hadn't recognized that sooner, it was half due to denial of her own feelings and half due to the fact that being with Cam had been *so much better* than anyone she'd ever dated before. The conversations, the laughter, the underlying buzz of attraction—it had all been better.

For Jackie's part, if she decided to view tonight as a date, it would be a matter of finally calling their time together by its real name.

Would it be that way for Cam too? Did she want to take a chance on dating Jackie? Did what they have together truly mean more to her than friendship and casual intimacy?

Jackie didn't know for sure, but deep down, she knew what she wanted the answer to be.

At 6:30 on the dot, a knock on Jackie's front door interrupted her last-minute preparations, making her stomach flutter.

She smoothed a shaky hand over the dark green velvet wrap dress she'd chosen for the evening. With its rich color that looked nice against her complexion, it was one of her favorite purchases in recent years, but she'd barely worn it because the V-neck dipped a tad lower than what she normally wore. The fact that she hadn't worn it much made it feel special, though, as did the French twist she'd styled her hair in.

She doublechecked that the straps of her shoes were secure then hurried to the door. As soon as she opened it, her heart skipped.

Cam stood on the other side wearing a dark suit, perfectly tailored to her long, lean frame.

Oh wow.

"Cam—" Jackie paused when she caught the look in Cam's eyes. Her expression was intense, full of passion but also affection.

"Jackie, you look stunning," she said with a note of wonder in her voice.

Even though her throat had closed up, Jackie managed to rasp out, "So do you."

The color in Cam's cheeks deepened, and she grinned. "Thanks."

When Jackie realized they'd been standing there staring at each other for a while, and Cam was still on the porch, she hastily stood aside. "I'm sorry. Come in for a second while I grab my jacket."

Cam crossed the threshold and pulled something from behind her back. "These are for you."

Jackie's breath caught. Cam was holding a bouquet of deep red roses.

She brought me flowers!

All those questions that had stirred up inside Jackie when Cam had first asked her to the theatre began to settle.

"Thank you, Cam. They're lovely." Jackie reached out, allowing her fingers to brush Cam's hand as she accepted them. Their eyes met again, and Jackie lost track of what she was doing.

"I-I'll put these in some water, and then we can go."

Once she'd done that, she retrieved her jacket, and Cam helped her into it.

On the way to the theatre, their conversation flowed as naturally as it always did, but the air between them was charged. There was a newness and excitement that hadn't been there before.

That energy remained as they found a parking place at the Majestic and took their seats for the show.

The Sapphire Hourglass was an entertaining, dramatic production, full of evocative dance numbers, stirring music, and intense dialogue. During one particularly enthralling scene in the third act, Jackie found herself searching out Cam's hand in the darkness.

When their hands met, Cam's body jerked, as if she'd been startled, but then she entwined her fingers with Jackie's and held on firmly. She stared at Jackie through the shadows, but Jackie couldn't make out her expression. Still, a glow of happiness and acceptance radiated from her. They continued holding hands for the rest of the performance.

Once the show had ended and the house lights came back on, Jackie sat back down after the standing ovation and tried to take it all in. "Wow! I'm going to be processing that for a while."

She looked at Cam as she sat back down. "I re-read the novel yesterday in preparation for this."

"So did I," Cam murmured, before sitting up straighter so a few people could squeeze past them to exit the row.

Jackie leaned closer to Cam. "What was that?"

Cam's face changed color. "Well, I didn't re-read since I hadn't read it before, but I downloaded the e-book for *The Sapphire Hourglass* and read it. I figured you'd want to discuss it once we saw the show, and I didn't want to be totally lost."

Jackie melted inside. "You did?"

"Yes, and I'm glad because there were a lot of things in the show that I wouldn't have gotten the full nuance of if I hadn't."

"I'm sure. Can you give me an example?"

"Well—" someone else on the row jostled their way in front of them, and Cam chuckled. "Maybe we should continue this somewhere else. I booked a reservation at the Mexican place down the street, if you want to go?"

"Definitely!" Jackie stood and held out her hand. Cam accepted it, her face brighter and happier than Jackie had ever seen it.

Jackie helped Cam to her feet and held on as they exited their row and made their way to the theatre lobby.

I can't believe this.

As Cam walked with Jackie, hand in hand, into the theatre lobby, she was tempted to pinch herself with her free hand. This entire evening had been like a dream, starting with the moment Jackie had opened her front door.

She was breathtaking.

Her dress, hair, and makeup were gorgeous, of course, but what stunned Cam even more was that Jackie had put so much effort into her preparations for tonight.

She dressed up like this to go to the theatre with me.

With me!

Cam's heart rate went into outer orbit every time she thought about it. And now they were holding hands. Here in public like a real couple. Unbelievable. She'd never dreamed it would be this easy.

As they made their way through the crowded lobby, Cam's mind was already half on the dinner ahead. Yes, she wanted to hear Jackie nerd out over the show, but she also wanted to broach the topic of their relationship. Hopefully, the restaurant had heeded her request for a quiet corner table and—

Jackie came to an abrupt stop, nearly causing Cam to collide with her. Cam chuckled over the near miss, but Jackie was staring straight ahead.

Cam frowned. "Jackie, what's wrong?"

Her face had gone paler than normal. "My brother and sister-in-law are here."

"Oh." Cam's heart plummeted to her stomach, but she wasn't sure if it was because of the news or Jackie's reaction to it.

"Shit. I think he saw me." Jackie dropped Cam's hand like it was a hot coal.

Cam flinched but quickly dissembled. She looked in the direction Jackie was staring, but couldn't make out which of the many faces might be Jackie's brother. "It's okay," she soothed. "Nothing to see here, right? Just two friends at the theatre."

Jackie's head jerked toward Cam, and she looked her up and down.

149

It was so different from the heated, admiring perusal Cam had received when Jackie had opened her door. This look was appraising. Critical. And it chilled Cam to the core.

"That hardly seems likely," Jackie snapped.

Cam's body jolted as if she'd been punched.

Hardly seems likely?

Right. As if the poised and perfect Jacqueline Webster would ever have a friend like Cam.

"No. I guess it doesn't." Cam said stiffly. "In that case, I'd better leave. You can say hello to them, and I'll wait for you in the car so I can take you home."

No way they were making it to dinner after this.

There wasn't time to wait for a response, not that Cam particularly wanted to hear one, so she swiveled around and stalked toward the exit.

God, I'm such a fool.

She repeated the phrase over and over to herself on the way to the car, like a password she was trying to memorize. It was an apt comparison, since she'd obviously forgotten far too much already.

She'd forgotten the pain of Tina's rejection all those years ago so much that she'd put herself in the exact same situation all over again.

Jackie wasn't her girlfriend, and she never would be! Even when she'd been submerged in the chaos of discovering her sexuality, Jackie had made it one hundred percent clear she had no intention of being in a real relationship with Cam or any other woman. Her plan was to marry a man and be the perfect respectable daughter to her family. Never mind that family had lied to her. She still belonged to them more than she ever would to herself or anyone else.

Tonight was proof of that. As soon as Jackie had spotted her brother, it was like a switch had been flipped. Cam had watched her transform from the sweet, easygoing Jackie she was used to spending time with into Jacqueline Webster, the politician's daughter who cared more about appearances than anything else.

And Cam had actually let herself believe that Jackie could learn to move past all that enough to return Cam's feelings and choose to be with her.

I'm such a fool.

Cam got in her car and started the engine, letting it idle as she stared out the windshield without really registering the activity of the busy

28

On Saturday morning, Jackie awoke after only a few hours of sleep, buried beneath an avalanche of sadness and dread.

All she could think of was the wistful expression on Cam's face as she'd dropped Jackie off in front of her house the night before.

"Take care of yourself, Jackie," she'd said before leaving.

Even when breaking up—if you could call it that when they'd never really been a couple—and even after Jackie had treated her so badly, Cam had shown her kindness.

She didn't deserve Cam. Not even her friendship.

Jackie rubbed a hand over her eyes, which were still swollen from crying most of the night. Never in her life had she felt so frozen and helpless as she had ever since spotting Conrad in the theatre lobby. She'd panicked so badly that she'd all but shoved Cam out the door, pushing her away like she'd carried a horrible plague. In the emotion of the moment, Jackie really hadn't absorbed Cam's reaction, but now it was seared in her memory. Cam's face had shown shock, pain, and betrayal.

Betrayal from Jackie.

Then on the car ride, when Cam had calmly but honestly expressed her hurt, Jackie had been speechless. What could she even say or do? 'Sorry' was so useless; it wouldn't undo anything.

Jackie could protest that how she'd responded to seeing Conrad and the prospect of him seeing her and Cam together wasn't a true reflection of her feelings for Cam, but so what? Feelings meant nothing if actions didn't back them up. And Jackie's actions had been hurtful and cowardly.

So cowardly. Her whole body had been trembling with apprehension as she'd stood beside Cam and watched Conrad and Lisa approach. How could she explain Cam? Would they guess the truth about her and Cam without Jackie even saying anything?

What would her brother say? What would he think? Would he accuse her of embarrassing the family the way Dad undoubtedly would have? Would he say he never wanted to speak to Jackie again?

The questions had incapacitated her. So she'd let Cam go, thinking Jackie was ashamed of her and their friendship.

Nothing Jackie could have said would have made that right. The relationship imploded right before her eyes, and she had been powerless to stop it.

Jackie turned on her side and buried her face in the covers of her bed. Her empty bed.

This was so wrong!

She should have been waking up with Cam beside her this morning. They should be talking, laughing, maybe even making love. They had been on the verge of something last night. Something that was more wonderful than anything Jackie had experienced in the past. Jackie had known it. *Felt it.* What she and Cam could have had was real.

Real.

If she hadn't been crying again, Jackie would have laughed at the word. What did she know about real?

The night before, she had done what she'd always done. She'd been the person she'd always been: cautious, careful about appearances, deferential to the family image. But it was all so fake! The 'family image' she'd always known wasn't even an accurate picture!

She'd been lied to. For her entire life, she'd done everything she could to win the approval and esteem of a father who would never give her those things for reasons she'd had no control over. And even after learning all that, she'd fallen back into the same pattern. She'd chosen appeasing her brother over her own wellbeing and, more importantly, over the feelings of the amazing, gentle woman she cared about.

Why?

As she sobbed out her heartache and frustration, Jackie wished she had her mom here now as she'd wished so many times before. Would she have been sympathetic to Jackie's situation? Would she have taken her to task for hurting Cam? Or would she have considered the breakup a necessary sacrifice for the good of the family?

That last option was unlikely since her mom had died while running away to be with her lover.

Not for the first time, Jackie wondered what sort of a man Doug McCurdy had been. And the more she wondered, the more aggravated she got with herself. Why was she content to walk around with so many unanswered questions about her own past?

As far as Jackie could tell from her internet research, Doug's sister Peggy was still alive and well. The last time she had searched, she'd even found an email address for Peggy. Maybe she couldn't do anything to fix the rest of the wreck she'd made of her life, but she could at least try to contact this woman and look for some answers.

Jackie resolved to do exactly that…as soon as she finished crying.

So much crying. She'd never felt so shattered after a breakup before. Were relationships between women always this intense?

An hour later, Jackie had managed to get herself up and showered. She'd even prepared a cup of hot tea, although her stomach was still churning too much for food.

Once she'd gathered her resolve, she sat down at her laptop with her cup of tea and composed an email to Peggy McCurdy or Hines, which was her married name.

After several false starts, she typed a simple message explaining who she was and expressing her desire to know more about Doug. She also assured Peggy she would understand if she didn't want to speak with her. Then she'd left her cellphone number at the end of the message and sent it.

Seeing the words "Message Sent" pop-up gave her an unusual sense of satisfaction. It could be weeks before she received a reply, if she ever did at all, but this was a step forward.

Now, if she could only figure out another step.

It was Christmas Eve, a fact she'd forgotten until she'd turned on her computer and seen the date. Although holiday cheer was the farthest thing from her mind, she did need to wrap the presents she'd bought for Conrad, Lisa, and Riley. They hadn't set a specific time to get together, since Christmas Eve and Christmas Day were always public-facing days for Conrad, but Jackie knew she'd need to get the gifts to them at some point.

She forced herself to go to the spare closet where she kept them and pulled out her wrapping paper and ribbon.

As soon as she opened the closet door, a sharp pain stabbed her chest. The first gift she spotted was already wrapped. It was the present she'd gotten for Cam. She'd been so excited to give it to her, and now she'd probably never get that chance.

God, she'd made such a mess of things.

Fighting the urge to melt into tears again, she pushed the package aside and retrieved the rest of the gifts.

Jackie took her time wrapping the presents, measuring and cutting the sheets with precision and making elaborate bows for each package. Making gifts look nice was always something she took pride in, but today, she was more fastidious than usual. Concentrating on each detail helped keep her mind occupied…at least for a short while.

When she finished that task, she resumed the lesson plans she'd begun preparing for the next semester. But she'd only gotten through a few when her phone rang.

For one wild moment, she thought it might be Cam, but her heart sank when she looked at the screen and saw a number she didn't recognize. She answered anyway, finger hovering over the End Call button in case it turned out to be a spam call.

"Hello?"

"Is this Jackie Webster?" a woman's voice asked.

"Yes. May I ask who's calling?"

"My name is Peggy Hines. I'm Doug McCurdy's sister."

Jackie sank against the back of her chair under the weight of her shock. Peggy had already read her email and decided to call!

"That was fast," Jackie said. It was a silly way to begin the conversation, but she had no idea what else to say.

A watery chuckle filtered through the phone's speaker. "I suppose it was, but I've been waiting thirty-one years to meet you."

Jackie swallowed. "Y-you have?"

"Yes," Peggy said gently. "Ever since my brother told me about you not long before he died."

"As I said in my email," Jackie continued in a shaky voice, "I only found out the truth a couple of weeks ago. But I would really like to talk to you in person sometime."

"I'd like that too. I'm sure you'll be busy tomorrow, but if not, we'd love to have you over for dinner."

Jackie pulled the phone away from her ear and stared at it for a second. Then she returned it to her ear. "But tomorrow is Christmas Day."

Peggy chuckled again. "That it is. But we would be glad to have you at dinner. My daughters and their families will be here too."

Jackie's mind reeled at the invitation, at the whole situation, really. She was talking to her estranged aunt for the first time in her life and was already being asked to meet the entire family.

When Jackie didn't respond, Peggy said, "Oh, I realize that would be an awful lot to absorb for the first meeting, and I don't want to pressure you at all. I just wanted you to know that you're welcome, and that the family would be thrilled to get to know you. But I only want you to do what feels comfortable."

The corners of Jackie's mouth lifted the slightest bit. Peggy's kind reassurance reminded her of something Cam would say.

Why did everything have to remind her of Cam?

Only the night before, Cam had said she would never ask Jackie to come out until she felt safe and comfortable to do so. Yet, at the same time, Cam had been on the cusp of offering Jackie something wonderful...if only Jackie had been willing to take the leap and accept it. Was that what love looked like?

Jackie gulped in a lungful of air. "Thank you, Peggy. I'd love to come to dinner. What can I bring?"

29

Jackie wiped her damp palm on the side of her slacks as she stood outside the modest but attractive two-story house that belonged to Peggy Hines and her husband. As she approached the front door, she looked over her outfit one last time. She'd chosen a simple pair of gray slacks and a green sweater. Nothing too dressy. She hoped it was appropriate for the gathering.

She also studied the cherry pie she was carrying. Even though Peggy had insisted Jackie only needed to bring herself to dinner, Jackie couldn't fathom the idea of arriving as a guest empty-handed. There hadn't been time to get anything fancy, so she'd dusted off her baking skills and prepared a pie. You could never have too much dessert, right?

Once she'd steadied herself, Jackie rang the doorbell. She only had to wait a minute before the door swung open, and a woman about Jackie's height in her mid-fifties with reddish brown hair appeared on the threshold.

"Jackie!" Peggy beamed at her. "It's so good to see you."

She felt the sincerity and welcome of the greeting all the way to her bones.

Peggy extended her hand to Jackie. When Jackie accepted it, Peggy pulled her into the house, which was toasty warm in contrast to the cool December temperature outside.

"Come here, everyone," Peggy said, once she'd led Jackie into a good-sized living room dominated by a tall Christmas tree adorned in red and green. "Jackie's here."

Several people stood from the room's various sofas and chairs to greet her. The first to approach was a jovial-looking middle-aged man with a bald head. "Hi, Jackie. I'm Peggy's husband, Stan."

She'd barely had a chance to shake his hand before a woman who appeared to be a few years older than Jackie introduced herself as Peggy and Stan's daughter, Sarah.

Their other daughter, Susan came in from the kitchen, introduced herself and took the pie from Jackie. Next, she met Sarah and Susan's husbands and children. There were four kids, ages ranging from seven to seventeen.

For once, Jackie was glad she grew up being forced to attend so many social gatherings, as it had made her good at remembering new names. Otherwise, she might have been overwhelmed.

Before long, they were all sitting down to dinner. The family had a policy that every member had to contribute something to the meal, except the smaller kids, who helped the adults. Consequently, the dining room table was overflowing with the feast.

As she sat down, it occurred to Jackie she'd never actually been to a casual family holiday meal like this before where everything was homecooked. Christmas meals in the Webster household were always much more formal affairs.

Conversation around the table was easygoing through most of dinner. The adults talked about work or home improvement projects; the kids shared what they'd done at school in recent weeks. Some might have found it mundane, but to Jackie, it was like witnessing a completely different culture. The openness and affection among the family members was so foreign to her own experience.

The youngest grandchild, Cathy, was still regaling the rest of the family with stories from her school year when they all moved to the living room for coffee and dessert. But midway through an already lengthy description of how great her teacher was, she got distracted by pie.

Susan laughed at her daughter's sudden distraction and turned to Jackie. "I'll bet you're glad you teach high school instead of having a room full of rambunctious first graders like this one."

"Mommy, what's ram-bunc-tious?" Cathy asked. She was now sporting a dollop of ice cream on her nose. Her dad was trying to wipe it off despite her squirming.

"It means hyper," Susan answered.

Jackie smiled. "Oh, they're still rambunctious when they get to me; it's just a different kind of energy."

"You know, Jackie, I think Doug would be so pleased to know you're a teacher," Peggy mused. "Our mother was a mathematics teacher."

"Really?" Jackie asked.

"Yes." Peggy turned to her oldest daughter. "Sarah, go get that picture of grandma from the hall."

Sarah returned with a photo in a wooden frame and handed it to Jackie. It was a black and white image of a tall woman in glasses and her hair in a bun standing in front of a chalkboard.

For the first time since Friday night, Jackie felt a wide grin spread over her face. Her grandmother had been a teacher too! She looked at Sarah and Peggy. "Thank you for showing me that."

"Okay, kids. Time for clean up!" Susan said. Her children and nephew whined, but they all headed toward the kitchen.

Jackie started to stand too, but Peggy stopped her and gestured at the kitchen where her kids and grandkids were assembling. "They've got this. Have a seat so we can chat."

When Jackie took her seat again, Peggy relaxed back into her own chair. "So, do you have a boyfriend?"

"Grandma!" Connor, the seventeen-year-old, chided as he scooted by them to gather up dessert plates. "You shouldn't assume."

Peggy patted his shoulder. "You're right. I'm sorry."

She returned her attention to Jackie. "Do you have a boyfriend *or* girlfriend?"

Jackie's face grew hot at the correction. "Uh…not to sound cliché, but it's complicated."

"Love is like that sometimes, I'm afraid," Peggy said with a solemn nod. "It certainly was for your parents."

Jackie's nerves began to hum. Now they were getting down to it. All the questions she'd been storing up rushed to the front of her mind, each clamoring for attention. "Was my mom going to run away with Doug? When the car crashed, I mean."

Peggy frowned. "Is that what you heard?"

"My aunt Constance said that Dad found out about Mom and Doug not long after I was born, and when he confronted Mom, she ran to Doug. But I didn't know if she meant to get a divorce and elope with Doug or what."

"I'm fairly certain your dad only found out about your mother and Doug's relationship *because* of the car crash," Peggy said.

"What?"

With a sad shake of her head, Peggy continued. "Florence stopped seeing Doug when she learned she was pregnant with his child. Only she didn't tell Doug. She broke things off with him. He was so upset that he quit his job as campaign manager. But then when the news came out that Florence had given birth to a baby girl, Doug realized what had happened. He wrote Florence a letter saying he wanted to be with her, and that he wanted to raise you together.

"Florence wrote him back saying she couldn't walk away from her marriage and life. Doug wrote her several more letters and called her until she finally agreed to meet with him somewhere out of the way. Then he brought her back to his house to talk."

Peggy's hand was shaky as she took a sip of her coffee. "I was there when it all happened. Stan was out of the country for work, you see, so the kids and I were staying with Doug. It was terribly sad.

"Doug begged and pleaded with Florence, but she refused to change her mind. She said there was no way she could upend the life she'd built with Clive like that. It would be best for Clive to keep believing you were his daughter. There was no reason for anyone to find out differently."

Peggy paused for a moment, to give herself or Jackie time to breathe. Maybe both. Jackie's hands were throbbing, which made her realize she'd been gripping the cushions of the sofa as she listened. Relaxing her hands, she met Peggy's eyes, letting her see she was ready to hear the rest of the story.

"I don't think for a second it was easy for Florence," Peggy continued. "Please know that. She found herself in a complicated situation, and in the end, she believed staying with Clive was the best thing. When Doug saw he couldn't change her mind, he agreed to drive her back to wherever they'd met. And that's when the car crash happened."

Jackie chewed her lip. "I'm sure it looked strange for them to be in the car together, but was that really enough for Dad to figure out they'd been having an affair?"

"No, but Doug's letters were still in your mom's purse."

"Oh, wow." Jackie closed her eyes. She couldn't help but pity Clive Webster in that moment. In a single day, he'd found out his wife had died, she'd been unfaithful to him, and the baby he thought was his daughter had been fathered by another man.

Peggy pressed on. "Clive managed to keep the details of the accident a secret."

"Yes, I could see him bribing whomever he needed to so the story wouldn't make it into the news." Jackie drew in a deep breath and slowly released it. "Did he bribe you to stay quiet too, Peggy?"

Peggy looked away. "No, not exactly. But I've told you so much already today. There's no need to go into that right now."

Judging by Peggy's evasive response, Jackie suspected she wasn't going to like what came next. Not that everything that came before was particularly pleasant either. "I've been living with lies my whole life. I think I deserve to hear the truth."

Peggy heaved a heavy sigh. "You're right. You do. Well, not long after Florence and Doug died, I went to see Clive. I told him I understood why he didn't want anyone to find out about the affair and that I had no intention of telling anyone. But I also asked if he would allow me to visit you from time to time."

When Peggy went silent, Jackie leaned forward. "And?"

"And…he told me if I ever contacted him again or attempted to see you, he would make sure Stan got fired from the oil rig he was working at the time. Not only that, he'd ensure Stan wouldn't get hired for any other oil and gas work in this state."

Peggy turned pleading eyes on Jackie. "I'm sorry. I should have pushed back. Or tried again later. Clive was still dealing with the fallout from everything. He might have been more reasonable later. But I didn't do any of that. We had two young kids to support, and I was afraid Clive would make good on his threat. Then the years went by and I figured it might be better for you to grow up not knowing too much about the past."

"You don't need to apologize," Jackie said. "He put you in an impossible situation, and you had to do what you could to take care of your family."

"Yes, but you are family too, Jackie. Please know we never forgot about you. Stan and I followed you in the newspapers when we could." Peggy's voice waivered. "And it's so good to see what a wonderful young woman you grew up to be."

Jackie's throat closed. She couldn't remember when, if ever, anyone in her family had said something like that to her before. Reaching over, she placed a hand over Peggy's. "As difficult as it has been to find out the truth, I'm glad we reconnected."

Peggy smiled at her through shining eyes. "I am too."

30

"Are you volunteering today, my heart?" Mama asked when Cam answered her call.

"No. I volunteered yesterday since I had the day off, but the museum isn't open on Christmas Eve. I'm free today," Cam said.

"Good! Then why don't you come home and stay the night? It will give us all more time together."

"But Mama—" she started to protest.

"You have other plans?"

"No, I don't," she admitted with a sigh. "Okay. I'll finish up a few things here and then drive up this afternoon."

"I'm glad. We've barely gotten to talk to you the last couple of months."

"I'm sorry, Mama. There's been…" Cam forced her voice to stay calm and steady. "There's been a lot going on. I mean with work and all."

"Yes, with work," Mama repeated with the same skeptical tone she'd used when Cam had been six and tried to blame her older sister for the spilled paints all over the bathroom. "Well, you can tell us all about *work* when you get here. Drive safely, my heart."

The call ended, and Cam sank back onto her bed where she'd spent most of the morning, still in her pajamas. She wasn't about to admit it to Mama, but she had wanted a day to wallow before facing her family. She'd never even told them about Jackie. Now how could she explain showing up looking like the living dead over a breakup?

She'd spent a mostly sleepless night and the entire morning second guessing her entire relationship with Jackie.

Being around her had been so incredible. Cam had told Jackie the truth the day she'd gotten her promotion: something about her had made Cam feel confident and bold.

But now Cam was filled with pain and questions. Had Jackie had any real feelings for her at all? Cam had thought she'd sensed it. Like when Jackie had come to her the night she'd found out about her dad. Or the night less than a week ago when she'd come to dinner at Cam's apartment, and she had invited her to the theatre.

Cam had started to believe they could have something real together all the way up to the moment Jackie had seen her brother. The way she'd looked at Cam when faced with the prospect of introducing her to family had left Cam feeling empty and cold.

Had Jackie ever even found Cam attractive? Or had Cam merely been the warm body that happened to be present when Jackie had her sexual awakening? Why would she be interested in someone like Cam anyway? Like Tina, Jackie had come from an entirely different world. A world where Cam was an embarrassment.

Cam buried her face in her hands. Whispers of shame and doubt began seeping into her brain. She'd been foolish to get attached to Jackie. Why had she never learned to stay in her place? Tina should have been the only lesson she'd needed in a lifetime, but no! She had to go reaching for the unattainable yet again. And yet again, she sat here in the aftermath nursing a broken heart.

Maybe it was best she was going home today. Right about now, she could use her Mama's soothing presence, her auntie and grandmother's busy chatter, and a hug from her nephew and niece. And, with any luck, the holiday meal preparation would keep them all too busy to notice Cam's heartache.

Cam knew something odd was going on as soon as she pulled into Mama's driveway and saw her sister walking toward the front door. Mari was an assistant manager at a retail store that stayed open late on Christmas Eve.

Mari turned when she saw Cam approach and waited for her. When Cam hugged her, Mari's coat was cool from the windy December air.

"Why aren't you at work?" Cam asked.

"I shifted around some of the other staff who wanted extra hours so I could get off early today." Mari leaned closer and studied Cam's face. "Mama asked me to because she said you needed to talk to us."

"She did?" Cam gaped at Mari.

"Yeah. Is everything okay?"

"Everything's fi—" The front door swung open before Cam could finish a statement that wasn't exactly true anyway.

Grandma stood in the doorway frowning at them from behind her glasses. "Are you children going to stand in the cold all day, or are you coming in?"

They obediently shuffled inside and took off their shoes and coats.

Once she had greeted and hugged everyone, Cam headed into the living room to admire the Christmas tree. She smiled at the several new handmade ornaments that sported Cody and Jo's names written in crayon.

When Mama approached, Cam asked, "Where are the kids?"

"Jake is bringing them later." She wrapped an arm around Cam and pulled her toward the sofa. "Come sit down."

Once Cam did, Mama, Mari, Grandma, and Aunt Nat all took seats around her. Mari and Aunt Nat pulled their chairs in closer until the family formed a loose circle.

Cam chewed her lip when she realized everyone was watching her. "Is this some kind of intervention?"

Mama folded her arms. "Something's wrong, my heart. I can tell. What is it?"

"Why does something have to be wrong?" Cam asked, even though she'd learned a long time ago that arguing with Mama's intuition was futile. "I've been busy with work. But that's no excuse not to call more. I'm sorry about that."

Aunt Nat, who was sitting on Cam's right reached over and took Cam's chin in her hand and tilted it toward her. "Is it work that's giving you these dark circles under your eyes?"

If it were anyone else, Cam might have resented the observation, but Aunt Nat's dry, wrinkled hand was soothing as she held Cam's face. She studied Cam with that tender ferocity she'd always had when Cam or Mari got sick as children. Then she'd always go to the kitchen and whip up some kind of remedy. Wistfully, Cam wondered if Aunt Nat had anything for a broken heart.

"It's nothing. Not worth all this questioning. I just—" Finally, Cam looked around at the women surrounding her. Each face was attentive and concerned.

Her thoughts flashed back to Jackie's descriptions of her cold family dinners and the way her aunts treated her. Compared to that, Cam was the fortunate one. Why was she holding back from the people who cared about her?

Cam took a deep breath. "I sort of met someone."

"Ooh, finally!" Mari interjected, which earned her a light smack on the arm from Grandma.

"How long ago did you meet her?" Aunt Nat asked.

"About six weeks ago."

Had it only been six weeks? The way Cam ached inside; she would have thought it had been six years.

"Why didn't you mention it before?" Mama asked, her expression grim and maybe even wounded.

"I wasn't trying to keep it a secret," Cam hurried to explain. "It was supposed to be a casual thing and then it grew into more. At least it did for me."

Then she recounted the whole story from the first meeting to Friday night's disaster. She glossed over the spicier details, of course. There was no point in scandalizing Grandma and Aunt Nat.

It felt good to talk about all of it. Apart from her mini meltdown at Shiloh's coffee shop, Cam hadn't spoken about Jackie or her feelings to anyone. Surprisingly, many of the memories made her smile or even laugh, with the grief over losing it all slipping into the background in the form of a dull ache.

"So, that's why I didn't talk about it," Cam concluded. "Jackie and I were never girlfriends. And after Friday, I've started to wonder if Jackie ever wanted more."

"For what it's worth, I suspect she really did want more, but she got scared," Mari said. "I mean, it sounded like you were both treating Friday night like a date, but it's a huge, scary leap to go from one first maybe-date to meeting the family. And that's if you're straight. I can't imagine how intimidating it must have felt in Jackie's situation."

"You have a point," Cam mused.

"But Camryn was understanding of that," Grandma said, looking disgruntled. "She told Jackie she only had to introduce her as a friend. And that wasn't even good enough?"

"Maybe Jackie didn't feel right introducing Cam as only a friend when she knew it wasn't true," Mari argued.

Whoa.

In her agitated state, Cam hadn't thought of that. Maybe Jackie had felt trapped between two difficult alternatives: completely owning up to being involved with a woman or lying about who Cam was to her.

"I guess I still have some thinking to do about all this," Cam murmured. "I jumped to the conclusion that Jackie was embarrassed to be seen with me and would never consider a romantic relationship."

She sent Mama a sheepish grin. "Maybe I should have talked with y'all earlier, huh?"

Mama tried to scowl as she shook her head, but the corners of her mouth twitched. The rest of her family chuckled.

Aunt Nat elbowed Mama, "Come on, Sandra, don't pass up your chance for a good 'I told you so.' What kind of mama are you?"

Everyone laughed again. The sound was a balm to Cam's soul.

Mama's face grew serious again. "I understand how you didn't tell us about this Jackie sooner because you thought it was only a casual relationship. But there's something else. You've been quiet, even vague about your life for a while now, and I don't understand it. You barely even talked about your promotion!"

"I know. I didn't mean to make you feel cut off." Cam squirmed in her seat then swept her gaze over everyone. "Any of you."

She hesitated, gathering her thoughts. As usual, neither Mama nor any of the others prompted her to continue. They simply waited.

Cam returned her focus to Mama. "I guess I struggle to talk about my career or how things are going for me in Dallas because of the way I moved off and left this life behind when I know that's not what you wanted for me."

Mama studied Cam for a long moment. Then she shook her head. "We've missed you ever since you moved away, my heart, but you had bright, beautiful dreams that couldn't be contained in this little town. I know this. I never wanted to hold you back.

"Sometimes I worry all those white-collar men you work for will try to exploit your gifts and quench your passion, but that doesn't mean I think you belong here."

She leaned closer to Cam. Maybe it was Cam's imagination, but Mari, Aunt Nat, and Grandma seemed to scoot in too, tightening the circle. "Whether you're here or there, we are still connected. You'll always be my strong, wild, and colorful child, and all I want is for you to share your heart with us."

Hot, unexpected tears began to slide down Cam's cheeks as Mama pulled her in for a hug. Cam wasn't normally much of a crier, but she'd needed it. She'd needed *this*: Mama's loving, affirming words and her family's supportive presence. Why had she kept her distance?

The rest of Christmas Eve and Christmas Day were full of food, laughter, and sharing for Cam and her family. They'd exchanged presents after lunch. As it had been when Cam was growing up, gift giving was a fairly modest affair in her family, but it was always heartfelt.

Cam had been surprised to receive a set of paints from Mama. Art supplies weren't exactly something Cam had a scarcity of, but when she'd opened the box and sent Mama a questioning look, Mama had said, "You can keep them here so you can paint when you visit."

The not-so-subtle nudge to visit more made Cam smile.

Most of the family grew sleepy and napped after eating lunch and exchanging gifts. Even the kids had passed out in the middle of playing with their new toys. Cam, on the other hand, took her paints to the bedroom she'd shared with Mari as a child and found a small canvas to work on.

As she began to paint, she got lost in the act of creating. It was so nice to be making art again…just because. There was no assignment, no deadline, no marketable concept for her to produce. It was only Cam, her tools, and her imagination.

The canvas gradually filled with color, and peace washed over her. When her thoughts inevitably turned to Jackie, the peace remained.

She hadn't been foolish to lose her heart to Jackie. And she had no reason to be ashamed for taking a chance. It had shown healing and courage to ask Jackie out with the hopes of turning their relationship into something more serious. She could be proud of herself for that. Jackie was an incredible woman and completely worth the risk. She only hoped Jackie would realize that about herself one day too.

31

Jackie returned to her house late on Christmas Day. After the revealing conversation with Peggy about the past, it might have made sense for Jackie to make her escape to process everything, but she hadn't done that. She'd stayed and chatted with the family and gotten to know them better. They seemed every bit as eager to get to know her too.

It had been such a surreal feeling to spend time with people who wanted to know Jackie for no other reason than that she was family. Peggy, Stan, and their children had made it clear that they did consider her family and would like to stay in contact with her, if she was comfortable with it. Jackie still didn't know what to do with all the events that had led to this, but she knew she wanted to foster the connection too.

It wasn't until she'd changed to her pajamas and sat down on her sofa with a cup of peppermint hot chocolate that the sadness from earlier that day returned in full force.

She wished like hell she could tell Cam about everything that had happened today. And even more, she wished she could hear how Cam had spent Christmas. She would have loved to see more pictures of Cam's family and heard more of her funny stories about her niece and nephew.

But that wouldn't happen now.

Jackie set her mug on her coffee table then curled up on the sofa. Thoughts of facing even more days without Cam stretched before her like one of those long, sparsely populated Texas highways her family had traveled when she was young.

Cam would be starting her new job duties in earnest this coming week, and Jackie wouldn't get to hear how it was going or give her a pep talk, if need be. They wouldn't be getting coffee at Shiloh's either or exchanging random texts throughout the day or making dinner before spending the night wrapped in each other's arms.

Jackie had ruined all of that.

As she reached for her mug again, her eyes fell on a photograph Peggy had given her. According to Peggy, it had been the only photo of Doug and Jackie's mom in Doug's belongings.

Picking up the photograph, Jackie studied it longer and better than she had when Peggy had first given it to her. In the picture, Doug and her mom were sitting side by side on a porch swing, presumably at Doug's house. Instead of facing the camera, they were looking at each other.

It wasn't difficult to see they were in love. Peggy had said that Florence had once confessed to her that there was both comfort and passion in her relationship with Doug, two things she'd never really experienced with Clive. And yet, she had chosen to walk away from all of that and cling to her old life, breaking Doug's heart in the process. If it weren't for the car crash, she might have ended up staying married to Clive for decades.

Would she have been happy? Who knows? But she would have had the life she'd always been used to. She would have had security in keeping the status quo, even if her own heart had been broken in the process.

Jackie would never fully know or understand her mom's motivations, of course, but she couldn't help but draw uncomfortable parallels to her own life.

When Jackie had admitted to herself that she was attracted to women, she'd been adamant that it would change nothing about her public life or her future plans. Her growing feelings for Cam had made her rethink those plans, but when the time came for her resolve to be tested, she had folded like a marquee tent in a windstorm.

Jackie had chosen her own version of the status quo over love.

Love?

She sat up so fast, she nearly kicked her coffee table over. Her breath grew shallow, and her heart thumped so loudly she could practically hear it.

It was obvious, wasn't it? She was in love with Camryn Durant. Her solid, sweet, and impossibly sexy Cam. She made Jackie laugh, made her think, made her feel…so many things. Safe and warm one minute then breathless and on fire the next.

But above all else, Cam had made Jackie feel cared for and *wanted* simply because she was Jackie.

All her life, Jackie had smiled and posed and turned herself inside out for her family's approval. Cam hadn't asked for any of those things. All she'd asked was for Jackie to accept her as she was.

Jackie could do that. Hell, she could do more than accept; she could *adore* Cam for who she was, if Cam would only give her another chance.

She stood and began to pace her living room. It would be asking a lot of Cam after everything Jackie had put her through. And she couldn't show up with empty words or vague promises. It wasn't enough to *say* she wanted Cam and was willing to come out and be with her openly. Tina had probably said that same thing dozens of times, and she'd still broken Cam's heart.

No, words meant nothing. Jackie needed to take action.

For the first time since she'd decided to become a teacher, she knew exactly what she wanted. Not what she told herself she wanted so she could make someone else happy. Jackie knew what *she* wanted.

Taking a deep breath, she reached for her phone. It was after ten o'clock at night, but this couldn't wait. She scrolled through her contacts and tapped the one she needed.

When the ringing stopped, she spoke up without waiting for an answer. "Conrad, I need to tell you something. It's important. Can we meet tomorrow?"

32

The Friday before New Year's Eve was the quietest shift Cam had seen since she'd started volunteering at Wolly again. She didn't mind, though. She took the opportunity to study some of her favorite exhibits along with the ones she'd overlooked. It was like connecting with old and new friends alike.

She stopped in front of a radiant watercolor depicting a field of sunflowers. An ache materialized in Cam's chest, but she smiled anyway. The flowers in the painting reminded her of the flower crown she'd bought for Jackie at the Christmas festival.

How was Jackie now? Had this first holiday after her dad's death and learning the truth about her family been painful for her? Had she spent it with her brother's family, or had that been too much for her?

Cam's heart clenched at the thought of Jackie spending the day alone in her house with no one to hold her as she dealt with everything that had happened. Knowing she hadn't been the one to fill that need and, most likely, never would be again drilled a deep well of sorrow inside Cam.

A sudden nearby shuffling sound interrupted her reverie. Cam turned. A small boy ran through the hall adjoining the room where she stood, and a woman who was probably his mother called after him.

The door behind the mother and boy swung open and a woman stood in the doorway, her figure outlined by the afternoon sunlight.

Cam blinked.

Jackie?

Cam's heart raced as she watched Jackie enter the building. Before

173

the door could close, a man who appeared to be several years older than Jackie entered behind her.

A sharp jolt hit Cam's stomach. Jackie was here with a man. Was she dating someone already?

Before Cam could decide what to do, Jackie's focus zeroed in on her, and she stood still and gazed at her. Then she approached. The man didn't follow her, though. He paused and put his arm around the shoulders of the woman who had been chasing the little boy.

Jackie stopped a few feet away from Cam and sent her a small, shaky smile. "Hello, Cam."

Cam's throat was dry.

Even bundled up in a coat and scarf to ward off the uncharacteristically cold weather, Jackie was so beautiful. Why did it feel like it had been months since she'd seen her instead of a week?

When Cam didn't respond—she couldn't find her voice—Jackie's smile faltered. She bit her lip then took a deep breath before beckoning to the man who had come in with her. "Cam, I'd like you to meet my brother Conrad."

The man stood beside Jackie, and Cam looked from one face to the other. Now she saw the resemblance between them. Not only that, she'd seen Conrad Webster on the news a time or two.

"Conrad," Jackie said, "This is my friend Camryn Durant."

When she said "friend," Jackie's eyes met Cam's with a wary expression.

Cam stared back. Jackie was introducing Cam to her family and asking to be friends again.

Remembering her manners, Cam extended her hand to Conrad. He shook it with a polite smile. "It's very nice to meet you, Camryn."

"Please, call me Cam," she said, finally managing to speak.

Before Cam could say anything else, the energetic boy and his mom joined them.

"And this is my sister-in-law Lisa and my nephew Riley," Jackie said.

Lisa swept an appraising gaze over her, but Cam refused to squirm. Cam offered her hand once more, and Lisa accepted it in her own smooth hand with long, manicured nails.

Cam looked down at Riley then and smiled. He had dark brown curls and a round face that looked prone to mischievous laughter. "Hello, Riley."

"Hi. Where are the dinosaurs?" he asked.

"Dinosaurs?" Cam rubbed the back of her head.

Conrad and Lisa laughed, which made both of their faces relax some.

"The last museum we visited was the Perot Museum of Nature and Science, so now Riley thinks *every* museum should have dinosaur fossils," Lisa explained.

"Oh, I see," Cam said with a chuckle. She returned her attention to Riley. "We don't have any fossils, but we do have an exhibit about the petroglyphs in Seminole Canyon. Those were drawings made on rocks by people around seven thousand years ago. You wanna see?"

Riley's eyes widened. "Yeah!"

"Come on!" Cam gestured for him to follow.

"We don't want to take up your time," Conrad said.

"It's almost the end of my shift. I don't mind."

After that reassurance, all the Websters followed Cam to the petroglyph exhibit.

Cam's nerves were strung as tight as the skin covering the indigenous frame drums in the exhibit they'd just passed. Had Jackie really brought her family here to make amends and prove she wasn't afraid to acknowledge her friendship with Cam after all? Was repairing the friendship her *only* goal, or did she want more?

There was no doubt in Cam's mind or heart what she wanted with Jackie. Once, she'd thought being platonic friends with Jackie was possible. But that was before she'd gotten to know her better. Before they'd spent hours wrapped in each other's arms. Before she'd realized she'd completely lost her heart to Jackie. If Jackie wanted to go back to only being friends, Cam didn't think she could do it.

But this was absolutely not the time to discuss or even fret over it. Not with Jackie's family watching. Cam gave herself a small shake and forced herself to focus on the tour. The museum was familiar territory, and she loved to see kids become fascinated with the art.

Despite his rowdy nature, Riley was also attentive and boundlessly curious. In the space of an hour, he must have asked at least a hundred questions as they moved on from the petroglyph exhibits to others that Cam knew to be popular with the little ones.

Conrad and Lisa asked a few questions too, but mostly, they hung back and let Cam show Riley around. Jackie was comparatively quiet.

Cam kept sneaking glances at her, but Jackie's face didn't reveal much. That stung. Cam liked to think she'd become skilled at reading Jackie. Dread tugged on Cam's heart. Would they ever be that close again?

By the time they arrived back at the museum's lobby, Conrad and Lisa were much more relaxed and affable than they had been at the start.

To Cam's surprise, Lisa even gave her a light hug as they prepared to leave. "Thank you for taking time to show us around. I don't know when I've seen Riley this engaged in anything."

"Except in dinosaurs, of course," Cam said.

Conrad approached and shook Cam's hand. "It was great to meet you, Cam. I hope we see you again sometime."

He glanced at his sister then back to Cam. "In fact, I hope you'll accompany Jackie tomorrow night to the New Year's Eve party Lisa and I give every year."

Cam stared at the man. She heard the words coming from his lips, but her brain was struggling to absorb them.

"N-new Year's Eve party?" she repeated dazedly.

"Yes, it's always a lovely time," Lisa said. "It's only a few of our closer friends, but we all dress up and welcome the new year in style. Goodness knows we could use a fresh start after this year."

Cam thanked them…or something. She really wasn't sure what she was saying or doing by that point, but she did manage to look at Jackie. Would she say goodbye and leave now too?

As if in answer to Cam's silent question, Jackie said, "You all can go. I'm sure Riley is ready for dinner by now. I'd like to stay and talk to Cam."

Jackie turned to Cam and searched her eyes. "That is, if it's okay with Cam."

Cam nodded. Her heartbeat was practically thundering in her ears by now.

As they walked to Cam's car to make the short drive to Shiloh's, Jackie's knees were shaking. Literally shaking. She didn't know that was something that really happened. It always sounded like something made up in stories.

When she'd first caught sight of Cam in the museum, Jackie had been momentarily stunned, even though she'd gone there with her family with the express purpose of seeing her. But she hadn't been prepared for the way everything inside her had come alive at seeing Cam again.

The woman I love!

The euphoria was short-lived, though, as Jackie became overwhelmed by the fear that had plagued her ever since she'd come up with the plan to go to the museum to see Cam.

What if Cam didn't want to see her?

Jackie wouldn't have blamed Cam if she'd told her to get lost.

Instead, she'd dealt with the awkwardness of seeing Jackie again and meeting her family all at the same time. She'd been her usual wonderful self with Riley, patiently answering his questions and showing off the exhibits in a way that made sense and appealed to him. It may have looked effortless, but as a teacher, Jackie knew what an impressive feat that was.

Cam hadn't even gotten mad or run away at the end of the visit, when Conrad and Lisa had embarrassed Jackie by acting like she and Cam were already a couple.

Jackie still couldn't believe that had happened. When she'd made up her mind to come out to Conrad, she'd expected him to react the way Dad probably would have: with anger, disappointment, or shame. She'd been prepared for Conrad to think, first and foremost, of how her news might affect his image.

But that's not what he'd done. He'd been surprised. He'd asked a few questions, but he had been supportive, even to the point of agreeing to meet Cam. Then he and Lisa had invited Cam to their New Year's Eve party, of all things. No, they hadn't invited. They'd *assumed* Cam would come as Jackie's plus one.

And to think, one of the reasons Jackie had sabotaged her relationship with Cam was her fear about how her brother would react.

As Jackie and Cam drove, Jackie stole a glance at Cam. Her face was calm except for the way her dark eyebrows dipped low, as if she were puzzling over a problem. Jackie suspected she might be processing everything that had just happened in the museum. If that was the case, she wanted to give Cam the space to do that before they talked, even if it meant sitting with her own barely-contained nerves a while longer.

The heavy silence between them lasted all the way until they got to the coffee shop counter to order. When Jackie and Cam approached the register, Shiloh grinned at them. "Heyyyy, guys!"

Cam appeared to flinch. "Maybe this was a bad idea," she muttered.

The comment wasn't directed at Jackie, but it made her shaky all over again. Did Cam not want to talk after all? Did she want to go home and leave Jackie and their connection in the past?

But Cam gestured for Jackie to go ahead and order, so she did. This time, Jackie got a cup of chamomile. The last thing she needed right now was caffeine.

When they both had their drinks, they sat at their usual corner table. Jackie frowned. Was it still *their* table?

Cam picked up her drink then set it down without taking a sip. She finally met Jackie's eyes. Her expression reflected some of Jackie's own nerves and uncertainty. "You introduced me to your family. I-I don't understand."

"Cam, I am so, so sorry for the way I treated you at the theatre," Jackie said as she scooted closer to the table. "I panicked when I saw Conrad, obviously, but that was no excuse. The last thing in the world I wanted was for you to feel like I was ashamed of you, but that's what happened."

Cam's deep brown eyes filled with warmth. "I know you would never hurt me on purpose. And, while maybe you didn't handle the situation the best way, I realize I probably overreacted."

"No! You didn't," Jackie hurried to assure her. "You stood up for yourself, and set a boundary. God, I respect that. I was the one who needed to get my act together. That's what I was trying to do today. I'm sorry if I made things awkward for you showing up with my family like that, but it was the best idea I could come up with to prove to you that I'm getting over my fears and hang-ups and that...I-I'm proud to know you."

A small, shy smile played across Cam's lips. "So you told them about our friendship."

"I told them everything, Cam."

Cam's jaw hung open. "Everything?"

"Well, maybe not *everything*," Jackie said with a smirk. "I left out a few of the hotter details. There are some things you shouldn't discuss with your sibling."

The color in Cam's face deepened in that cute blush she always got whenever Jackie made a suggestive comment. Jackie couldn't help but chuckle.

It only took a second to grow serious again, though. "But I told them the important part."

"The important part?" Cam pressed.

Jackie drew in a shaky breath. This was scarier than she had imagined. But seeing Cam's face with its earnest, concerned expression gave her the strength to suppress her fears. After that disastrous night at the theatre, Cam deserved to be on the receiving side of this equation for a change.

"Yes. I told them I was falling for a woman." She searched Cam's eyes. "A remarkable, funny, gorgeous woman who completely turned my world upside down. Only I messed things up with her and was hoping she'd give me another chance."

Cam went completely still as she stared at Jackie. It was hard to tell if she was even breathing.

Tentatively, Jackie slid her hand across the table and took Cam's. She didn't pull it away. That was a good sign, wasn't it? Even the small touch felt wonderful. "I'll do whatever it takes to earn your trust. If that means starting over as friends, completely platonic, until you know if you want something more with me, that's okay."

"I can't," Cam said with a firm shake of her head.

Jackie's heart plummeted all the way to her shoes. She stared down at the table.

She had tried to prepare herself for this, but it was still hard. Clearly, Cam had too many old heartaches to take a chance, especially on Jackie after she'd hurt her.

Cam squeezed her hand, making Jackie look up. Cam murmured, "I meant that I can't *only* be friends. Not with the way I feel about you."

Now not only her knees, but Jackie's whole body started to tremble. "H-how do you feel?"

Cam's handsome features relaxed into a radiant smile. "I'm falling for you too. And I want something real with you."

Cam's bold, confident statement took Jackie's breath away. "Like girlfriends?"

The term sounded novel to her ears, but also right. So right. She and Cam belonged to each other.

Cam nodded, the color in her cheeks getting darker again. "Like girlfriends. If…that's what you want too."

Jackie sprang from her chair so fast she nearly knocked it over and threw herself at Cam, wrapping her arms around her firm shoulders.

Then she pulled back and gazed down at Cam. "That's exactly what I want. *You* are what I want. Can I kiss you now?"

Cam's eyes widened. She glanced from side to side before refocusing on Jackie and nodding. Then she leaned down and placed her lips on Cam's, eyes closing in joy and relief. She'd come so close to never experiencing this again.

In some ways, though, she never *had* experienced this. This kiss was more intense, more meaningful than all their past ones. They were both all in on this now. It wasn't casual, and it certainly wasn't friendly. This kiss was passionate, loving, and real.

Cam's arms slid up her back and pressed Jackie closer as the kiss deepened. They kissed until Jackie went breathless and saw stars.

When they finally broke apart, Jackie was interrupted from staring into Cam's eyes by the sound of…applause.

She straightened fast and gaped at a nearby table where Shiloh stood clapping, along with the two women who were seated at the table. Jackie recognized them as regular customers. Her face grew hot.

Cam glanced at their cheering section and shook her head. "Okay, guys. That's nice but wholly unnecessary."

"We're just happy y'all finally came to your senses," Shiloh called out.

Jackie's eyebrows went up. When had Shiloh and their customers gotten so invested in this relationship? She sent Cam a look.

"Long story," Cam said with a small grin and shake of her head.

Jackie wanted to hear the story, but right now, she wanted Cam's lips on hers even more. She stroked her fingers over Cam's jaw and leaned in for another kiss. This one was shorter, since they had an audience.

Cam pulled away first. "Maybe we should continue this discussion someplace else."

33

Talk about déjà vu.

Exactly eight days after the ill-fated theatre trip, Cam found herself getting dressed up once again. Tonight, she chose a velvet, midnight blue dinner jacket she loved but had never actually worn because she rarely had anywhere fancy to go.

Like last time, Cam's anxiety was giving her heartburn but for entirely different reasons. Before, she'd been nervous in anticipation of asking Jackie if she would ever consider a serious relationship with her.

At least she had an answer to that question now.

Cam couldn't contain the grin that spread over her face as she thought of it. Jackie had shocked her by showing up at the museum with her family the day before and even more so by admitting she was falling for her.

The thrill of astonishment and joy that had pulsed through Cam's chest as Jackie had told her how she felt—there were no words to describe it. If she could paint her feelings, the canvas would be an explosion of vibrance and light and rainbows.

And she had shocked herself with her own bold declarations. Somewhere along the way, she had finally learned to put away her fears and dare to take chances with her heart again. It was exhilarating and scary all at the same time.

Tonight, Cam was taking another chance by going with Jackie to her brother's New Year's Eve party, and her nerves were telling her about it even though Jackie had assured Cam there was nothing to worry about.

When they'd left Shiloh's the day before, Cam had driven Jackie home. They hadn't even made it out of the car before they were making out again. Cam's body had vibrated with longing. She'd desperately longed to go with Jackie into her house and make their reunion complete, yet she had held back.

"I can't believe I'm saying this, but I think we should talk some more before we...do anything else," Cam had said while catching her breath.

Jackie's cheeks had been a lovely shade of pink. "You're right. We need to talk. I want to make sure we start our relationship on solid footing."

Cam's heart had given a tiny skip at how much they were in alignment. "Exactly, so I think I should go home and call you."

"What, why?"

"Because I don't trust myself to keep my hands off you once we're inside," Cam had confessed.

That statement had resulted in more irresistible blushing and a few more hot kisses, but Jackie had agreed.

Then Cam had gone home and they'd ended up talking on the phone well into the night. They'd discussed their feelings more and how they wanted their relationship to be. Jackie had never had a girlfriend, of course, so she had been full of questions.

Jackie had also told her about spending Christmas with her biological father's family, and Cam had talked about her holiday. Then they'd discussed Conrad's invitation to the New Year's Eve party and agreed that they would go together.

Now, as Cam fussed over her white shirt collar and straightened her jacket, she fretted over the decision, even as she knew she couldn't take it back.

A light knock on her apartment door reinforced that fact, and Cam's heart skipped a beat.

Jackie

Cam hurried to the door and opened it. All she could do was stare and drink in the sight of Jackie in a silk burgundy dress. It was long and tasteful, but the neckline dipped, showing off a hint of cleavage. Also, there was a slit in the skirt of the dress that gave Cam a peek at Jackie's incredible legs. "Damn, woman. I'm glad I didn't see you in this yesterday, there's no way I could have kept my distance."

Jackie's hazel eyes sparkled. "You're one to talk."

She slid her fingers up and down the lapels of Cam's jacket, making Cam's skin tingle, as if Jackie's long fingers were caressing her skin and not the fabric. "No one should look this sexy in a suit. It's unfairly distracting."

Before Cam could even blush, Jackie's fingers curled over the lapels, and she pulled her into a heart-stopping kiss. Cam's arms glided around the silk of Jackie's dress and tugged her closer until their bodies melded together.

They stayed locked in a fiery embrace until Cam slowly backed away, panting the slightest bit. "It's probably best you don't ravish me in my hallway. There are kids on this floor."

"Me?" Jackie laughed. "Me ravish you?"

"Anytime, babe," Cam growled before backing out of the doorway so Jackie could enter the apartment. "But not in the hallway."

Jackie's giggles followed Cam inside, but she paused before entering. "Hold on a minute. I didn't bring you flowers, but I do have your Christmas present."

She stepped back into the hall and returned with a wide, flat object wrapped in bright red and green paper.

Cam looked from the gift to Jackie. "What in the world?"

"Open it!" Jackie handed over the package and somehow managed to bounce on the balls of her feet while wearing high heels.

"Okay. But let's sit down first."

Once they were seated on the couch, Cam carefully unwrapped the package. Then she let out a low whistle.

Underneath the paper was a dark brown portfolio case. She could tell from feel and smell that it was made of genuine leather. "Wow."

Cam ran her hand over the case from the top, all the way down to the front bottom right corner, which sported her initials. "Thank you, Jackie. This is absolutely beautiful."

Jackie beamed. "Your art is beautiful. It deserves a beautiful case."

Cam couldn't respond over the sudden lump forming in her throat, so she leaned in and planted a thorough kiss on Jackie's lips. She responded immediately, and they got lost in each other once again.

Several minutes later, Jackie scooted back and traced Cam's face with her fingertips. "So, you really like it?"

"Like it? I love it!"

"I'm so glad. I actually had it commissioned from one of the leather craftsmen we met at the Christmas festival."

"Well, there's a coincidence," Cam said with a laugh.

"What do you mean?"

"Hang on." She jumped up from the couch and hurried to her room to retrieve Jackie's Christmas present from the bedroom closet.

When she returned to the living room, she handed Jackie the deep cardboard box adorned with colorful holiday designs.

"What's this?" Jackie asked.

"I commissioned something from one of the festival artists too."

Jackie lifted the lid off the box to reveal a small painting. It was a swirling abstract design in warm colors. "Max did this, didn't he?"

She studied the painting closer and traced the script that overlaid the colors. Her head jerked up, and their eyes met. "Wait a minute...this is a Hilda Spaulding quote!"

"That's right." She sat down next to Jackie. "There are four of them."

Jackie pulled the paintings out of the box and examined them one at a time. "These are some of my favorite quotes from her books. How did you know?"

"I snooped through your copies of Spaulding's novels and found the passages you marked with sticky tabs. Then I messaged Max and asked if he could do a collection of pieces with the quotes." Cam brushed a hand over the edge of one of the paintings. "He asked me about color inspiration, and I suggested some of these since you wear them a lot and have decorative accents in your house with them too."

Jackie fell silent as she stared down at the painting in her lap.

Cam's nerves returned. "Was that okay?"

"You supported one of my former students by commissioning him to do these, you incorporated the words of my favorite author, and you thought about how to make it coordinate with my color preferences? I'd say this is the most thoughtful gift anyone has ever given me." She leaned over and wrapped Cam in a tight embrace. "Thank you, darling."

"You're most welcome."

Cam held Jackie close, convinced there was no better feeling in the entire world. They stayed like that for several minutes, as if they'd both be content to remain there all night.

Unfortunately, they had somewhere else to be. Cam sighed, her breath ruffling Jackie's hair. "We should probably get going. I don't want to make a bad impression right away by arriving late."

Some of Cam's lingering anxiety must have seeped into her tone, because Jackie leaned back and studied Cam's face. "Are you worried about tonight?"

Cam looked away. This was a new beginning for them, one where she and Jackie were honest about their feelings for one another. It didn't make sense to pretend about this. "I'm nervous, yes. For both of us. I'm sure I don't have to tell you I'm not used to this kind of setting, and I can't imagine how stressful it must be for you getting ready to go to a social event with a girlfriend for the first time."

"Yeah, it's a lot," Jackie conceded. "I can't pretend it's not. And, when you asked if I wanted to go tonight, I said I was in favor of it mostly because it was important for you to know that I'm proud to go anywhere with you by my side. But if you're not comfortable with this, that's completely okay."

"You don't have to prove anything to me. I mean, you came out to your family. That was huge, and I guess that was the catalyst for our relationship." Cam reached down and took Jackie's hand. "But I stand by what I've always said: you have to do what's right and safe for you in your own time. I don't need you to rush into making this public just to show me you're serious about us. I trust you."

Jackie squeezed Cam's hand and beamed at her. "See, that makes me even more proud to claim you as my girlfriend. And I'm ready to do that tonight. Yes, it's making me nervous, but it's exciting too. All my life, I've tried to fit other people's expectations of me, but now, I feel like I can finally start learning to be myself."

"You don't know how happy I am for you." Cam's heart swelled, and she kissed Jackie's cheek.

"Thank you. But what about you? We've talked about why I want to face down my nerves and do this, but why are you willing to go? I don't want you to feel obligated."

"I don't!" Cam said quickly. "I know you're not pressuring me. It's just…I've been thinking: Conrad and Lisa, they're your family. And this party tonight is part of the world you came from. I know you didn't stay there, but it's still your background. It's part of what makes you the person you are."

Cam took Jackie's hand in both of hers. "When you first told me about your family, I was rude. I let my own prejudices and bad experiences get in the way. That was wrong. Going forward, I want you to know I accept all of you, and I want to get to know you as much as possible. If that means going to events like tonight's party now and then, if that's what you want, then so be it."

Jackie shook her head and let out a watery chuckle. "If you're really ready to go to this party, why do you keep saying things that make me want to kiss you senseless?"

Cam chuckled. "That wasn't my plan but—"

Jackie surged forward and planted her lips on Cam's until Cam did, indeed, lose all her senses for a few minutes.

34

Jackie made a point not to leave Cam's side for most of the evening. That was partly due to an overwhelming feeling of protectiveness she'd never experienced in a romantic relationship before. She wasn't really worried anyone at the party would be unkind to Cam, but she knew Cam was nervous and could probably use the extra reassurance.

Mostly, though, Jackie didn't want to be away from her. Maybe it was the newness of being Cam's girlfriend, or maybe it was how devastatingly hot she looked in her dinner jacket and tuxedo pants. In any case, they stayed close together except when Lisa took a few minutes from her other guests to show Cam around the house.

Lisa and Conrad had both been just as welcoming and attentive to Cam as they were with their friends. They made a point to include her in conversations and ask her about her job, volunteering, and artistic pursuits. They had been similarly polite to Jackie's boyfriends in the past, but it had never mattered this much to Jackie. For one thing, Jackie's feelings were much more involved and, for another, she knew her brother and sister-in-law's behavior would set the tone for how everyone else in their circle treated Cam and the relationship.

The example they set must have been working because the other couples at the party were courteous too. Most of the people at the gathering were familiar to Jackie. It was a mix of Conrad and Lisa's longtime friends and newer connections formed through Conrad's political career.

She and Cam found things to discuss with everyone they interacted with, and Jackie was beginning to relax and enjoy the evening until a shrill voice she hadn't heard in several years called out behind her.

"Jacqueline Webster! It's been sooo long."

Jackie and Cam both turned to face the newcomer.

Payton Foster. Jackie barely managed not to wince.

She and Payton had been friends in high school, although it wasn't easy because Payton had always been snooty and prone to too much gossip. Her family and Jackie's had known each other for decades, so that may have solidified their connection more than any real camaraderie.

"Payton, hi," Jackie said. "You look nice this evening."

It wasn't a lie. She'd always dressed like a beauty contestant, and tonight was no exception. Her sparkly silver dress hugged her rail-thin body, and her blond hair was swept up in a stylish twist.

Payton charged up to them and stared from Jackie to Cam, a salacious smirk on her lips. "I'd heard about you, but I didn't believe it!"

Jackie's shoulders tensed. She didn't have to ask what Payton had heard. *Okay, let's get this over with.* "Cam, this is my old friend Payton Foster."

She placed her hand on Cam's arm. "Payton, this is my girlfriend Camryn Durant."

Payton's mouth dropped at Jackie's candor. Then she swept a long, curious look up and down Cam.

Dear God. Why did I decide to bring Cam here to subject her to this?

But Cam held up well to the scrutiny. She assumed that charming, friendly grin that had caught Jackie's eye from the very first and extended her hand to Payton. "Hello, Payton. It's so nice to meet you."

Payton took Cam's hand in what appeared to be a loose, disdainful grasp and shook it once.

"We went to high school together," Jackie explained.

Cam's smile brightened. "Oh, really? Then maybe you can answer something about Jackie that I've been wondering about."

Payton frowned and finally looked Cam in the eye. "What's that?"

Leaning in closer, Cam asked, "Was she the teacher's pet?"

"I couldn't say," Payton huffed. Then she paused as she processed the question. "Well, actually, yes. She was insufferable!"

Jackie snickered under her breath. Cam had stumbled on the only thing Payton liked more than gossiping, which was complaining about other people's behavior.

"She always got the best grades," Payton continued, "always knew the answers to the questions when teachers asked. No one else even bothered raising their hands. They'd just look at Jackie and wait for her to answer."

Cam chuckled. "I knew it!"

Payton shook her head and sent Jackie a reproachful look. "I always told her to tone it down around the boys. They hate it when their girlfriends are smarter than they ar—"

Payton froze. Her eyes darted between Jackie and Cam, and her mouth clamped shut.

Cam winked at her. "I guess everything worked out, then."

Payton's eyes widened. "I-I guess so." Then she burst out laughing. "It worked out perfectly!"

After a second, Cam laughed too and so did Jackie.

Most of the tension dissipated, and Payton chatted away about some other scandal that had occurred within their graduating class.

When Payton finally moved on to refill her drink, Jackie stepped close to Cam and squeezed her arm. "You handled that well. Do they teach stuff like that in Coming Out School? If so, where do I enroll?"

"There's no school, I'm afraid." Cam caressed the hand Jackie had placed on her arm. "Everyone develops their own bag of tricks for awkward situations like that. Mine includes deflection and humor. Unless someone is a complete asshole, that's usually enough to move them off the topic and on to something else."

"Ooh, sexy *and* smart," Jackie whispered in Cam's ear. "That's quite a combination."

Cam shivered before dropping a quick kiss on Jackie's nose. "Now behave, please. It's almost midnight."

Sure enough, Conrad and Lisa were handing out noisemakers and confetti to all their guests in preparation for the countdown.

Jackie's heart raced as everyone began to count in unison.

"*TEN,*

NINE,

EIGHT…"

Her focus zeroed in on Cam, who was beaming back at her while the countdown continued.

When the year started, there was no way Jackie could have predicted the way the last couple of months would play out: meeting Cam, coming to terms with her sexuality, discovering the truth about her parents…falling in love.

None of it was expected. But overriding all the other complicated emotions was a solid, deep sense of gratitude. Jackie was so much happier with the person she was tonight than the one she'd been a year ago.

"HAPPY NEW YEAR!"

As everyone shouted and cheered, Cam swept Jackie into her arms and held her tightly. Jackie's eyes closed, and she savored Cam's scent and heat and tenderness.

Pulling back, she raised her hands to cup Cam's face and bring their mouths together. Without hesitation, Cam kissed her back with enough passion to put all the New Year's Eve fireworks in the world to shame.

35

Jackie sat beside Cam on the sofa and watched her long, skillful fingers flutter over her keyboard as she signed into her laptop.

Reminiscing about what those fingers had done to her the night before when they'd returned to Cam's apartment after the New Year's Eve party was almost enough to distract her from the matter at hand.

Almost.

"We don't have to do this today, if you're not ready," Cam said, bumping her shoulder against Jackie's.

She shifted to study Cam. "What makes you think I'm not ready?"

Gently, she tapped Jackie's hands, which she only now realized were clutching the fabric of her jeans in a death grip. "You look like you're waiting to get a root canal, babe."

Jackie relaxed her fingers. "Okay, maybe I'm kind of nervous, but I really do want to meet your mom. Besides, you've already met my family…"

She paused. "Well, you've met Conrad, Lisa, and Riley. I think I want to wait a bit before exposing you to Constance and Joan. I'm trying not to scare you off."

Cam reached up to stroke Jackie's cheek, her touch warm and soft. "You're not going to scare me off."

She sent Jackie a playful grin. "But given everything you've told me about them, I fully support your decision to wait."

Laughter bubbled up from Jackie's chest, easing her anxiety a little.

When Cam had left the cozy cocoon of the bed this morning, Jackie had been disappointed until she had explained that it was almost time for her weekly video call with her mom. Then she had shyly asked if Jackie would like to join her on the call to say hello.

Jackie had eagerly accepted. She'd been looking forward to meeting the woman who could raise someone as wonderful as Cam.

But then her nerves had kicked in.

It was odd. She had met former partners' families before without being anywhere near as tense as she was right now.

Of course, she hadn't been as madly in love with those past partners as she was with Cam either. Not that she'd told her that yet.

Cam might have said she wouldn't be scared off, but Jackie wasn't ready to test that resolve with a declaration of undying love. It was probably too much this early in their relationship when she was still working to build Cam's trust.

"There's nothing to worry about," Cam assured her, interrupting her amorous reflections. "It will be a brief call with Mama, and she'll like you. Why wouldn't she?"

Maybe because I hurt her daughter?

Jackie gulped. She didn't know if Cam had told her family about the breakup, but judging by how close they seemed to be, it was a strong possibility.

Before Jackie could fret any longer, Cam opened her video call application, and a window flickered to life on the screen.

Cam's mom appeared in the window and smiled. "Happy New Year, my heart!"

"Happy New Year, Mama."

She put her arm around Jackie and pulled her close. "Mama, I want you to meet my girlfriend, Jackie Webster."

Hearing Cam call her that sent currents of joy rippling through Jackie, as she smiled at the screen. "I'm glad to meet you, Mrs. Durant."

A small grin played across the older woman's lips. "Well, hello, Jackie. I'm glad to meet you too." She glanced off screen and called, "Mari, you were right. Cam is introducing me to Jackie. Come on."

To Jackie's astonishment, Mrs. Durant was immediately joined, not only by Mari, but also by Cam's grandmother and great aunt. The two elder women huddled beside Cam's mom on her sofa, and Mari stood behind them.

Cam started to sputter. "Mari! When I texted you about Jackie and me getting together, I didn't mean for you to organize a whole family convention the first time I called up to introduce Jackie to Mama."

"What convention?" Mari asked with an overly innocent shrug. "We were all here, so why not say hello to all of us?"

Cam mumbled something under her breath, but she made the rest of the introductions, squeezing Jackie's shaky hand as she did.

As she surveyed the four faces looking back at her, she felt the pull to slide into her charming and genteel Jaqueline Webster mode, but she resisted. Cam had always made her feel like it was okay to be her authentic self, so it was important to be honest. "I have to admit, I wasn't expecting to meet everyone today, and I'm kind of overwhelmed, but I've been looking forward to this. Cam has told me a lot about all of you."

Before anyone else could respond, Cam's grandma stared at the screen. Her eyes were inscrutable behind her glasses, but her mouth was set in a stern line. "Camryn told us about *you* also."

A shiver ran down Jackie's spine. "I—"

"Oh, Marion, be nice," Cam's Aunt Nat chided. "They obviously worked things out. Look how happy Camryn is now."

The intimidating grandma's fierce focus shifted from Jackie to Cam, and her expression softened.

Jackie turned to look at Cam too. It was her new favorite thing to do.

When their eyes met, Cam's held a glow of tenderness, and Jackie nearly forgot where she was. Cam pulled Jackie's hand to her lips and kissed it. "Yes, I'm very happy."

"There, you see?" Aunt Nat's sharp voice made Cam and Jackie jump. "No sense in dwelling on the past."

Mari and Mrs. Durant murmured their agreement.

Jackie faced the screen again. "I don't want to dwell on the past either, but I do want to say something. You all love Cam so much and want her to be safe, so you deserve to hear it. I hurt Cam, and I bitterly regret it. But I soon realized what an incredible person I was losing by letting her walk away, and I got myself together."

She squeezed Cam's hand. "I'll always be grateful that Cam gave me another chance, and I promise I'll do my best not to squander it."

Jackie looked into each face before her. "I care about her so much. And I care about her dreams, her future, and her happiness…maybe even as much as you do."

"Jackie," Cam murmured, her voice huskier than usual. She pulled

Jackie into her arms and held tight.

When the embrace ended, Jackie thought she saw a few sets of glistening eyes on the screen.

"Thank you for that," Cam's grandmother said. Her face was tranquil now. "That's all we ever wanted for her."

"You're welcome, ma'am."

A faint smile lifted the corners of the older lady's mouth. "You'd best just call me Grandma."

Jackie's heart gave a jolt then fluttered happily. "Okay."

36

Cam couldn't stop whistling "Auld Lang Syne," even though they were already three days into the new year. Since Jackie was still on winter break and January second had been a vacation day for Cam, they'd spent all weekend and Monday together.

A large, satisfying chunk of that time had been spent in bed.

Steamy memories flooded Cam's brain as she continued to whistle while brewing coffee on Tuesday morning.

Because she had to get ready for work, Cam had reluctantly left Jackie sleeping in her bed, but hopefully, she would stir in time to have a cup of coffee with her before it was time to go.

As if summoned by Cam's hopes, a long pair of lily-white arms wrapped around Cam from behind. Her eyes closed, and she reveled in the feel of Jackie's warm, shapely body pressed against her back.

"Good morning," Jackie whispered in Cam's ear. The sensation of Jackie's breath on her skin and the sound of her voice, still husky from sleep, sent shivers through her.

"Good morning." Cam twisted around so she could give Jackie a proper greeting. But, for a moment, she could only stare into Jackie's eyes.

She was so gorgeous, especially in the mornings like this before she'd put on her makeup or going-out clothes. She looked soft and serene…and happy.

Words of love and devotion gathered inside Cam, longing to pour out, but she held them back.

It's way too soon.

Rather than speaking, Cam leaned in for a kiss in hopes of *showing* Jackie some of what she felt.

Several minutes later, they ended their passionate embrace so Cam could attend to the coffee.

"Mmm. That smells divine," Jackie said.

Cam poured a cup of the brew and doctored it the way Jackie liked it: with one scoop of sugar and a dash of cream. Then she handed it over.

"Thank you, darling."

"You're welcome," Cam answered with what felt like the world's goofiest grin on her face. She loved it when Jackie called her that.

While preparing her own cup of coffee, Cam said, "I'm afraid I can't make a big breakfast like I usually do. *Someone* kept me too busy to get groceries yesterday."

Jackie smirked. "Is that a complaint?"

"Never!" Cam laughingly assured her. "Anyway, I do have a couple of Shiloh's cranberry scones, so all is not lost."

"Ooh. Cranberry? Those are my favorite." Jackie rubbed her hands together.

Cam swallowed another laugh. "Yeah, I…think I remember your saying that."

"That's because you're such a considerate girlfr—" Jackie paused and frowned. "I'm pretty sure the only time I mentioned my affinity for cranberry scones was the morning after our first night together."

"Really?" Cam tried to play it cool.

"You remembered that?" Jackie opened her eyes wide in exaggerated surprise. "Wow. You must really be hung up on me."

Cam barked out a laugh. "You have no idea."

As Cam heated the scones, she asked, "What are you going to do today?"

"I'm way behind on preparing my lesson plans, so I need to work on that. Then I thought I might call or visit Peggy, if she's free."

"I'm glad you plan to keep in touch with her." Cam carried the scones to the table. "It will probably be good for both of you. It sounded like her family was welcoming too."

"They were," Jackie agreed. "I can't wait for you to meet them."

Cam's heart gave a skip. "Me neither."

The rapid yet smooth way their lives were already intertwining left Cam breathless. Like the call with her family on Sunday. Mama, grandma, Aunt Nat, and Mari were already set to wrap Jackie into their fold after she'd been so open and honest about her feelings for Cam.

Everything inside her pulsed with wonder and joy as she recalled Jackie's tone and expression when she'd told the family how important Cam was to her.

Maybe it wasn't too soon for that four-lettered word, after all.

"What about you?"

"What about me?" Cam asked, wondering if she'd lost track of the conversation with her musing.

"This is a big day, isn't it?" Jackie pressed. "You and Mr. Bolton are meeting with the Open Air Hill people today, right?"

"Don't remind me," Cam said with a groan. The last few days had been a welcome distraction from the upcoming meeting. "I still can't believe Mr. Bolton wants me to lead the whole presentation."

"I can believe it, and I think it's wonderful." Jackie beamed at her.

"I think the only reason he decided to let me lead was because he still feels guilty about not figuring out that Logan was stealing my work sooner."

Jackie crossed her arms. "Or he realizes you busted that nice ass of yours on this project."

Cam snickered at the colorful compliment, but she shook her head. "If he thinks he needs to reward me, that still means he's doing it out of obligation."

"No, that's not what I meant," Jackie said. Her face grew serious. "Cam, why did you work so hard on this project? Why did you volunteer for it in the first place?"

"Well, I thought it was an interesting campaign. And I had all these ideas in my head about how it would…" Cam stopped and pondered for a second. Then her eyes met Jackie's. "Because I was passionate about it."

"Exactly!" Jackie bounced in her chair. "From what you told me, Bolton and his team were struggling before you came on board with the project. But you helped turn it around with a fresh perspective and, more importantly, your enthusiasm for the campaign. That makes you qualified to present on it. Any good leader would see that."

Cam leaned back in her chair and mulled over Jackie's words. She was right. Maybe Cam had earned her place on Bolton's team with her passion for the project. That, and her willingness to swallow her fears and go after it in the first place.

Her attention refocused on Jackie. Her lovely, wise, and encouraging girlfriend.

Maybe it was time to put aside her fears once again and be completely truthful with her.

Jackie was worth it.

"Darling, is something wrong?" Jackie leaned forward to study her. "Are you still worried about the presentation? It will be great. I know it."

"No, no. There's nothing wrong. Thank you for talking me through that," Cam murmured.

"Anytime. I know how you appreciate my…insights," Jackie said with a playful toss of her hair.

A chuckle escaped Cam despite her pounding heart. "I do. I really do. But I don't just love your insights, Jackie. I love you."

The coffee spoon in Jackie's hand dropped to the table with a clank, and she stared at Cam with wide eyes. "You do?"

Cam nodded. "Yeah. I realize it's fast, and I hope I didn't make you uncomfortable. But I wanted you to know."

Jackie's eyes began to shimmer with moisture. She slid off her chair and walked over to kneel beside her. "Oh, Cam. Thank you."

Thank you?

Whatever she'd been expecting Jackie to say, it hadn't been that. "You don't have to thank me for loving you, Jackie."

"I'm not." Jackie's cheeks turned an appealing shade of pink. "Actually, I am grateful for that. But I'm thanking you for saying it. I was worried if I said it too soon, I might scare you away. It wasn't easy keeping it to myself, though, so I'm glad I don't have to anymore."

"Jackie, are you saying—"

"I love you, Cam!" Jackie's face transformed with a stunning smile. She grabbed Cam's hands and kissed the back of each one. "I love you so much."

Cam thought her heart was beating fast before, but now it felt like it could leap out of her chest. She linked her fingers with Jackie's and pulled her to her feet. Just before their lips met, Jackie murmured, "I'm so glad you walked into my life."

Cam was glad too. Glad for art museums, cranberry scones, Christmas festivals…and even crowded bars.

The End

ACKNOWLEDGMENTS

I want to thank my family and friends for encouraging me as a writer. In particular, thank you to the friends who were beta readers for this project. Your feedback made the story stronger and boosted my spirit in the process. To my friend and editor, Victoria Grant, I appreciate you so much. It's always fun to work with you from either the reading or writing side, and it's an honor to have you around to witness my author evolution and metamorphosis.

I need to give a big shoutout to my virtual morning sprint author friends. Not only are you all a boundless source of encouragement, expertise, and humor, you also accomplish the impossible by making me actually enjoy mornings.

Finally, I want to say how much I love the sapphic book community in general. I've been around readers and writers for most of my adult life, but none have been more positive, accepting, and generally awesome as so many of the sapphic readers and writers I've had the privilege of interacting with in the last couple of years.

ABOUT THE AUTHOR

Robin Clairvaux spends their time dreaming up soft-hearted sapphic stories, and sometimes...they even write them down! When they aren't daydreaming, Robin loves reading, especially sapphic romance and old school whodunnits, watching classic movies, and singing along with their vintage jazz playlist while commuting to their day job as a technical editor.

Robin grew up all over the (mostly southern) United States then went to college in New York City, but their roots are deep in the red dirt of Oklahoma, where they now live, work, and play.

Sign up for Robin's newsletter at their website: https://www.robinclairvaux-author.com/

Made in the USA
Las Vegas, NV
02 May 2025

21602391R00121